WHAT DIES IN SUMMER

Jim Beaudry, or Biscuit, as he's usually
known, is a teenage boy trying to stay out of
trouble. But trouble has a way of finding him,
first in his nightmares and then in his waking
life. When one summer afternoon Biscuit and
his cousin L.A. discover the savaged body of
a schoolgirl in the Texas wilderness, they are
pulled into a manhunt that will put both of
their lives in danger.

TOM WRIGHT

WHAT DIES IN SUMMER

Complete and Unabridged

CHARNWOOD
Leicester

First published in Great Britain in 2012 by
Canongate Books Ltd.
Edinburgh

First Charnwood Edition
published 2013
by arrangement with
Canongate Books Ltd.
Edinburgh

British Library CIP Data

Wright, Tom, *1953 Apr. 28 –*
What dies in summer.
1. Suspense fiction.
2. Large type books.
I. Title
813.6–dc23

ISBN 978–1–4448–1415–6

Published by
F. A. Thorpe (Publishing)
Anstey, Leicestershire

Set by Words & Graphics Ltd.
Anstey, Leicestershire
Printed and bound in Great Britain by
T. J. International Ltd., Padstow, Cornwall

This book is printed on acid-free paper

MP. First Believer

EXILE

EXILE

1

Mothers

I did what I did, and that's on me. But there's no way to make sense of what happened without figuring L.A. into it too. That was the thing with her — she never tried to change anything or anybody, but nothing she touched was ever the same again, including me. I think one reason was that whatever she did — and don't get the idea I'm forgetting she was a girl — she did absolutely balls-out. No warnings, no explanations and no particular interest in whether you understood or not. The way we got her in the first place was a perfect example.

Supposedly I have a touch of the Sight, which Gram says is some kind of throwback that crops up in her family every so often. In my case it's unpredictable and generally useless, but this time it was dead on, flashing inside my head like heat lightning just as we were finishing the breakfast dishes in the kitchen. Something was wrong on the front porch. Nothing dangerous or necessarily spooky, but definitely out of whack. I dried my hands to go out and take a look.

It was the first Saturday in February, summer as gone as it ever gets and Oak Cliff just beginning to wake up under a frost blanket that looked like diamond dust. Thin orange blades of sunlight stabbed through the bare crape myrtles

3

along the driveway and angled across the frozen lawn and the porch, outlining L.A. where she sat scrunched down inside her old Cowboys jacket with her back against the wall and her arms locked around her knees. Her face was almost dead-white except for her raw nose. She was shaking and rocking and staring ferociously at nothing, the pale poofs of her breath trailing away through the slatted light like miniature smoke signals.

Two of the St. Mary's sisters, out unnaturally early for some unknown reason, had stopped on the sidewalk across the street and were eyeing us like a couple of penguin detectives. Because of their tendency to appear only at the most awkward times it was certainly no surprise to see them now, but it shook me a little anyway. The presence of witnesses in ambiguous circumstances always did unless I was ready with a good solid cover story, and at this point I was still trying to rough out some sort of explanation for L.A. being here that clearly ruled out guilty involvement on my part.

L.A. was my only cousin, in fact the only kid I was related to in any way as far as I knew, which was one of the reasons I didn't have a baseline of normalcy to measure things like this against. What I did know from hard experience was that with her in the picture the sky was the limit when it came to how much trouble we could actually be in here. For starters, I had no idea why she would run away from home, but naturally my first thought was that it must be the problem with her folks, my aunt Rachel and her

4

husband Cam, who could get pretty nasty when they were drinking. Which, when you got right down to it, was all the time.

But I didn't really get it, and right there you have the difference between being smart and being intelligent. I probably have enough IQ for most routine purposes, but being smart is another thing entirely. That means having the knack of locating the center of gravity of a thing, finding the balance point of meaning and importance in it, and that's exactly where I generally mess up. But it didn't take a genius to recognize how out of the ordinary this situation was, and even at that moment I think I knew L.A. had just taken us across a line we were never going to come back to.

Even though I knew better than to think she would ever make things that easy, I still took another look around for some clue that might make sense of this situation — Aunt Rachel's car disappearing around the corner, L.A.'s bicycle, tracks through the frost, anything. But except for the ever-watchful sisters and the plumes of their breaths, there was nothing to see but the silent, sparkling neighborhood itself.

I helped L.A. up and got her inside.

'Good Lord,' said Gram as we came in. She dropped her dish towel on the counter beside the sink and came over to us.

'She must have been out there a long time,' I said. 'Look how hard she's shaking.'

'Well, what in heaven's name,' said Gram. She brushed L.A.'s dark tangle of hair back with her hand to get a better look at her eyes, saying,

'What is it, dear? Are you hurt?'

L.A. shivered on, saying nothing.

Gram gave her the expert parental once-over for cuts, bruises and broken bones, saying, 'You're cold as a frog, young lady.' She examined L.A.'s fingertips and *tsked*. 'But I don't believe it's hypothermia just yet.'

She got the blue comforter, wrapped L.A. in it and sat her in the window chair at the kitchen table, then heated milk for hot chocolate. I went to the cupboard for a cup and the bag of small marshmallows and got a spoon from the drawer, L.A. vigilantly tracking our movements from inside the blanket like some kind of captured night animal.

When Gram set the chocolate in front of her she stared at it for a minute without moving. Then her hands came slowly out from the folds of the comforter and she picked up the cup to take a sip, then set the cup back down, making no effort to wipe off her marshmallow mustache.

Her shaking eventually stopped, but she still had nothing to say. She'd never been much of a talker in the first place, but now she was silent as the grave. For me this went straight past weird and all the way to the outskirts of scary, her just looking at me like that with those big wild eyes.

Gram on the other hand was a regular female, meaning there was pretty much no silence in her. She got Aunt Rachel on the phone, skipped her warm-up and went directly to the fastball, popping them in high and tight: 'immature,' 'irresponsible' and 'self-indulgent,' just to name a few. It wasn't hard to picture Aunt Rachel at the other end of the line — pretty like Mom but a little taller, darker and drunker, probably wearing her usual boots and jeans — pacing back and forth, smoking and running her hand through her hair as she yelled back at Gram. Early or not, if she didn't already have a drink in her hand it wouldn't be long before she was into the vodka.

Gram summed up: 'As usual, Rachel, you've contrived to make the worst of a bad bargain. But at least Lee Ann is safe here with us, and that is a deal more than I can say for her in your care.'

Because of her excessive intelligence and her Yankee education, Gram actually talked like this all the time. To me the most impressive thing about it was the accurate way her words nailed you without leaving any room to maneuver or defend yourself. Aunt Rachel was no slouch herself as a yakker, but she couldn't keep up with Gram, especially when she was sozzled, and when the dust finally settled the verdict was clear — L.A. was ours.

Gram was big on the idea that the best strategy against fear and confusion was counter-attack, her method being to lock in on what had to be done first, do it no matter what, then move on to the next thing, and then the thing after that. Now that L.A. was more or less okay for the moment and wasn't going anywhere, the next order of business was retrieving her clothes and stuff from Aunt Rachel's house, including her dog Jazzy, a bug-eyed little shag that Gram called a shit-zoo. But L.A. refused to go with us, shaking her head energetically when Gram tried to persuade her by pointing out — pretty reasonably, I thought — that we needed her there to make sure we got the right things.

'Come on, L.A., it'll be okay,' I said.

She just backed away, one eye on the hallway, staking out her line of retreat.

'Oh, well,' said Gram, grabbing her purse.

We ferried everything over from Aunt Rachel's in the Roadmaster, L.A. brightening up a fraction when she saw me climb out of the car with Jazzy under my arm, running up to snatch her from me as I came around the camellias from the driveway.

Gram and I lugged the stuff down the hall to what used to be the sewing room, where there was a spare bed. As we worked, Gram explained that in ancient times in China dogs like Jazzy were officially designated as cats to allow them to enter the Forbidden City, where apparently only cats were allowed to go.

Like a lot of what Gram said, this had the peculiar effect of filling my mind with odd ideas and new angles on things while actually seeming to leave me more ignorant than ever. For instance, I couldn't understand how a place could be called a city if nobody could go there. Or at least nobody but cats and certain funny-looking little undercover dogs. But maybe it wasn't that you couldn't go there exactly — maybe the city itself was forbidden in some way, possibly by reason of having been built against orders or out of illegal materials. I wanted more information about this, but I didn't ask Gram, for the very same reason you don't blow up the dam to get a glass of water.

With a little scrounging around we found a nightstand and dresser and some old but kind of nice-looking lace curtains for the window. Fresh sheets on the bed, a few knickknacks here and there, and just like that it was a girl's room.

Gram squared off against the unknown, put her hands on her hips, said, 'There,' and the deal was done. Whatever L.A.'s reason was for being here, this made it fully official. Whatever was coming, we were going to face it as a family of three.

2

Adjustments

I don't mean to make it sound like everything just snapped into place, though, because it didn't. L.A. never really got all the way back to being her old self again and there were certain things I had to learn, like being more careful than ever about touching her when she wasn't looking. What I got in return was her remembering not to make any sudden movements at the edge of my vision, which gives you some idea of how we got through those first days.

Meantime, I was gradually coming to terms with the possibility L.A. was permanently done with talking, even taking a certain off-beat pride in my ability to handle the idea. I doubted there were very many guys out there who could even grasp the concept of a speechless girl, much less get comfortable with it.

But then Dee Campion whispered to her.

Dee was a friend of ours, one of those kids who's always around but doesn't usually say much and never really seems to be completely in on things. At the time I didn't understand how much he and I had in common, and for a while I wasn't sure what to make of him. Gram called him a 'gentle boy,' something I never heard her say about anybody else. He was an artist. His

10

specialty was watercolors, things like apples, onions and wineglasses, and he painted them so well that I couldn't distinguish what he did from straight-up magic. He was thin and blond and seemed to catch more light than other people, which made him look beyond ordinary, maybe a little tragic, like a saint or a doomed poet. There was just something about him, and whatever it was made me feel like a bear at a tea party when I was around him.

Plus we didn't actually see eye to eye about much of anything, so even watching TV with him could be kind of an obstacle course. He was polite about it but you could tell he had no use for sports, whereas I didn't care much for stuff about romance, relationships and other female ordeals. If I ever did get him to watch a game with me, he tended to ignore the count and the infield adjustments and veer off into speculation about things like whether the team colors agreed with a particular player's personality or how the guy's relationship with his father might have affected his batting average.

But even though Dee wasn't the kind of kid you'd ever think of offering a smoke to or going out to hit grounders with, there was still something kind of likable about him and I considered him basically okay. In fact, he was one of the favored few allowed in on the secret of Gram's supernatural once-a-month raisin cookies, and this month when the day rolled around he dropped by.

But this was no ordinary cookie day, because after a little polite munching and idle chitchat with Gram and me, Dee got up and without any fanfare walked over to the green chair where L.A. was sitting in her usual stony silence. No cookies for her. Just that thousand-yard stare in the general direction of the TV, like the rest of the world didn't exist. Dee leaned down so that his lips were by her ear and whispered something to her that lasted about as long as the Pledge of Allegiance. When he finished, they looked at each other for a couple of beats, then he lightly touched her arm, went back to his place on the couch and reached for another cookie.

As much as I wanted to know what he'd said to her, I knew I never would, recognizing this immediately as one of those little loose ends the universe was always dangling in front of me, especially where L.A. was concerned. I took the only sensible course, telling myself it probably wasn't that important anyway, and tossed it in the same mental bin where I kept questions like how many angels could dance on the head of a pin.

But then the next night when I was studying for my U.S. History test, flipping through the pages without finding what I needed to know, I said more or less to myself, 'What the hell's the Missouri Compromise?'

And without looking up, L.A. said, 'Missouri washes, Kansas dries.'

I almost jumped out of my socks. I watched her and waited for a while to see if there was going to be anything else, but she'd said all she was going to for that day. Still, I took it as a breakthrough. And sure enough, the next morning at breakfast she spontaneously asked me to pass the milk, and by the end of the day she was talking again, not exactly a mile a minute, but almost back to what passed for normal with her.

As far back as I could remember, Aunt Rachel had never stayed at home longer than a few hours at a time, meaning she constantly needed a babysitter for L.A. And since Gram never turned her down when it came to taking care of L.A., and did it for free, L.A. was always overnighting either at our house when I was still at home or later here at Gram's. So even though she and I were technically solo kids, we were used to each other, and now that we had no place left to fall we did what it took to get along, including wrangling out a morning bathroom schedule and getting the chores divided up more or less equally. I wouldn't call it wall-to-wall harmony, but we did manage to hammer out some kind of mutual deadlock on most points.

Then Gram started getting serious about L.A. going back to school. 'We simply have no alternative, dear,' she said in that law-of-nature tone of hers.

But L.A. shook her head and went silent again. It was their first major standoff, and it got me thinking about whether truant officers actually existed in reality or were just another parental figment like the tooth fairy. I'd never personally seen one or heard a reliable eye-witness report and wondered what the uniform would look like and whether they'd

13

carry special undersized handcuffs and night-sticks and arrive in small paddy wagons painted in cheerful colors.

But I wasn't truly worried, because of my experience with Gram's rock-solid belief in education and the unbreakable will behind it. There was also the simple reality of L.A. being a girl, with the kind of backhanded, diabolical intelligence that implies, plus her well-established history of dazzling teachers and showing me up in class. In other words, school was her natural turf, and I knew she couldn't stay away from it forever.

Sure enough, less than a week later she gave in, coming out of her room at seven-thirty that morning dressed and ready as I was about to leave. We hoofed it over to Lipscomb just like nothing abnormal had ever happened, and that was the end of her educational strike. This returned us to a certain level of regularity at Gram's, and by the time school was finally out for the year L.A. and I were back in the old groove, kicking around town like we always used to, like we owned the streets and summer was just for us.

I guess it's proof of how unreliable the so-called Sight was that it didn't tell me what was coming. I've wondered a thousand times how things might have turned out if it had only given me a heads-up about what was going to happen, and what I was going to do, before this summer was over.

3

Old Stories

It surprised me a little that Gram was actually in favor of L.A. and me running around loose.

'You both need the lollygagging,' was how she put it.

The way I took this was that if we stayed out of any kind of high-profile trouble and got home by suppertime we were in the clear. By now I had been living with Gram a long time — since back in junior high, in fact — so I knew what she considered high-profile trouble and how to steer clear of most of it. With L.A. this part could have been tricky, but because her special relationship with disaster was so mysterious and unpredictable that it was useless to worry about it, I decided to leave that whole issue to the universe's discretion and put it out of my mind.

Today we were on our way to Beauchamp's Liquors over on Lancaster to throw the football around and maybe practice some pass routes, and we were making our next-to-last stop behind the old Keogh place back under the big oaks and pecans across from Herndon Park. L.A. had gotten down on her hands and knees and was peering into the crawl space under the house.

'Here, Fangbaby,' she said, clicking her tongue softly. You could've fried meat on the street itself, but with the light breeze it was almost cool here in the deep shade at the back corner of the house. Across the street I heard the bobwhite chirp of the seesaw in the park, and for a second I caught the old-shoe smell of the crawl space. I held my football under one arm and watched L.A.

'I hear something,' she whispered, reaching into the pocket of her blue jeans, where I knew she had a fried chicken gizzard wrapped in foil.

All I could hear besides the seesaw was the *birdy-birdy-birdy* call of a cardinal somewhere in the bushes behind us.

'Most likely a rat,' I said.

But then Fangbaby materialized out of the darkness and edged forward: pink nose, long twitchy whiskers, bright green eyes watching L.A.'s hands carefully. There was no way you could mistake her for any other cat. She had a white head and neck, orange stripes the rest of the way back and only three legs, like somebody had thrown her together at the last minute out of spare parts. She was what Gram called feral, meaning everything scared her. One day she'd gotten half eaten by a couple of bird dogs from over on Alabama Street before I could kick them off her, and now she couldn't hunt to feed herself.

Trying to watch L.A. and the gizzard at the same time, she pickily sniffed it over the way cats do, like she hadn't completely made up her mind about it yet, then took it carefully in her teeth and went front-hopping back under Mr. Keogh's house, where she turned around and watched as we eased away.

16

'Bet she lets me touch her pretty soon,' L.A. said as we pushed back through our break in the hedge to the sidewalk. This part of Elmore was paved with concrete that had seen better days, the cracks mended with thick worms of dirty tar that divided its surface into a mystery map of some hot, unknown world. I glanced up at the high cirrus clouds streaking the sky and saw a silvery commuter plane slanting down toward Love Field across the Trinity. I wondered who was on it, where they'd been and what it would feel like to fly away.

'Probably bite the shit out of you,' I said, tossing the football up with one hand and catching it in the other, not really believing my own words. Wild cats are a tough sell, true, but L.A.'s magic with animals wasn't something you wanted to bet against.

'We'll see,' she said. She unwrapped a sucker, popped it into her mouth, then balled up the wrapper and threw it at me. We angled across the concrete to Beauchamp's, a one-story yellow crackerbox with a wide empty lot beside it that we used for a practice field.

An old green Fairlane two-door with the windows cranked all the way down sat tucked into the shade under the big-leafed catalpa at the back corner of the store. From the rearview mirror a little black shrunken head with stringy hair and stitched lips dangled like a piece of rotten fruit.

This meant our friend Froggy, the lady who owned the store, was here.

Inside, it was cool and dark, with a smoky

17

spilled-whiskey smell and neon beer signs in various colors shining down like alien moons. Froggy was perched on her stool by the register, where she sat all day smoking Chesterfields and watching the customers with those spooky pooched-out eyes of hers.

'Hi, Froggy,' said L.A.

'Junebug!' croaked Froggy. 'Jasper! Come on in here and get you a couple RCs. There's plenty in the cooler.' Probably not realizing we'd gladly stay anyway, she usually bribed us with stuff like this or maybe pickled eggs or chunks of fried boudain to hang around and listen to her yarns about three-day parties and gunshots in the dark and famous uncontrollable people she'd known, like Meyer Lansky and Ava Gardner and Ernest Hemingway. She seemed to use as many different words as Gram did but hers were quicker and edgier, going off like strings of firecrackers in her stories.

L.A. went into the cooler, came back with two cans of RC and handed me one. When it was later in the day we could sometimes get a beer out of Froggy if she was in a good mood and had a broken six-pack in the cooler, but I figured this time the sun was still too high for that. For some reason Gram wasn't happy about us coming down here, but we liked the place and naturally we liked Froggy because she took us seriously and seemed to get a kick out of talking to us. We brought the returnable bottles we found to her for the refunds because we enjoyed the way she always messed up her count and argued with us that we had a dollar's worth more than we really did. She also pretended not to notice the occasional Chesterfield we filched from her pack.

'What are you two shady characters up to today?' she said. Her hair was like orange steel wool and she wore heavy flashing rings on her little crooked fingers. Her nails were long and lacquered blood-red.

'Pass routes,' I said, sipping cola. I noticed a man working his way up the middle aisle behind us. He wore a Celtics muscle shirt and was kind of hollow-bellied, with big knuckly white hands that had freckles on their backs. He was looking at all the different kinds of liquor bottles, like he couldn't make up his mind whether he was a whiskey drinker or a gin man. Like he thought it didn't show when you're looking for a chance to steal something. I figured him for a bum, or maybe a transient, like Gram would probably say — anyway a white man without a job — but to me he didn't really seem very old for a bum in his sneakers and baseball cap turned backward. There was a big gap where his two upper front teeth should have been, and even though he had a mustache and a pointy Adam's apple and needed a shave, something about him reminded me of the kid on the cover of *Mad* magazine.

Froggy blasted off into a story about some hairy-eared husband she used to have.

L.A. said, 'I didn't know you were married, Froggy.'

'Why, hell, Junebug, one time or another I married about every knuckle-draggin' potlicker and swingin' dick in Texas,' she said. 'Sucked 'em all dry as gourds too!' She cackled herself off

19

into a long coughing fit.

When she was recovered enough she took another drag on her cigarette, then suddenly her look went hard as she watched the man coming up behind us. I turned around in time to see him raise both hands in surrender and disappear toward the back of the store. L.A. saw this too, and I could tell she was having one of her mysterious thoughts as she watched him go, but of course there was no telling what it was. Not then, anyway.

What I did know was that something significant, something I myself couldn't see, had just happened, and that we were a long way from being through with this guy.

4

Catches

After we finished the RCs and heard about how Froggy had caught one of her husbands, the guy with the hairy ears that she told the most stories about, in bed with her manicurist and shot off one of his thumbs with her derringer — 'Ain't what I meant to shoot off!' — we walked back out into the blazing sunlight.

When our eyes readjusted, we set up at the back of the lot with me at quarterback and L.A. at flanker, going out on my count for the timing pattern and playing it like she played everything, like her life plus the fate of the galaxy depended on it. She had just reached back on the run for a bad throw when, sure enough, the guy we'd seen inside came around the corner from the front of the store, stopped and smiled when he saw us. He stood there in the sun for a while, not even seeming to feel it, just smoking and watching us like somebody who didn't have anyplace in particular he needed to be.

And naturally with an audience on hand L.A. and I started hot-dogging a little, heat or no heat. It was one of those times when things come together for you. I was getting a lot on the ball and L.A., with the sucker in her mouth, was pulling the ratty old Wilson in from every kind of impossible angle. When I led her too much on

21

one route she dove and got the pass anyway, doing a tuck-and-roll as she hit the ground and coming up with the ball. The guy put his Camel between his lips and slowly applauded as L.A. raised her arms to the imaginary fans and bounced around in her victory dance. A trickle of red had started from the road rash on her elbow, but I knew she'd bleed out altogether before she'd show her pain to anybody, much less this character.

'Y'all pretty damn slick,' he said. 'Reckon you could hit me with one a them bullets?'

I looked at him for a second, then said, 'Sure, come on. You can run a post.'

'Post.' He nodded, moving the pack of cigarettes from the waist of his jeans to his sock. 'You got it, podner.' He leaned out over the line of scrimmage, dangling his arm down and shaking his fingers to loosen them up, exactly like a real wide-out.

'On *two*,' I said. Looking over the defensive set, I yelled, 'Hut! Two!' and slapped the ball. The guy dug out, juked left once and then cut in the afterburners, showing hellacious speed for an adult. He looked back after a dozen strides with the cigarette still in his mouth, and when I let the ball go he watched it spiral up, made a little adjustment to his route, got under it and cradled it in thirty-five yards downfield.

'Yeehawww!' he crowed, strutting like a rooster as he came back to the huddle.

'Where'd you learn to play?' I asked.

'Cornhole U.,' he said, leaning aside to spit. 'Down Huntsville.'

We ran a few more patterns and the guy only dropped one ball.

Finally he said, 'You troops wanta go out for a couple? See if I still got a wing here?'

'Sure, okay,' I said. L.A. looked down for a second and then nodded, dusting off her Levi's.

'Okay, y'all, this here's Niggers-Go-Long. Wide right,' he said with a strict look at each of us. 'We are fixin' to go down*town*.'

We positioned ourselves to his right, and when he called, 'Set!' then, 'Hut! Hut!' and slapped the ball, we hauled ass. I did a little juke of my own to the outside for show, giving L.A. just enough of a jump to beat me downfield. The guy put everything he had into it, grunting as he let the ball go. Running all-out, L.A. got her fingertips on it and pulled it down just before she ran out of field at the edge of the sidewalk.

'Hey-hey, Hall of Fame, man!' the guy yelled.

L.A. wrinkled her nose as she walked back with the ball. We lined up again, and I caught the next couple of passes. We kept running routes until all of us were sweaty and winded.

'Hoofuck in HAHH!' the guy said. 'Jeez, that was great!' He sidled over to me, dropped his cigarette and ground it out in the gravel with the toe of his sneaker. He flicked a couple of sweat drops from his eyebrow with his thumb. 'So hey, what's your name, podner?'

'James.'

'More like Biscuit,' said L.A. from the milk crate against the wall where she had sat to retie her sneaker. My father had called me that years

23

before because he said when I was little I'd do anything for a biscuit, and ever since then L.A. had taken an evil pleasure in doing the same, to the point that I didn't waste energy anymore resisting it. Concentrating on her shoelace, she didn't look up.

'Well, fuckin-A, Colonel Dogbiscuit, I presume.' A quick left-handed salute. 'Permission to address the colonel as Biscuit, sir?'

'Sure.'

'My name's Earl. Hot Earl, the Peckerwood Pearl.'

We shook hands. L.A. showed no interest.

'Where you from, Biscuitman?'

'Jacksboro.'

'Jacksboro. Good. Good town to be from.' He licked along the bottom of his mustache, still a little out of breath and looking thoughtful. 'How about Miss Sweetmeat there, she with you?'

'Yes sir,' I said, realizing I wasn't really answering the question the way he meant it. From the corner of my eye I saw L.A. picking at the seam of the football, frowning.

Earl twisted back over his shoulder toward L.A. 'What's your name, little sister?'

'Lee Ann,' she said. 'We're cousins. I'm not anybody's sister.' She tossed her stubborn ponytail and unwrapped another sucker, a green one this time.

'Well, okay, then,' said Earl, winking his red-rimmed eye at me. 'So, you got family in Jacksboro, Biscuit?'

'Not anymore. My dad's dead.'

For some reason this news seemed to lift

24

Earl's spirits a little. By now L.A. was moving away along the store wall, tossing the ball up against the yellow brick and catching the carom, paying no attention to us.

'And what about her?' Earl said. 'Where's she from?'

'She's from here,' I said. 'Is your name really Hot Earl?'

Earl was pulling at his lower lip. His mind was somewhere else. 'Say what?' he said. 'Oh. Yeah, Daddy used to call me that. When I was a kid.' He smirked. 'Called me other things when I got older.' Taking another look at L.A.

'You know, that ain't bad stuff there at all, Biscuit.' He took me farther aside, threw his arm over my shoulder and gave me a squeeze. 'You noticed the way she wears them little jeans like that?' he said softly. 'I know you did.'

'No sir,' I said, wondering if he saw the lie in my face.

'How-dee-doo,' said Earl. His lunch-meat-and-cigarette breath was getting a little hot. I tried to pull back, but he just held on to me and stayed right there in my face.

'Won't be long at all, young man like yourself be gettin' some ideas,' he said, jerking his head toward L.A., who had stopped tossing the ball and was checking out her other sneaker. 'Just lookie there.'

Earl obviously didn't know much about my head if he thought we were going to have to wait for me to get ideas. I looked at L.A. bending over in her white Fair Park T-shirt with the red Ferris wheel on the front.

25

'You can see them little titties real good, can't you?'

I flinched slightly because that's exactly where I'd been looking.

Earl got more conspiratorial. 'Listen, you guys like movies?' Talking now for L.A. to hear too.

'I guess,' I said.

'Some movies maybe,' said L.A., drifting our way.

'Fact is, I know how to make movies myself. Done made a bunch of 'em.'

I thought about this for a few seconds, beginning to show a little interest.

'Tell you what,' said Earl. 'I could put you two monkeys in a movie.' He pointed at us with two fingers.

L.A. was listening to Earl now, seeming to shake off some of her attitude.

'No way,' I said.

'Damn straight,' said Earl.

It occurred to me I had no idea how movies actually got made. But surely it was more than just a one-man operation.

'A *movie* movie, or just some home movie or something?' L.A. said, continuing to sidle in closer. She took the sucker out of her mouth, inspected it for a second, then put it back. Making up her mind.

'Nothin' but the real deal,' said Earl. 'True Hollywood all the way. Guys and gals doin' ever-what comes natural.'

L.A. kind of made a face, but Earl wasn't looking at her. He was looking right into my eyes.

'Well, so where do you make the movies?' I said.

'My place,' Earl said, beginning to look excited. 'Wanta check it out?'

Glancing at L.A., I saw a little glint come and go in her eye. She was always surprising me one way or another, but not today.

I said, 'Where's your place?'

'Right down the alley here,' he said. 'Over the garage.'

L.A. shrugged and gave me the *let's do it* look.

'Sure,' I said. 'Let's go.'

5

Showtime

Earl bowed and swept his arm through the air to usher us into the alley. He whistled quietly through his teeth and cracked his knuckles as we walked along. The tune sounded like maybe something of Fats Domino's. He dug his elbow into my ribs to demonstrate that we were into something good together.

We came to a leaning double garage with an unpainted apartment above it. The garage was empty and smelled of dust and old lawn mowers. Earl started us up the chancy-looking stairs on the outside wall, L.A. first, then me, then himself. He sang a line about somebody's baby being called *Shoo-Ra* under his breath as we climbed, and halfway up the stairs he leaned forward and bumped his forehead lightly against the small of my back.

On the landing at the top of the stairs L.A. looked down over the railing and then back to Earl, and when he nodded she opened the unlocked door. We all went in. There wasn't much light but I could see a small square wooden table, a chair and a bed with no sheets, just an army-green blanket and a bare pillow. The little kitchen had a gas stove and a short refrigerator on the counter, and between the bed and the table was a window with a roll-up shade pulled most of the way down. A million little stars of light sparked through the brown shade from the sun behind it. All over the floor, on the table and bed, everywhere, there were dozens of pint and half-pint empties, all rum bottles with the caps missing.

Mom's boyfriend Jack was a whiskey guy when he wasn't drinking beer. The bottles he brought it home in were generally bigger, and he got rid of them when they were empty. I watched L.A. pick up one of Earl's flasks and sniff it.

'What does this stuff taste like?' she said.

'Never mind that,' said Earl. 'Here, let me make you a place to sit.' He pushed the blanket and a couple of empty bottles back from the edge of the bed. He ignored L.A., but she came over and sat beside me anyway, rolling the football back and forth along her thigh. She looked around at the room.

'This is a nice place,' I said dishonestly. The bed smelled kind of like fish and wet dogs, which started a tickle of queasiness in my stomach. There was an old calendar on the wall over the table that showed a couple of naked boys on a wide stone porch with a lake and snowy mountains in the background.

'Oh, you ain't seen nothing yet,' said Earl, planting himself in the chair with his back to the door and his knee against mine.

'Where's your TV?' I said.

'Don't need that,' he said. 'Plenty to stay entertained with.' He scratched at the black spider tattooed inside his left forearm, then

29

pinched and pulled at his crotch. 'We can make our own fun.'

'How about the movie?' said L.A., cocking her head at him.

'Sure,' he said. 'But listen, you guys want something first? Maybe a little Thunderbird to start us off right?'

L.A. shook her head. I said, 'No, thanks.'

Earl seemed disappointed. He walked over and got a foil-wrapped package from the freezer compartment of the fridge and came back to sit down. He took a small twisted cigarette from the foil, used a Zippo to light it and took a long drag. He held the smoke down for a while and then kind of groaned it out through his mouth and nose. The smoke smelled like burning rope.

'Want a little hit?' he said, holding the cigarette out first to L.A., who shook her head again, then to me.

I took it and tried to draw on it as he had done, which made me cough. My eyes watered. Then I tried again and this time managed to control my cough reflex.

Earl had a tiny gob of white spit at each corner of his mouth. 'Maybe we ought to have a little game first,' he said. 'I can think of some good ones. Y'all know Yellow Dog?'

I drew in smoke again and had no trouble at all this time. Earl was looking back and forth from L.A. to me. He seemed anxious to get started.

L.A. twirled the football, shaking her head and glancing at Earl out of the corner of her eye, saying, 'That's pretty dumb.'

By now my stomach had somehow settled down completely, but I noticed the world was getting kind of cockeyed and I seemed to have dislocated my mind somehow. I began looking around Earl's place, smiling and wondering if he had any Twinkies.

'Hey, okay, you're right,' said Earl. 'That is dumb. I know what'd be good! Strip poker! How about that?'

I just couldn't stop grinning, but L.A. was serious as Saint Peter. So was Earl, only in a frustrated kind of way. By now he was beginning to pay more attention to L.A., and it seemed to bother him a lot that he couldn't get her interested in anything. He was sweating harder than ever, and he kept looking from her to me and back again as if he were running out of ideas. The time for Twinkies seemed to be about over, and I could sense L.A. silently changing gears.

Then Earl suddenly hunched forward and grabbed my leg, jamming his hand hard up along the inside of my thigh.

'Whoa,' I said.

In half a beat L.A. was up and over to the dirty window. She jerked the little doughnut on the string at the bottom of the shade and released it, letting it roll the rest of the way up, where it whapped around a few times before stopping. Outside, there were treetops in every direction, and among them a few green-shingled rooftops.

'Hey, look, Bis!' said L.A., pointing. 'You can see Gram's house from here!' She looked excitedly back at me.

'Hah? What?' said Earl, standing up, turning his head to the window, bending to take her line of sight.

'Right there,' said L.A. 'You can see Daddy's new truck and everything. He must be going back on day watch this week. You should see, Bis, it's like being up in a tree.' She turned and caught my eye. I looked out the window.

'Day watch?' said Earl. 'What day watch?' He stared at L.A., who just gazed innocently back at him. He scratched his neck, thinking. He walked over to the sink, then back to the window and looked out again.

'Isn't it neat?' said L.A.

Earl shivered. He was starting to get a constipated look. Finally he shook his head.

'Ratfuck,' he said under his breath, the gap in his teeth making it sound like 'ratpuck.'

L.A. was finally beginning to show some enjoyment, and of course I was still seeing the humor in everything, but now Earl seemed to be getting more miserable by the second.

'Double-dog ratpuck,' he said. He gave his head a last shake, took off his cap and ran his hand through his oily-looking dark blond hair. Then he moved over toward the door. 'That's it,' he said tiredly, reaching for the knob to open the door and let us out.

But L.A. said, 'Wait.'

He jerked his head around. 'Huh, what?'

'Did you forget about the movie, Mr. Earl?'

'Tell you what, little sister, I think we're gonna just forget that whole deal.'

32

L.A. was beginning to look a little put out with Earl. I heard the last of her sucker cracking between her teeth.

'But we had it all planned,' she said.

'Yeah, well, that's off now. Come on, let's go.'

'Not yet,' said L.A.

Earl's expression tightened. 'Hey,' he said. 'Don't bust my nuts, all right? Y'all need to just cut right on out of here.' He glanced at the window. 'Your Gram and them'll be waiting on you.'

'But it was all set,' said L.A., laying the stem of her sucker on the pile of Camel butts in the mayonnaise jar lid on Earl's table. 'All we wanted was a chance to make a little money. You know, like real actors.'

'Money?' squeaked Earl in disbelief.

L.A. watched him, looking sensible and composed. I cleared my throat. We heard the refrigerator compressor come on.

'For chrissake,' Earl said. It looked like the air was going out of him a little at a time. 'Money.'

'Daddy always says people should be reasonably compensated for their efforts,' L.A. recited. Her eyes, without actually moving, seemed to flicker slightly toward the window. Earl's did the same.

Which caused me to picture Uncle Cam, who as far as I knew never owned any kind of watch. Plus I would have considered it a toss-up whether it was more likely L.A. had ever in her life called him Daddy or the sun was going to stand still in the sky. I didn't think he had any theories about kids getting paid either, but then I admit I wasn't exactly clear in my head at the moment. I did know he didn't have a new truck and never showed up at Gram's house at all, any more than that was actually her house we were all thinking about outside Earl's window.

'I don't have no money, man,' Earl told L.A., putting his hand on his hip pocket and looking wearier than ever.

'Let me see,' she said in a friendly tone, setting the ball on the bed next to me and holding out her hand for his billfold. 'I bet you were gonna buy some more cigarettes and rum.'

Earl let out a long breath and handed over the billfold. L.A. dug around in it for a few seconds. Behind a thin leather flap she found a ten and two folded fives. She took both of the fives and looked up at Earl. 'This should be fair,' she said. 'Five for Biscuit and five for me.' She handed back the billfold. Earl just blinked sadly as he took it from her hand. L.A. picked up our ball, and we went to the door. She kind of straightened herself up and in her most serious voice said, 'Thank you very much, Mr. Earl. We do appreciate you.'

But Earl didn't answer, just kept staring at her.

A minute later we were down the steps and out to the alley. The sun was lower now and looked redder behind the trees, the world gradually squaring up and losing some of its funniness. Looking back, I saw Earl watching us through the crack of his door.

L.A. watched him watching us for a minute, then turned to me. 'He really should be more careful,' she said.

34

I shrugged. 'What's for dinner?'

'Meat loaf,' L.A. said as she tucked my five inside the waistband of my jeans. 'I know what you're thinking.'

'We've still got an hour. I can do both,' I said. 'You?'

She shrugged. 'Why not?'

We started off along the alley to head north on Lancaster toward the Dairy Delite, the idea of Twinkies losing some velocity but still bouncing around in my mind.

6

Unknowns

I woke up in a cold sweat, knowing for a definite fact that death was a teenage girl and that she had been standing silently by my bed during the night. For a few seconds I felt paralyzed, physically and mentally, smothering under the weight of my inability to protect Gram and L.A., or even myself, in case of attack.

Looking around me in the gray morning light, I couldn't see anything wrong or out of place, so I pulled on my Levi's and went to check the house. Gram was in the kitchen heating water for tea and humming along with the radio, which was quietly playing some old Bob Wills number. L.A. was asleep under her mound of pillows, snoring softly. One of the pillows lifted an inch or so and Jazzy peered sleepily out at me from underneath it.

There was nothing suspicious in any of the other rooms, and now that I was all the way awake I was beginning to forget why I needed to protect Gram and L.A. The house itself felt all right. I decided to see if a shower would get the last of the dreams off me. I stood under the hot spray until I was pretty sure I'd gotten all the benefit possible from it, then as I was drying off noticed the can of Colgate shaving cream I'd bought at the grocery store the week before and decided to shave, whether I needed it or not. Finishing with no nicks or scrapes to deal with and feeling a little smug about that, I dressed and went out to the kitchen. Cornflakes, orange juice, a little hot tea with honey, Gram shaking her head sadly at something in the paper.

She looked up at me, saying, 'What is that smell?'

'Aqua Velva.'

She leaned forward and inspected my cheeks and chin. 'I suggest lighter strokes, but more of them,' she said. 'Do you have a styptic pencil?'

'Yes ma'am.'

'Good. And if you must use that aftershave concoction, I'd suggest you be more sparing with it.' She sat back and eyed me. 'As a courtesy to others.'

'Okay.'

'Is there an occasion?'

'Yes ma'am. They're showing all the old Elvis movies at the Crest this week. I'm taking Diana.'

'Ah, the lovely Miss Chamfort,' Gram said, going back to her newspaper. 'I trust you will comport yourself as a gentleman.'

The way Gram said 'gentleman' made me think of a man in a tuxedo and top hat, with muttonchop sideburns and spats. But my instincts told me she really meant I should keep my hands strictly off Diana, an idea that made each and every molecule in my body vibrate with resistance.

I decided silence was my best bet.

After the movie, when Diana and I were walking home from the Crest, my usual random curiosities started to kick in. One of my theories was that getting to know a girl required understanding how she felt about rock stars, so I made up my mind to ask Diana what she thought of Elvis. I wasn't sure what I wanted to hear, though, and I ended up waiting until we'd walked all the way to Skillern's, where there was an *EXCITING SALE!* on trusses and mineral supplements, before I actually said anything, the whole time thinking about the different ways she might take the question. But since she and I were sort of going together — meaning we had dry-kissed a few times and I'd let her use my handkerchief during one of the weepy movies she dragged me to, after making sure it was clean, and then actually accepted it back afterward — I didn't see where I had any real choice. One of the main principles Gram was always trying to drum into my head was that knowledge is power, and I figured understanding Diana as completely as possible was my best shot at getting the relationship up to a higher level.

Diana had always been L.A.'s buddy, which made us acquaintances from way back, but most of that time she'd been just another skinny girl who thought boys had cooties. Then, before I knew it, the three of us were hanging out together, or maybe us and Dee, or Hubert Ferkin if he wasn't off somewhere jamming with some guitar accomplice of his. Then gradually it escalated from that to Diana and me actually going places on our own.

Lately I had really been warming up to this and therefore trying to maintain my poise, but it could sometimes be a challenge. In fact, the first time the two of us went out alone I strangled on my Coke to the point of practically coughing up my socks right there on the marble floor of the theater lobby. Diana slapped me on the back and offered me Kleenexes, which naturally did nothing to help my embarrassment, but I was hoping this one humiliation hadn't damaged the overall dignity of our relationship beyond repair.

Diana was fascinating in a lot of ways. For one thing, she tended to give people and animals semi-mysterious nicknames. She was satisfied with mine but she called Jazzy 'Muttkin,' which actually made sense, and her little brother Andrew 'Fubbit,' which as far as I could tell didn't. Neither did 'Porkchop' for her dad or 'Harpo' for L.A. If you asked her why she called them that, all you got was some loopy answer like, 'If I don't, who will?'

Sometimes she could be too intelligent for comfort. Once when we were watching a TV show about some kid whose parents had died, she started watching me instead of the show. I may have gotten something in my eye, but I definitely wasn't crying. Diana seemed to think I was, though, and she said, 'You're thinking about your mom and your dad, aren't you?'

I tried to clear my throat. 'I miss them,' I admitted.

Diana thought about that for a minute, finally saying, 'I don't think that's really true.'

I just looked at her.

'I think what you miss is how you think things used to be.'

In spite of her quirkiness Diana was intelligent and beautiful like L.A., but in almost everything else they were opposites, L.A. being sort of dark and solemn and never wasting any words, especially nowadays, whereas Diana was sunny and a lot of fun and of course always had something to say. She had easy-looking brownish blond hair that came down to her shoulders, and if you looked closely you could see a few light freckles scattered across her nose. Her eyes, which seemed to be smiling most of the time, were as big as L.A.'s but instead of almost black they were green with some blue mixed in, and little coppery specks around the edges.

Diana's relationship with L.A. was one you'd never expect to happen, but now that it existed it was impossible to imagine them not being friends. They were so close it didn't bother them to be apart.

One day when my nosiness got the best of me, I said, 'How'd you and L.A. get to be such good buds?'

Diana shrugged the way she did when she was being patient with me. 'She's the only girl I know who's smarter than I am.'

'Smarter than you?' I said. 'You're like a calculus magician or something — you're gonna be an architect.'

Another shrug.

I said, 'Doesn't really matter, I guess. You're both smarter than me, that's for sure.'

She took a long look at me, then said, 'You really believe that, don't you?'

I didn't answer, because I was still thinking

about how friendship works and where it comes from.

Diana said, 'Harpo could be anything she wanted. But that's not what I'm talking about.'

'So what are you talking about?'

'I guess it's the way you never have to explain anything to her. Or maybe because it's impossible to lie to her.'

'How do you know? You don't lie to her.'

Diana gave a little snort, saying, 'I've seen it tried.'

'Well, she trusts you, I know that,' I said. 'And she remembers stuff you said and did even way back when we were little kids.'

Diana thought about that for a minute. She said, 'I was a kid — I mean, I guess I still am — but I don't think she ever really was.'

This was a new idea for me, but I immediately felt the truth of it. I said, 'It's weird — I live with her but you know her better than I do.'

Diana didn't answer right away, and when she did there was a hint of sorrow in her voice.

'Maybe,' she said. 'But I think it's what I don't know that really matters.'

'I don't understand.'

'I know,' she said.

At this point I hadn't exactly lost track of the conversation, but I was a little preoccupied with pretending not to look down at Diana's legs. I knew better than to say so, but one of the reasons I liked her so much was the way she looked in her summer shorts, like the white ones she was wearing today. She had long legs for a girl, and I really enjoyed the way she'd cross one over the other when she and L.A. were sitting around talking. Once when I mentioned their smoothness to L.A. she looked at me in a way that left no doubt I'd just run the flag of my ignorance up the pole again.

'They'd be about as hairy as yours if she didn't shave them every week,' L.A. said, inflicting on me a whole new gallery of mental images I could have done without.

Anyway, the movie Diana and I had just seen had been about Elvis in the Army, and I was remembering his song about not having a wooden heart. But Diana apparently wasn't too impressed with him, which struck me as uncanny.

'Don't you think he's good-looking?' I said.

Without looking at me, she dug her elbow into my ribs. 'You tryna be funny, Biscuit?'

'Hey, really.'

'Sure I do. He used to be almost as pretty as Paul Newman. He's kinda fat now.'

'Okay, so how come you're not impressed?'

'When I see Elvis in a movie?'

Like we might run into him at Piggly Wiggly.

'Anywhere,' I said.

She thought about this for a while, which was another thing I liked about her — she actually considered things. She shook her hair back as we walked along and kind of frowned. Finally she said, 'Because he doesn't seem real.' She glanced at me. 'Like Batman.'

'The cartoon?' I asked, wanting to make sure she didn't mean the guy who played Batman on TV, who seemed entirely real to me because he looked exactly like my shop teacher from last year.

'Yeah, like that.'

She opened her little patent-leather purse and offered me a Certs, which lifted my heart because I knew it meant that when we got back to her house I was going to get another kiss to go with the two or three quickies I'd had during the movie. During one of these I'd opened one eye and seen several kids in the balcony leaning forward to look down at us, and, being unsure whether they thought we were doing it right, I hadn't known whether to be embarrassed or not.

Thinking about this, I noticed Diana smelled kind of spicy at the moment, halfway between the sudsy smell she came from the shower with and the salty one she had when she was sweaty. Wait, not sweaty, I corrected myself, remembering Gram's rule: horses sweat, men perspire, ladies glow.

'What about Aquaman?' I said when I got my thoughts back in order.

'Mackerel breath,' she said, popping a Certs into her own mouth.

'Know what'd be good?' I said. 'Living underwater like that — the cool and quiet and just plants waving in the current and a few fish going by. A whole 'nother universe.'

'I'd rather be in the clouds.'

'What, like an angel?'

'No, a fighter pilot.'

I visualized Diana diving on a MiG, cutting loose with the machine guns, the tip of her tongue out for concentration.

'Do they let girls fly jets?' I said.

'Probably not. But I'd do it if I could.'

'You'd really shoot down a Russian?'

'I didn't know you actually had to shoot anybody.'

'Fighters have to shoot *somebody* down. What else can they do?'

She chewed her lip and reflected. 'I'm not sure about that part,' she said. 'Maybe they'd just let me fly around and watch for troop movements and stuff.'

'Balloon'd be better,' I said, thinking of the silence.

Diana didn't say anything.

'Holy shit!' I yelled, jerking her into the doorway of Woolworth's, causing her to yip in protest. 'It's Jack!' I said, the words coming out in a kind of desperate hiss.

Getting it now, she followed my eyes. A block down the street Mom's boyfriend and another man, a thin bald guy in a black Harley T-shirt, were having a conversation on the sidewalk, looking almost like a mirage at this distance in the heat haze. Jack was dressed in starched jeans and a bright green cowboy shirt.

'Did he see you?' asked Diana. 'Is your mom around?'

As if hearing her, Jack looked our way. I felt a sensation like swallowing a chunk of ice. It sounds strange now, but in those days I actually thought I understood what danger was.

'I don't think so,' I said. 'C'mon.'

We ducked into the store, negotiated a couple of aisles, found the rear door and pushed through it. Walking along the alley toward the next street, I said, 'I can never figure out where the hell he's going to be.'

Diana took my arm. 'He wouldn't do anything to you out in public like this, would he?'

'I don't know,' I said.

'It'll be okay, Bis.' She squeezed my arm. 'Just stay away from him.'

Neither of us said anything else for a while. The locusts filled the atmosphere with their zinging. We walked along the hot sidewalk, in and out of the shade of the old maples, pecans and sycamores that overhung Madrid Street, the sections of concrete occasionally tilted one way or the other or cracked across to accommodate the thick roots knotted up under them. Diana had complained to me of having big feet, but I didn't see it that way at all. In fact I thought they looked pretty delicate next to mine, and I enjoyed the light little stepping sounds they made as she walked along beside me. She was about L.A.'s height, which meant she was almost eye to eye with me and could keep up without any trouble even when I was in a hurry.

I was still thinking about how all-around good it was to walk with Diana when we saw Colossians Odell. We weren't too far from the bus station and the Salvation Army, definitely still in bum country, so it was no surprise to run into him here. He was halfway down the alley with his red Radio Flyer wagon, looking into a trash can that stood against the wooden fence behind a gray-roofed house. When we caught up to him, he flinched at the sound of our footsteps.

45

We took his upwind side.

Diana said, 'Hi, Mr. Moog.'

'Why, how do,' he said when he saw who we were, giving us the whole keyboard of his smile. 'Proud to see you, miss, and you too, Mr. Biscuit. This a fine day the Lord done made us.'

Along with his big cream panama hat, Colossians was wearing his usual all-weather outfit today, baggy old khakis, brown tweed sports jacket with no collar or lapels, and his holey black high-top tennis shoes. I figured he'd have his rat Caruso in his pocket too because he never seemed to go anywhere without it.

Of all the walk-around people I knew, Colossians was my favorite, one of the reasons being the songs he sang. They always came without warning, Colossians just spreading his arms out wide, throwing his head back and letting go, singing up into the trees about the fell tide or the Negro jubilee or other strange, tragic things in a voice so huge, dark and unbelievably powerful that it made dogs bark a block away and started the squirrels chattering in the trees. Hearing it for the first time, Diana had blurted, 'Oh, geez,' and taken a quick step back before she could stop herself.

Gram had said, 'He must be a basso profundo. That's quite a rare voice — I wonder if he's been trained.'

Generally Colossians only sang in the middle of the afternoon.

'It's according to how much wine he's had,' L.A. had pronounced.

When she and I had first met him we asked

46

why he sang to the trees. He took off his panama, ran his long hand over the smooth dome of his eggplant-colored head and said, 'Now you darlin's, right there you done ast me the veriest thing I doesn't know.' Then he put the hat back on his head, scooped out his rat and held him up for us to admire. He told us the rat's Christian name was Caruso, but he usually called him Honey or Lagniappe.

'How'd you get him?' I asked.

'Outquick him down Salvation Army last year. Took a little gettin' used to, both sides, but we finest of frens now.'

Today Caruso let Diana stroke him between the ears with the tip of her finger, his whiskery nose twitching. Colossians took a raisin from a box he carried in his back pocket and gave it to Caruso, who sat on his haunches on Colossians' palm and held the raisin in his miniature hands like an ear of corn as he ate it. With the sun behind him, the veins glowed red in the pink shells of his ears. We messed with Caruso for a while longer, then when we were sure Colossians wasn't going to sing today we told him goodbye and walked on, me thinking about everything and nothing, Diana thinking no telling what, neither of us saying anything.

7

Beliefs

Eventually my thoughts brought me around to something I wanted to ask even though I wasn't really sure I wanted an answer. I said, 'Is Dr. Kepler out of the hospital yet?' Her house was on Fernwood, not far from here, but it had been at least two months now since I'd seen her.

'Yeah,' said Diana. 'Mom said she'd probably be able to stay at home for a few weeks, but then she'll have to come back to the hospital again.'

I didn't like the sound of that. It's not that I was necessarily that big a fan of old people other than Gram, it's just that Dr. Kepler was a nice lady. Even now that she didn't have hair anymore, I actually thought she was pretty in her own way, with her soft skin and dark eyes full of thoughts. She was so thin you could see her shoulder blades and the bones down her back, but I knew from listening to the talk on Wednesday nights when the book club met at Gram's that she was still a fighter. And I found out scientific people can have pretty strict opinions about literature.

'We are Vladimir and Estragon!' she hollered in her sketchy voice one night. She'd made everybody read *Waiting for Godot* even though it was really a play instead of a book, because it was her turn to choose. When she said what she did, the other women kind of stiffened. They were mostly Baptists and Methodists, but she was a physicist, which meant that even though they liked her, none of them except Gram really understood her thinking. Diana and I were playing double solitaire at the kitchen table just through the archway from the front room, where we could hear everything. L.A. was at the pool practicing dives, so I felt like it was up to me to listen on her behalf too.

'Explain, Joan,' Gram said, setting her glasses on the lamp table, where they focused two little half-moons of concentrated light on the white cloth. She picked up her cup of tea and took a sip.

'Such folly!' Dr. Kepler said. 'And such a fine metaphor for the entire human race — Vladimir and Estragon, waiting and talking, talking and waiting, endlessly deluding themselves and accomplishing nothing!'

'Well, I don't see how that applies,' said Mrs. McReady.

'Dear, dear,' Mrs. Pynchon said from the green chair. She was always a step or two ahead of Mrs. McReady, and she did see how it applied.

'I smell a theological debate,' said Gram. 'Why don't I get us some cookies?'

Dr. Kepler thumped her doilied chair arm weakly with her little fist and said, 'Only our deeds matter. Man must *do!*'

' . . . *be-doo-be-doo*,' sang Diana to herself as she turned over a card.

49

'Love matters,' said Mrs. Pynchon, setting her own cup aside. 'Hope. Certainly faith.'

'Ah, yes, there is the magic word,' Dr. Kepler said. 'Belief without evidence. With it we can justify anything.'

'How'd she ever get so smart?' Diana asked softly.

'Gram says they had different ideas about education in Europe.'

For me Dr. Kepler's words carried a certain kind of excitement even when they sounded discouraging, but Diana saw it a different way. 'That's too scary,' she said. Not many things troubled her, but she had a certain concern for the fate of her soul. When Mrs. Pynchon said, 'Nothing in this world means much to me if I can't believe in something greater than myself,' Diana nodded without looking up.

Dr. Kepler said, 'No one has brought us more unspeakable cruelty, more wars, more death, than the Prince of Peace and his peers with all their holy warriors. Perhaps we should look for greatness somewhere else.'

Diana shook her head unconsciously as she laid down the club five.

But now I was remembering when Dr. Kepler had come back from seeing her internist, the year after I came to live with Gram. Listening to her, Gram had said, 'Oh, Joan, no!'

'Now, Miriam, the last thing I will have is you saying there is some higher meaning in this, that I am being called home to Jesus and we will understand it all in the sweet bye and bye, or any of that happy nonsense.'

'But Joan,' Gram had said, 'is there no comfort for you?'

'My comfort shall be in seeing to the completeness of my life and trying to be worthy of my friends.'

Gram had hugged her and sniffled, and, watching from the hall, I'd felt a chill that seemed to go all the way down to the atoms in my bones.

Now I thought of Colossians, who had no problem believing in things greater than himself because, on account of being off-and-on insane, he seemed to hear from them on a regular basis. I was the one who had introduced him to Dr. Kepler, and they had hit it off in spite of the different things they thought were real. She hired him to do some yard work, but she seemed to enjoy his singing in the same amazed way that I did. She said that in Europe before the war he might have been a luminary of the continental operatic stage, which I took to mean he could have been a singing star. But she said he wouldn't be the headliner very often because, always and everywhere, the best parts were written for the tenors.

'But what a splendid villain he might have made!' she said.

One day Dr. Kepler, in her straw sun hat and gardening gloves, was watching Colossians at work when L.A. and I arrived to deliver Dr. Kepler a loaf of dill bread Gram had baked for her. Colossians was planting bulbs in the front garden and I got interested in the process and left the bread presentation to L.A. Watching him

51

on his knees in the soft, dark earth, smoothly turning aside a thick curl of the soil with his trowel, slipping a bulb from the sack beside him under it and moving on to plant the next bulb with no waste motion, his big hands barely seeming to move, I realized for the first time how much more there was to raising flowers than just throwing out a few seeds, how if you wanted to do it right it was a matter not only of understanding but of somehow joining with the soil and in a way befriending it.

'Perennials are so wonderfully appealing,' said Dr. Kepler. 'Something that will come again each year, almost a way of going on oneself.'

'These amaryllis and hyacinth do you proud, missus. They faces be gloryin' the Lord ever spring of the world.'

'Let them glorify your strong hand, Colossians — there is nothing in the sky I wish to exalt.'

'Why, land sakes, missus, you not believin' on the good Lord?'

'I believe in what I know,' she said. 'I know the damned gangsters burned up my mother and my father and my three sisters in big ovens, and I know the smoke went away into the sky. There must have been a great deal of it; maybe the good Lord saw it. Now I am only smoke that is waiting its turn to go up to the sky, and soon enough the gangsters will have their way with me too. Their bones, and the murderers who walk among us, can inherit the earth without any further protest from me.'

I doubted that Colossians knew much about the smoke or the ovens, but he took off his hat, wiped his head with his bandanna and smiled at us all with a drop of sweat hanging like a jewel from the end of his nose. 'Well, that be all right, I reckon,' he said. 'Expect He go on try to keep a good watch on us just the same.'

But it wasn't the Lord I saw keeping watch at my bedside again that night. It was the girl who was death.

Doo-be-doo-be-doo, she sang softly from her cold blue mouth.

8

Times

The last time I ever rode my bicycle was the day I learned something important about what the word *home* really means. Or maybe what it doesn't mean.

I had been thinking more and more about L.A., trying to make sense of her being here and figure out what had happened to make her leave home. Gram must have wondered too, but I guess we both had our reasons for not asking. With me it was not wanting to piss L.A. off, along with the absolute certainty that she'd never tell me anything she didn't want me to know anyway. And even though I told myself L.A.'s arrival had nothing to do with it, my night visitor had shown up right after L.A. had, and the feeling of connection wouldn't go away. I finally decided that if I was ever going to have any peace I needed to know.

But that's where I hit the wall. I didn't think Aunt Rachel or Uncle Cam would tell me anything, at least not anything I could be sure was true. Which didn't leave many possibilities. The only source I could think of who might know something and be willing to tell me was Mom, but that didn't simplify things much because of all the pitfalls talking to her could involve.

What finally decided it for me was a miracle. Maybe that isn't the right word for it, but then I can't think of a better one. You can judge for yourself.

The day it happened started with rain, which began coming down in earnest while L.A. and I were having breakfast with Gram at the kitchen table. It was a cornflakes morning, and along with her cereal, which she was mainly ignoring, L.A. was taking occasional sips of the coffee Gram had fixed for her — half a cup of fresh-brewed Folgers filled the rest of the way up with milk and sweetened with a spoonful of brown sugar. Like always at this time of day, her eyes were wide and blank and her hair had what Gram called that freshly dynamited look. Jazzy was curled up asleep by her feet.

Since the municipal pool was open this morning and it was an Adult Day — which meant they only allowed swimmers old enough for you to have a reasonable hope they wouldn't pee in the water — this was supposed to be a swimming day for us. But when I heard the rain and wind and noticed how dark it was getting outside, I was forced to start thinking in terms of fallback plans. With a frog-strangler like this in the morning, a lot of times it's just the beginning of a whole day of start-and-stop rain, which would mean the pool would be closed on account of the possibility of lightning.

Gram looked out the window for a minute and said, 'Now, where was all this last month when we needed it?' She set her coffee cup down in front of her.

L.A. didn't speak, just stirred her cereal around, rubbed her nose with the heel of her hand and yawned. She was never in a hurry to eat anything, especially in the morning. On the other hand, I was into my second bowl of flakes with no loss of momentum as I listened to the rain roar and rattle outside. By now it was almost dark as night out there. I didn't know why, but I enjoyed the sound of the rain. Regardless of how bad they could sometimes screw up your plans, I liked rainy days almost as much as rainy nights.

Then, while I was gazing absentmindedly at something on the back of Gram's newspaper about a teen reported missing, and just as L.A. was finally getting around to taking a bite of cornflakes, I noticed out of the corner of my eye that her hair was sticking almost straight out from her head. Even the fuzz on the backs of her arms had begun to stand up. Feeling a tickle on my own skin, I looked at my arms and at Gram and saw the same thing happening to us. Jazzy's head came up.

'Well, my land,' Gram said, trying to smooth down her hair. I noticed a smell in the air that reminded me of a hot radio, and then the entire world seemed to explode with something completely beyond sound — like a gigantic fist somehow slamming into me from all directions at once. The accompanying flash half blinded me. The lights went out and the dishes went on rattling for a couple of seconds.

'Good heavens!' said Gram. 'I think it must have struck the old sycamore.'

I guess Jazzy had jumped into L.A.'s lap,

because now she was peeking up at me over the edge of the table between L.A.'s arms, trembling and making small cooing noises, like maybe the explosion was my doing and she was begging for mercy. You could see the whites of her eyes. I shook my head and put my hands over my ears. I had a problem with loud noises anyway, and this one had started millions of little bells ringing in my head.

L.A., who was damn sure wide awake now, said, 'Is there gonna be a fire?' She had a death grip on her spoon, her knuckles white.

'I don't think so, honey,' said Gram. 'Not in this much rain.'

We sat in the semidark for what seemed like a long time, the noise of the rain wrapped around us like a weightless blanket. You never seem to notice how much a house is doing until it stops, and it felt a little strange with nothing running inside. But after a while we began to hear something different out there, not just the rain anymore but something else falling, something solider than water but not as hard as hail. We all looked at each other.

'I guess we'd better just make sure it didn't actually hit the house,' said Gram, pushing her cup away. She patted Jazzy's head and gave L.A. a reassuring smile as she got up, then went over to the window and bent to look out and up at the tree.

I went and looked too. Outside the window just a few feet away we could see that the big speckled trunk of the sycamore had a steaming rip down its side, with long jagged splinters sticking out and lying around on the ground. And along with the splinters there were also hundreds of fish, little silver ones, all the same size, quivering and flipping on the grass everywhere I looked.

For once in her life, Gram was speechless.

'Hey, L.A.,' I yelled. 'Look at this!'

As I said this the lights and the fan on the counter came back on. The toaster was upside down and thoroughly dead, and the stove clock stayed locked on 8:04 from then on, but otherwise the workings of the house seemed to take up again exactly where they'd left off.

L.A. got up from her chair and put Jazzy down into her box at the end of the counter. She looked out the window next to Gram and me, then ran to the cabinet under the sink and got an empty mayonnaise jar. She banged out the front door about half a second later, and I ran out behind her.

The fish were everywhere, all over the street, in flower beds, even on the roofs of the cars and houses. The rain had almost stopped, but a few fish were still plopping down from the trees.

'This is crazy, Biscuit!' said L.A., looking around the yard and up at the sky. 'Where'd they come from?'

I couldn't think of anything to say. I tried to imagine how far the fish could fall and still be undamaged like this. L.A. knelt down and touched one that was still twitching on the grass, then sniffed the tip of her finger and licked it. 'It's salty,' she said.

She began picking up fish from the lawn and

dropping them into the jar. When she had five or six, she went to the spigot and filled the jar with water. The fish seemed perfectly normal to me, darting around behind the glass like magnified eyes.

Gram was standing on the porch holding a dish towel, her mouth open and her eyes blinking as she looked around at all the fish. 'Lord, Lord,' she said.

A blue jay slanted down from a tree overhanging the street, lit on the wet sidewalk and cocked his eye at one of the fish. Then he grabbed it in his beak and flapped back up into the tree. Next door, Mrs. McReady's cat Beth stuck her head out from under the porch.

'Pharaoh, let my people go!' Gram said.

Jazzy looked out from behind her ankles on one side, then the other. The sky was getting lighter by the minute, the clouds beginning to thin and break up. Gram walked across the yard with her arms held out at her sides, laughing and shaking her head. Jazzy followed her closely.

'Minnows from heaven!' Gram said.

Several nuns had gathered in front of St. Mary's and were whispering to each other and crossing themselves, and all along Harlandale people were coming out of their houses, resting their hands on their hips, looking up into the trees and turning their faces to the clearing sky. There was a faint smell of iodine in the air.

Gram stopped beside L.A. and reached for the jar with a puzzled expression. 'Why, I know what these are,' she said. 'I saw fish like these out in Carolina when I was a girl. They're alewives.

They come from the sea.' She held the jar up for a better look.

By this time you could tell there was something wrong with the fish. They seemed to be swimming desperately but barely getting anywhere in the water. As we watched, one of them rotated slowly over onto its back and floated to the top of the jar.

'Hey,' said L.A. She peered into the jar and shook it once. Another fish floated up, and in a few minutes they were all belly-up at the surface of the water. She reached into the jar to poke at the fish with her finger, but they were dead.

'They can't survive in fresh water,' said Gram.

Jazzy transferred from Gram to L.A., who was taking another turn around the yard. They seemed to be trying to inspect each fish individually.

I was through examining the blasted sycamore and was looking at Beth as she crouched on the edge of Mrs. McReady's driveway, eating the small fish. She took each one by the head with her teeth, shook it, growled, then chewed and smacked at it until finally the tail disappeared into her mouth, the whole time watching me with her yellow eyes. As if a million years had disappeared and I was suddenly back in a time where humans didn't belong.

Taking another look around, I decided to take all this as a sign. I made up my mind to go over to Mom's house and tell her about the fishfall, which would give me a chance to find out what she knew about L.A. I went inside and tore off a strip of tinfoil from the box in the cupboard, wrapped two of the fish in it and put them in my pocket.

I didn't have a regular driver's license yet, but that wouldn't have made any difference. Gram would never have let me take the car for what I was planning to do even if I had had ten licenses.

Which left my bicycle. I went around to the garage to get it, expecting bad news, since in my experience anytime you took your eyes off a bicycle for ten seconds disintegration set in — tires went flat, spokes came loose, the chain jumped the sprocket or whatever. But it turned out the bike's tires were hard and everything else about it seemed to be in working order.

I may even have gotten the demented idea this was my lucky day.

As I pushed the bike out of the garage under the dripping trees, Gram said, 'Where to, dear?'

'Mom's,' I said. The blue jay screamed its thin power-saw call.

L.A. frowned and found a sprig of grass that needed stomping.

Gram smoothed the front of her dress, looked down at the ground for a second and said, 'All right. You be careful crossing Lancaster, James.'

Last year some kid riding a bicycle, a kid quite a bit younger than me, had somehow managed to get himself torn completely in half by a watermelon truck over there, and now Gram seemed plagued with the notion that I was going to be next. It might have been false confidence on my part, but I had no fear of produce trucks. The trolleys that used to run downtown, with all that blue electricity groaning and snapping from

61

their overhead power arms, seemed more menacing to me.

But the real problem occupying my mind at the moment was the time. It seemed to me that right now I had a better than even chance of finding Mom at home alone, which was the best-case scenario unless you counted things like Jack going to prison for life or choking on his own tongue, to name just a couple of outcomes that I knew for a fact it did no good to pray for. Mom being there alone would leave open the prospect of having a Coke with her, showing her the fish and telling her the whole story of what had happened. The next best possibility would include both of them being there but with Jack sober and cutting the grass or working in the garage, which would allow me to back away before I was seen. Of course, there were plenty of other ways it could play out, but somehow I managed to steer my thoughts away from those. One more illustration of the difference between being intelligent and being smart.

As I rounded the corner of Elmore a few cold fat drops were still falling from the trees, and you could see from the leaves and branches in the street and the steam rising off the pavement where the sun struck it that it had rained hard here too, but I didn't see any more fish. There was almost no traffic and I was making pretty good time, thinking of the fish and dreaming up ways to describe the episode to Mom, when the dog came at me.

I knew from previous trips through the neighborhood that he was the worst kind, a biter instead of a barker, fairly fast and persistent, staying after you longer than most dogs considered necessary. Just an all-around shit of a dog. He was reddish and funny-looking, like maybe a dachshund-collie mix or something, with semi-floppy ears that he laid back tight when he chased me. Jack, who wasn't a big guy himself, had heard me talking about the dog one day and with a hard grin said, 'Collie and dash hound, huh?' A wink at Mom. 'Somebody must of put his daddy up to it.'

I had the advantage of the grade on this block, and, wanting to build as much speed as possible for the chase itself, I got up on the pedals for leverage as the dog was angling across his yard. He was pumping too, his head driving up and down and his tongue swinging out at the side of his mouth. His hind claws threw up chunks of grass behind him as he ran. When he caught up with me in the middle of the block I put my near foot up on the handlebar and with my off leg tried to keep up a rhythm on the pedal, really punching on the downstroke and trying not to kill my speed by wobbling. I could hear the dog's claws on the pavement and the sound of his breath beside me, but he was fairly stupid for a bad dog and he did what he always did — kept snapping at the pedal, even though my foot wasn't there.

This time it turned out worse than usual for him. The pedal happened to catch him under the chin on an upswing, and I heard a loud clack and a couple of yelps as the dog broke off the chase. I looked back and saw him shake his head and make chewing motions with his lips pulled back as if he had peanut butter in his mouth. Pedaling away, I hooted at him and pumped my fist in the air, full of victory and knowing now what a winning streak I was on.

9

Tries

I was still replaying the chase in my mind as I coasted around the curve of Alameda and into Mom's driveway under the old magnolia. The storm must have been a strange one in other ways than being full of fish, because it obviously hadn't rained here at all.

The house was painted white now instead of the light yellow it had been when I lived in it, and the windows were framed by new green shutters with curved shapes cut into them. The holly bushes that grew in front and along the side of the house looked the same, and so did the two middle-sized chinaberries in the front yard, but the skinny poplar Mom had planted beside the house the year we moved here seemed quite a bit bigger than I remembered it. At one end of the porch was a wide clay pot planted with dry-looking red geraniums. There was a vacant feeling in the air, but I couldn't see the garage around the corner toward the back of the house, so I wasn't sure if anyone was home or not. I leaned the bike against the porch rail and climbed the steps to the front door.

Knocking twice, I called, 'Mom? Hello?' but there was no answer, so I opened the door and stepped inside. I could smell old smoke from Mom's cigarettes and the little cigars Jack smoked, and fried bacon from earlier that morning.

The sense of emptiness continued in here, but I didn't entirely trust it. Houses usually feel different when people are in them, no matter how quiet the people are, but somehow I couldn't tell about this one anymore. Since Jack had moved in the second year after Dad died and we had moved up to Dallas from Jacksboro, I was a stranger here and the house no longer really made sense to me.

I looked down the hall toward what used to be my bedroom but was now Jack's weight room and wondered if any of my stuff was still in there. I visualized the red chili-pepper lamp I'd left on the dresser and my dartboard and the Cowboys poster on the inside of the door. Thinking about this caused a weird feeling in my chest, and I made up my mind that if it turned out there was nobody here I'd go in there and see if there was anything I could salvage. Maybe bust something of Jack's while I was at it. I called to Mom again but still got no answer.

I walked on into the kitchen. There were dishes drying in the rack and next to that on the white-tiled counter I saw a glass ashtray with three Kool butts in it. Each one had Mom's bright red lipstick on the filter and had been stubbed out half smoked. Reasoning back from that, I knew Mom had gotten up first and had a cup of coffee while she read the *Morning News*. Then she'd have made breakfast and eaten with Jack and after that cleared the table, washed the dishes and had another cup of coffee over the puzzle page before leaving the house. In my mind I could see her setting the ashtray beside the drain rack on her way out the back door, saying, 'I'll wash you when I get back.'

In the living room I noticed the dark green cloth-bound book with a little brass latch on it lying on the side table next to the old blue easy chair where Mom always sat. Her diary. She was the only person I had ever known who kept one, and she had always been faithful about it. It wasn't like her to leave it out in the open like this, but there it was. I stood for a while having a silent argument with my conscience, then walked over to pick it up. The house still felt empty. I carried the diary back into the kitchen where the light was better, intending to sit at the table and maybe read the pages dated around the time L.A. showed up on Gram's porch.

I had just found the right date and caught a glimpse of the words

. . . absolutely gave me the creeps . . .

when there was a loud rap behind me. I flinched like the thief I knew I was and looked around. Of course it was Jack. He must have whacked his can of Schlitz down onto the counter, his trademark move, closing in silently and then making some loud noise to scare the shit out of you. Now he walked around the table and was lowering his butt lightly into a chair across from me, a tense-looking guy with quick movements and a lot of dark hair on his chest and eyes that had a funny jitter in them.

'The prodigal son,' he said as he leaned back in his chair and looked at me. 'Your mama's not here.'

'Yes sir,' I said.

'Grocery shopping or something,' he said, taking a swallow from the can. He reached across to take the diary from my hands, closed it with a snap and dropped it on the table in front of him.

'Yes sir,' I said again, thinking about Jack's job repossessing cars and wondering why I couldn't for chrissake get it straight when he was going to be here and when he wasn't.

'Left me here by myself in the peace and quiet,' he said.

He was wearing only sneakers and track shorts and one of those undershirts without sleeves or a neck, just straps over his shoulders. His armpits were shaved.

'What brings you over here to our little domicile, Jim? Leah's mama kick you out too?'

I realized that the whites of his eyes weren't really white but light pink, with little veins in them that branched like red lightning. I thought of Caruso's ears. Jack looked out the window as he tipped the can up and I could hear the thumping sounds in his throat as he swallowed.

'No sir,' I said, feeling jammed, like the time in Jacksboro when I was four and somebody's big orange dog had come roaring out at me from behind a hedge. I'd been frozen in my tracks, completely unable to move, which I guess was a good thing because the animal had just stood in front of me barking for a while and then given up and gone away, leaving me stuck there on the sidewalk like a wad of gum.

'Guess I'll go on back to Gram's,' I said, edging toward the door.

'Naw,' said Jack. 'Stick around.' He stood up and took a long last swallow from the beer can, then tossed it into the sink, where it ricocheted around and shot some foam up into the air. I'd seen him do this before, and it wasn't a good sign.

'Yes sir,' I said.

Jack rolled his shoulders and sucked his teeth. 'C'mon,' he said, 'let's work out a little.' He motioned me toward the back yard, where he had set up a speed bag outside the toolshed.

I followed him out the back door, wondering if there was any chance of somebody else showing up. Jack told everybody he'd been a Golden Gloves welterweight, and he watched all the fights on television and explained everything the fighters did wrong. He liked practicing his skills.

We got to the shed and he brought out two pairs of boxing gloves. 'You can have the light ones,' he said.

As I was pulling on the cracked and faded red gloves, Jack said, 'What are you — about as tall as me now? Damn near.' He popped his gloves together. 'Looks like you're gonna have your old man's shoulders too. We'll just see what you got.'

I stood there with my hands at my waist while Jack started to dance around me. Usually he did this for a while before he got serious about throwing punches. But he had his own gloves up and was bobbing and weaving. 'Stick and move!' he said, bringing in a left hook to the side of my head that staggered me a little, then skipping away.

This was not my first boxing lesson with Jack, and I knew there was nothing to gain by not trying to defend myself. I got my hands up and tried to watch his shoulders. I could sometimes slip a shot if I caught his head fake and the slight push of his left shoulder just before he threw the right.

'Really shoulda gone pro,' he said, bouncing and feinting. 'Show all them niggers a thing or two.' He blew out his breath and shook his head.

I kept my gloves up and watched him. He had a tendency to come in hard after he said something like this, and I wanted to be ready.

But I wasn't ready enough. He floated in with a straight right, and I sat down hard. Stinging tears tried to come up in my eyes but as I got up I brushed them away, trying to make it look like I was just swiping at my nose.

'Make a man out of you yet,' Jack said. 'Here, come on in and take your best shot.' He dropped his guard and let his hands hang at his sides, counting on reaction speed to keep from being hit.

I knew things were going to get worse now but there was no good way to go from here, so I got my chin down and my elbows in and moved forward. Jack was just watching me with a little smile, waving me in.

Then something suddenly changed in me. Everything went red and started happening in slow motion, the universe shrinking down to a bloody target with Jack's grinning face right in

70

the center of the bull's-eye. I felt weightless and unreal. Without thinking about it or even knowing I was going to do it, I gave him my best imitation of his own head-and-shoulder fake and threw my right hand as hard as I could. I wanted the punch to land, wanted to destroy that face more than I'd ever wanted anything in my life.

And I did nail him. His head snapped backward and the jolt shot up along my arm to my shoulder and neck as he staggered a couple of steps to the side but didn't quite go down.

It was absolutely the best punch I could possibly hope to throw, much less land, but there was Jack, still on his feet. He got his balance back and shook his head again. A trickle of blood started down from one nostril toward his mouth. As I looked at him, things began to change back to their normal colors and I tried to catch my breath. Jack gave me a tight smile and said, 'Pretty good shot.' But he was white around the lips and a muscle roped up in his jaw.

He started dancing on his toes again, this time watching me more carefully. He did a little shuffle and sidestep and from the other end of the universe I heard Mom saying, 'What the hell'd you do to him this time, Jack?'

I opened my eyes and tried to get up but couldn't. Mom's voice echoed around in my head, not seeming to have anything to do with me. She was kneeling beside me, bending down to inspect my face. I could smell her cigarette and her flowery perfume as she put her hand on the grass by my head to balance herself. Above her the light coming through the leaves moved and sparkled in her golden-brown hair.

She looked back at Jack, who was lighting a cigar. His gloves were nowhere in sight. 'For chrissake, his eye is swollen almost shut!' she said.

'Just sparring a little,' he said. 'He walked into one is all. He's fine.' He looked at me. 'Arncha, Jim?'

Nothing seemed to have any connection with anything else.

'Whagga,' I said.

Mom helped me sit up. My gloves were gone.

'Oh, baby,' said Mom. 'You're just a mess. Here, let me clean up your face a little.' Shaking back her hair, she took a tissue from her purse and wiped blood and sweat away from my mouth and the side of my nose. It felt like my arms and legs belonged to somebody who wasn't here at the moment.

'Guess I coldcocked him pretty good at that,' Jack said, taking a drag from his small cigar. 'Need to learn to hold back a little more.'

'Hey, Mom,' I finally managed to get out, my tongue slow and thick. 'We're boxin'.'

'Yeah, I know, hon.' She gave Jack another look. 'Jack's quite the athlete. Are you okay now?'

'Sure,' I said, swallowing the blood in my mouth.

Jack said, 'Where you been, sugar?'

'Don't start, Jack,' Mom said. She pulled me up.

'Just saying,' Jack said. 'Reasonable question to ask, man wants to know where his lady's been.'

He tilted his head to pop his neck. 'You telling me there's something wrong with that?'

I managed to stand up. 'Go onna Gram's now,' I said to the ground.

'Oh, honey, you must've wondered where your mama was when you needed her, didn't you?' Mom said, kissing me on the cheek.

'No ma'am,' I said.

She didn't say anything else. She stood by Jack as I stumbled back toward the driveway to go around front and get my bicycle.

'I'm just asking you what's wrong with the question,' I heard Jack say before the corner of the house came between us.

On my way back to Gram's I threw the fish to the dog and pedaled away as he snuffled at them in the gutter.

10

Finger-pointing

As I walked in the front door I saw L.A. standing with her back to me on the little blue granny rug in front of the record player, listening to Sam Cooke with her eyes closed and her hands in the back pockets of her jeans, moving slightly with the music: 'Wonderful World.'

Her not turning around meant that as always she knew it was me who'd come in. Gram was in the kitchen at the sink and the house smelled of roasting chicken, rare for us in the summertime and one of my all-time favorites. But I had no appetite and wasn't looking forward to explaining to Gram and L.A. what had happened to my face. On top of that, my head felt funny.

Coming back from Mom's I'd stopped to throw up, and I started toward the bathroom now to brush my teeth and splash some water on my face. But before I got there the floor tilted up at me and I was watching small fish that jumped in every direction and became silvery coins rolling away in the dark. There were millions of them. I was desperate to keep them from getting away but no matter how hard I tried I couldn't get my hands on even one.

Then I realized that somewhere some kid was calling for his mother in a wailing voice that rose and fell in a weird, tragic rhythm. All around me

74

the red light was back, except this time it was flaring on and off and back on again. Everything shifted and bounced and roared. I was going somewhere in a hurry. L.A.'s girl-breath was in my face and I heard her yelling at me down a long echoing tunnel, 'Be all right, Biscuit!' She was nose to nose with me, gripping me by the ears. 'You hear me?' she screamed. '*You gotta be all right!*'

There was more noise and movement and different colored lights and pretty soon somebody else's breath, a man's this time, and a moving white light in my eyes.

'Okay,' said a masculine voice. 'I'd call that equal and reactive. Tracking looks pretty normal, conjunctivae nice and pink, no apparent fractures.' A long-fingered hand clipped the light back into the pocket of a short-sleeved green doctor shirt. 'Can you hear me okay, tiger?'

'Uh-huh,' I said.

'I'm Dr. Colvin. What's your name?'

'Biscuit.'

'Biscuit, huh?' He looked at Gram, who nodded.

'His father called him that,' she said.

'What's your last name, Biscuit?' asked the doctor.

'Bonham.'

'Who was it you wanted to kill?'

'What?'

'You were talking about killing somebody. Sounded pretty serious about it too.'

'I don't know,' I said. But of course I did, and a wave of angry memories broke over me, followed by a chilling remorse that paralyzed my tongue and drenched me with shame.

He raised his hand, saying, 'Okay, how many fingers do you see, Biscuit?'

I focused my eyes. 'Two,' I said.

'Stick out your tongue for me,' the doctor said. I did. 'Feel this?' he asked, running his fingernail down one side of my face and then the other.

'Uh-huh.'

He took off my shoes and socks and scratched the bottoms of my feet with his pen, seeming to be very interested in how my toes reacted.

'Can you sit up for me, please?'

'Yes sir.' As he was helping me up I noticed he smelled like Lifebuoy soap.

He looked at my eyes again and said, 'I need to see if you can keep your balance now, Biscuit.' Behind him I could see L.A. and Gram and a nurse with black hair and a little pointed white hat.

I stood up. The floor looked kind of far off.

'Any dizziness? Sick to your stomach?'

'No sir.'

'How about your noggin — that hurt?'

'Yes sir.'

'Where?'

'All over.'

He had me turn and tilt my head and close my eyes and touch my nose and tell him what day it was. 'Can you smell anything?' he said.

'Yes sir. It smells like alcohol in here.'

'Anything else?'

'You smell clean.'

He smiled at me and said to the nurse,

'Cranials are intact and we don't seem to have any decerebration or anything going on with the brain stem. Level of consciousness is continuing to come up. I don't think we're dealing with any kind of acute bleed here but let's go ahead and get a skull series anyway, just to be on the safe side.' He looked back at me. 'How'd this happen to you, Biscuit?'

'Uncle Jack did it!' blurted L.A. There was a hot look in her eyes as everyone turned to her. She put her hands in her pockets and looked away.

'We were boxing,' I said.

'That'd be you and Uncle Jack?' said the doctor with a glance back at L.A. She nodded. I nodded too but immediately stopped myself and put a hand on my head to settle the pain.

'So the two of you, you and Uncle Jack, were boxing and you happened to get knocked out. That right?'

'Yes sir.'

'Any idea how long you were out?'

'No sir. My gloves were off when I came to. Mom was home.'

Dr. Colvin didn't seem to like the sound of that at all. He peeled back my eyelid for another look, saying, 'And Jack, did he do anything to help you, call for help or anything?'

'No sir, I don't think so.'

The doctor nodded, but he wasn't happy.

'You look like maybe a welterweight to me — that about right?'

'I don't know.'

'Well,' he said. He clapped me on the shoulder

and turned to the nurse. 'Let's get this slugger admitted, make sure we don't have any slow leaks.'

The nurse nodded.

'Did you say there was already a chart?' said the doctor, and she nodded again, handing him a thick folder.

'Wow,' said Dr. Colvin, looking at me over his little glasses. 'Not your first visit with us, I see.' He took the file and sat on a small wheeled stool to read it.

'Spiral fracture, left humerus, three ribs, different dates,' he said to himself as he flipped through the folder, his neck gradually reddening from the collar up. 'Mandible, possible bruised spleen. Jesus Christ, who's been seeing him?' He checked. 'Ferraro,' he said, looking up and closing the folder. 'New York asshole.' He breathed for a while as he looked at the nurse. 'This goes back over three years,' he said to her, his teeth showing. She nodded as if she were somehow responsible. 'Get him an ice pack,' he said.

'Yes, Doctor.' The nurse squeaked away along the polished floor of the hall in her rubber-soled shoes.

Dr. Colvin gave L.A.'s shoulder a pat as he passed her, then walked off toward the nursing station. A couple of nurses glanced up at him and moved out of his way. We heard the front doors open and saw Mom and Jack coming in. Jack was now dressed in cowboy boots, starched jeans and a yellow polo shirt. Mom was wearing her weekend-shortest black skirt and high heels, her hair pinned back on one side like an actress. Dr. Colvin saw them heading toward the examining room I was in and stopped as they approached. They stopped too.

'Might you be the parents?' he said.

Mom said, 'Yes. How is he?'

Dr. Colvin looked Jack up and down, then turned back to Mom as he answered. 'He's had a concussion. Right now it doesn't look too serious, but he's going to have to stay with us at least until tomorrow. We'll need to see how he does over the next twelve hours.' He moved off again toward the nursing station as they talked, still shooting looks at Jack, and they trailed along with him. I lost track of what they were saying. The nurse came back with the ice pack.

L.A. poked me in the chest with her finger. 'Why the hell'd you have to go over there?' she said. 'You're just a dumb' — *jab* — 'fuckin'' — *jab* — 'numb-nuts, y'know that?'

'Lee Ann,' said Gram.

This kind of stuff was not what I wanted to hear. I wanted sympathy. I looked at Gram, saying, 'Think they'll let me have some aspirin, Gram?' I balanced the ice pack on my head with one hand.

'Shit-for-brains,' said L.A. Gram fired a look at her, which I knew would shut her up for maybe five seconds.

'I don't know, James,' said Gram, moving over to help me keep the ice pack on my eye and cheek. 'They might not, because it's your head that got hurt.'

'Nothing but a flesh wound,' said L.A. 'A fat wound.'

I could tell she was starting to cool off. Through the glass I saw Dr. Colvin talking into the phone and watching Mom and Jack, who had now moved into the waiting area, Jack slouching down into one of the green plastic chairs, cracking his gum. Then the doctor turned away from them with the phone still at his ear and said something else, punching three holes down through the air one after another with his finger as he talked.

Mom got a cola from the machine against the waiting room wall and walked over to us. 'Hey, honey,' she said. 'Hi, Mom. How ya doin', Lee Ann?'

'Hi, Auntie Leah,' said L.A., taking a step back.

Mom glanced back at Jack, then took my hand, saying, 'How are you, baby?' She ran her hand through what she could reach of my hair. 'I've just been so worried about you.' She took a sip from her drink.

'I'm pretty good,' I said, noticing that although Mom did look sort of worried, most of her attention was directed back at the nursing station and waiting area.

As the nurse was getting me into a wheelchair to go upstairs, a big cop in a brown uniform and a sad-looking woman in a dark dress suit came in through the main doors. The woman had several manila folders in her arms. Dr. Colvin motioned them over. As he talked he tipped his head toward Jack, who was now paging boredly through an old *National Geographic*. I couldn't catch what Dr. Colvin was saying from this angle but it looked like he was angry at the woman, who kept nodding along with his words.

Then the cop thumped his palm on the counter, nodded to Dr. Colvin and stuck a kitchen match in his teeth as he walked over toward Jack, who had stood up when he saw the cop eyeing him.

'Say, podnah,' said the cop, his voice carrying clearly. 'You Jack Ardoin?'

'Yeah,' said Jack, hitching up his belt.

'Cajun, right?'

'What about it?'

'Y'know, I'm thinkin' I might already be acquainted with you,' the cop said as the match traveled slowly over to the middle of his mouth and then back. 'Wrecker service and repo lot offa Harrison, id'n it? You and that joker with the glass eye, what's his name?' Now that they were standing face-to-face you could see the cop had at least fifty pounds and five inches on Jack, and he wasn't giving him any room. Jack had to crook his neck to meet the cop's eyes.

'Bailess,' said Jack.

'Yeah that's it, Lester Bailess. I do remember y'all. Old Lester's uglier'n a Arkansas hairball, ain't he? Scratches his ass all the time — wouldn't doubt but what he's got pinworms. Went up for something a few years back too, if I remember right. Lessee, what was it, forgery? No, wait, it was messing with little girls, wudden it?'

Jack swallowed. There didn't seem to be any

need for an answer.

'Oh, well,' said the cop, waving the subject off. 'Tell you what let's do, Jack. Let's you and me come to the altar here for a minute.'

The sorrowful woman took Gram and L.A. away to talk. I couldn't remember seeing her before, but it looked like they all knew each other already. As the nurse started to roll me away I could still see the cop talking to Jack, his voice now too low and soft for me to make out what he was saying. He'd laid his big hand on Jack's shoulder and seemed to be massaging and pinching the muscles at the base of Jack's neck as he looked down at the tip of Jack's nose and talked around the match in his mouth. He shook his head and made a couple of weed-cutting strokes in front of Jack's face with his finger, then put the end of the finger against Jack's breastbone. Jack had stopped chewing his gum and turned white around the lips but didn't say anything, just nodded.

As I watched them an understanding came to me. At that moment I knew that Jack wasn't seeing the cop at all anymore. He was blinking in a strange way, his hands opening and closing at his sides, and I knew he was looking up instead at his own drunken, raging father, wishing he could become invisible and doing his best not to piss his pants.

Trying, with no success and no hope, not to be weak.

11

Dreamland

Later, lying on the bed in my room, unable to find a comfortable position, listening to the hospital noises, I thought I wasn't going to be able to sleep, but I must have drifted off because when I opened my eyes Dee was there, talking quietly with L.A. in the doorway of the room. Then he was standing beside the bed with his hand on mine. Then Hubert Ferkin was there, saying something to L.A. about 'that fuckin' Jack.'

The next time I woke up it was dark outside the window. I looked around the room. L.A. was curled up asleep in the armchair in the corner. There was an open *Life* magazine and an empty paper cup on the floor beside the chair. She was lying with her cheek on her hands, and I caught the light sound of her breathing among the other noises of the hospital. I was thirsty, but not quite enough to get up for a drink.

And then I was crossing into and out of dreams, the long, involved, semi-real kind you sometimes get with painkillers, where it's not always clear whether you're thinking about something that happened or dreaming about it:

It is early afternoon at Gram's, me on the couch in front of the TV with nothing else to do, watching Daffy Duck harass Speedy Gonzales.

But really mostly thinking about Diana.

L.A. is sitting cross-legged in her blue jeans and an old T-shirt of mine at the other end of the couch with a bottle of cream soda in her hand and her nose in one of Gram's magazines. Earlier I saw her sneak a drink of the Madeira Gram uses for cooking, so the cream soda could be for camouflage. The cover of the magazine, which is the kind that has recipes and pictures of beautiful kitchens and quizzes about how to tell if you're a good wife, shows a lemon cake with one slice out of it, like all magazine cakes. It looks like it would taste great, but I can't focus on that because I can't stop thinking about Diana. The reason she is a problem for me right now is that I have a more or less major date with her coming up. Actually it's a road trip, and even though her parents will be there too, I still have my hopes.

Not that Diana would worry. Except maybe for the possibility of hellfire and damnation, she is mostly fearless, seeing the universe as basically a safe place and generally counting on things to turn out all right. That seems kind of sweet but contradictory to me, a smart girl like her thinking that way, but I envy her peace of mind. Actually her whole family is like that, which is surprising to me because of the work they do. Diana's mom is a nurse at Parkland, which is a place that is somehow both here all around me and also across town, and her dad is a police detective, which you'd think would make them both pretty serious-minded from constantly looking at people who are sick or dead or guilty. But it doesn't really work that way, and this is one of the things I love about all of them. They like to laugh, even Fubbit, Diana's little brother, whose actual, unused given names are Andrew Gaines. I've helped babysit him several times and know that although he can be a four-alarm screamer if you piss him off, like any baby, most of the time he is either chuckling and grinning or dead asleep and really almost no trouble at all.

The trip I'm worried about is going to be to the Chamforts' family cabin at a place called Duck Lake somewhere up near the Canadian border in Minnesota. L.A. was invited too but after talking it over we decided one of us should stay with Gram. Overcome by an impulsive burst of gentlemanliness, no doubt brought on by the fact I was already throbbing with guilt about leaving the two of them here unprotected, I actually offered to flip L.A. for it. But she just looked at me pityingly, shook her head and said, 'Try not to fall in the lake.'

The trip will be a completely new experience for me and I have endless fantasies about it, imagining myself swimming with Diana in the cold water or taking her out in the boat or maybe just walking in the woods with her. The more I think about the possibilities the better it all sounds to me. But I am still uneasy.

'What's a soul kiss?' I ask L.A. I know what a French kiss is but I'm not sure it's the same thing.

L.A. puts down her cream soda, saying, 'Where'd you hear that?'

I usually give myself credit for being about as smart as L.A., but that isn't always easy to hold on to.

'Hubert and them,' I say. 'What's it mean, really?'

She gives me the you poor ignorant child look and puts her magazine aside.

'Here, I'll show you,' she says, coming over to sit on my lap facing me, holding my hips with her knees. She brushes the hair back from her cheeks and says, 'Close your eyes.' She takes my face in both her hands, then puts her half-opened mouth on mine and pushes her tongue between my teeth. Her mouth is cool and sweet from the cream soda.

When she draws her head back and we open our eyes, she looks at me with a funny expression, like maybe she's a little surprised at something, and her breath is coming fast. I see that her nipples are stiff under the T-shirt, the way they get when she's cold. She looks down at my lap between her legs and back up at my eyes as I sit breathing through my mouth and feeling the blood thumping in my neck. My ears are so hot they feel like they're going to spontaneously combust, and I am wondering where L.A. learned this particular skill and whether she'd be willing to do it again.

Then suddenly she gives a kind of strangled sob and punches me in the face, then again and again and again, swinging with both fists. I'm almost too surprised to react. I try to cover, but she's getting them in there pretty good in spite of me.

'Hey, SHID!' I yell, throwing her off my lap. I grab my nose. 'Tha hurds, godabbid!' I feel my lip to see if it's split. 'Why the hell'd you do that?'

She doesn't answer, just stands there in the middle of the floor, white as death and shaking from head to foot. She's looking more or less in my direction, but her eyes are glazed and unfocused.

A nurse woke me up, and I saw L.A. had now turned the other way in her chair. The nurse asked me how I felt and what my name was and where we were. In the background I could faintly hear different people talking: a woman saying, 'No, she was a good kid,' and another saying something about what happens when people turn away from God, and Dr. Colvin's voice somewhere saying, 'Not on my watch.'

The nurse left and I went back to sleep.

L.A. and I have been at the pool all afternoon and now we're back home with a little time to kill before supper. Gram has fixed meat loaf, peas, mashed potatoes and corn muffins, nesting the hot rolls neatly in a straw basket with a cloth napkin over them, her way with fresh-baked bread whether it's a special

87

occasion or not. I don't notice that L.A. has gone in to take a shower because I'm concentrating on snatching one of the muffins without getting caught. Not that the penalty would be that bad — just some stiff talk about how it isn't dinnertime yet and only hooligans take up their food in unwashed hands — but I pride myself on stealth and try to stay sharp. Today is a good test for me with Gram right there in the kitchen fussing around, but I score.

I stuff the muffin in my mouth as I walk down the hall and open the bathroom door. I've completely forgotten about L.A., but there she stands in a steamy cloud, naked and wet, on the rug by the tub shower. There are droplets of water on her skin and in the dark tuft of hair I didn't even know was there between her legs. Following my eyes, she looks down at herself and then back at me. A trickle of water travels slowly down between her small breasts toward her navel. Without hurrying, she takes a towel from the rack on the wall and wraps it around herself. Neither of us says anything. She watches me as I back away and close the door, taking the muffin from my mouth.

Somebody shook my shoulder and softly said, 'James, wake up.' I opened my eyes and saw Diana's mom in her white uniform. For a second I thought she might be an angel. 'I'm sorry we have to keep bothering you,' she said. 'We need to make sure you're all right.'

'M'fine, Miz Chamfort.'

'I know you must be tired,' she said. 'I heard you had a headache. How is it now?'

'Lot better,' I said.

'Dr. Colvin says your X-rays look fine.' She lifted my wrist and took my pulse while keeping an eye on her watch.

L.A. got up, stretched and walked over to look into my face with her eyes squinted half shut. Then she went back to her chair and worked herself into sleeping position again. She didn't open her eyes when Diana's mom touched her arm on the way out of the room. I went back to sleep.

12

Gifts

L.A. saw the old woman who gave me the stone before I did. We'd walked almost a mile along the tracks to where they cut through the woods south of the river, our first major outing since I'd come back from the hospital. My head felt light and full at the same time and I knew I still looked pretty bad, but everything was finally in clear focus. As we walked along the rails I was watching my sneakers and thinking about death when L.A. said, 'Look.'

The woman was bending down near a wild plum thicket at the edge of the right-of-way ahead of us, digging out some kind of root with what looked like a sharp stick. She was almost a hundred yards away but the instant I saw her she stood up straight and turned like a music-box dancer to face us, her eyes touching me all over like dusty moth wings. She looked like a tall rag pile with a straw hat balanced on top.

'Come on,' said L.A. 'Let's go talk to her.'

The woman just watched and waited for us without moving, holding the stick in one hand and the root in the other. When we got closer I could see that there was only one button holding her old gray sweater together in front. She was wearing a long dirty green dress with some sort of scarf cinching the waist, and black high-top tennis shoes that looked a lot like the ones Colossians wore. A squirrel tail dangled from the string around her neck and a snakeskin bag hung at her hip. Her hair was braided into two thick black pigtails that reached almost to her waist.

'Hi,' said L.A. 'Whatcha doin'?'

The woman looked hard at my face and then at L.A.'s. Her nose was crooked and seemed to be pointing to a spot on the ground to the left of my feet. She had a faint mustache and bright little china-blue eyes that created their own light under the brim of her hat. Her face was sunburned and narrow and hot-looking. 'I seek essences,' she said, her buzzing voice making my face tingle. She held up the root in her long purple-veined hand. It was brown but otherwise it looked like a small bent carrot crusted with dirt.

L.A. bent forward for a closer look.

'It's a root,' she pronounced.

'It's tomorrow,' said the woman. 'It's thunder. It's the mouse you didn't see.'

Something made me look around. A mouse exactly the same color as the woman's sweater ran away down the far rail, hustling busily along the hot shiny steel. I couldn't remember ever seeing a mouse out in the open like this, especially in broad daylight.

'What's it for?' L.A. asked, still eyeing the root.

'It has uses. Too many to speak of.' The woman waved the question off. 'What are your given names?'

'Lee Ann,' said L.A.

91

'James Beaudry,' I said. 'What's yours?'

'Rain. Marsh. Bone and Flower.' She fixed her eye on me, then touched the bruises on my face one at a time with the cool tip of her long knobby finger.

'He who did this is a troll,' she said. 'But a turning will come.'

I looked at L.A., wondering what this was all about, but she only shrugged, apparently not concerned, though of course with her you never really knew. The woman put the root in her bag and gave both of us another stare. A blue jay swooped down from the top branches of one of the plums and fluttered in the air in front of my face for a few seconds, seeming to look directly into my eyes, then flapped back up into the tree and balanced on a branch, cocking its head to watch us.

'Two of you,' the woman said. 'That's rare. Where do you come from?'

'Harlandale Avenue,' I said.

'Where is that?'

I turned and pointed. 'About a mile over there.'

'What creatures do you keep?'

'Jazzy,' said L.A. 'She's my dog.'

'The Lion Dog of emperors,' said the woman, nodding. 'Do you eat grain?'

'Yes ma'am.'

'And flesh?'

'You mean meat?' I said.

'I do.'

'Yes ma'am.'

'Do you worship?'

'I guess,' I said.

'No ma'am,' said L.A.

'You are familiar with the stars?' the woman said to me.

'Sirius and Procyon,' I said. 'And Polaris, and the stars at the top and bottom of Orion, Rigel and Betelgeuse.'

She nodded, saying, 'The Beast will kill again before he bows to you, James Beaudry Bonham, but there will be peace for the one you find and the one you betray.' She turned to look at L.A. 'And now you. The other knower.'

'I don't know anything,' said L.A.

'Come with me.' The woman turned and led us along the edge of the plum trees to a grassy slope where there were a lot of different-sized white mushrooms growing in a big ragged circle. It was like we were miles from civilization, except that from here you could see the big red Pegasus at the top of the Magnolia Building downtown, rotating slowly beyond the treetops. I was thinking about the fact that we hadn't told the woman our last names, or what kind of dog jazzy was.

She showed us where to cross into the circle, then gathered twigs and dry leaves and stacked them in a small pile in the center of the ring. She did something with her hands over the pile and a wisp of smoke came up through the twigs. In a few seconds orange flames licked up. Then she took something from her bag and sprinkled it on the snapping fire, and the smoke got thicker and whiter. We sat cross-legged around the little blaze with our knees almost touching.

The woman took out a blue stone the size of a pecan, held it in the smoke for a few seconds, then put it in her mouth. 'Give me your hands,' she said, sounding a little drunk with the stone under her tongue. When we joined hands I thought I felt an electric shock through my arms. L.A. blinked a couple of times.

The woman said something in a language like nothing I'd ever heard before, and the blue jay flew down to land on the grass near us. It fluffed itself and looked at me with its bright black eye. Closing her own eyes and lifting L.A.'s hand, the woman said, 'This child bears what cannot be borne, and more there will be.' She took in a deep breath through her nose and threw back her head. 'Water and air, share her burden.' Then she looked into L.A.'s eyes. 'When the time comes, you must strike true,' she said with a funny little twisting flourish of her bony hand that for some reason seemed to mesmerize L.A. 'The darkness will take back its own.'

She turned to me and said, 'Close your eyes.'

I did, and saw the face of a bear. It opened its red mouth and said in a woman's voice, 'Dreamer, cast the stone.' Then the image disappeared with a small wet pop. I opened my eyes.

'Well, that should do it,' said the woman, dusting her hands together. We all stood up, and immediately the ground began to tremble. A train whistle screamed and I looked down the track, wondering what train could be coming at this time of day. The engineers didn't sound their whistles on this part of the track either, because there was no crossing. But here the thing came anyway, the big diesel engines rumbling and the whistle ripping the air.

I looked back toward L.A. and saw that the woman wasn't with us anymore. Somehow she was fifty yards away on the other side of the tracks, gazing at us with a sad expression. Then the train roared past, a dark metal storm crashing through the sunny space that separated us, racketing the earth with its end-of-the-world noise and gusting hot diesel smoke against our faces.

But loud as it was, the train wasn't very long for a Texas freight. The last car passed, and when it was gone the woman was nowhere in sight. Once again I looked at L.A., who was watching the train disappear around the bend, and then noticed there was something in my hand. I opened it and saw the blue stone, still wet, shining like an eye from another world. Above our heads the blue jay flapped away across the right-of-way and into the woods beyond the tracks.

We never saw the woman again, but I kept the stone. Because I knew it was the center of something, full of meaning and warm with power.

13

Discards

By now I was convinced the apparition that stood at my bedside as I slept was trying to communicate something to me. Night after night I would dream that I had woken up half a second too late, her words only a fading echo, but when I tried to ask her what she wanted I had no voice. Sometimes I had the dream several times in one night, and I racked my brain for days trying to figure out a way to rig Gram's Kodak to take a picture of the figure. I thought of strings and pulleys and weights but never solved the problem of how to trigger the shutter at the right time. Once I almost asked L.A. to watch me sleep, then came to my senses just in time to bite my tongue. All she or Gram needed at this point was to find out the only man in the house had lost his mind. I decided to keep working on the problem on my own and keep my mouth shut.

A lot of the time Gram seemed tired and sad, but she gave no sign whether it was the mystery of L.A. she was worried about, or something else. And tired or not, she had her routines. For her this was the time of vegetables, and at least twice a week now she drove all the way down to Farmers Market at Central to walk along the rows of tables piled high with bright summer produce, coming home hours later with paper bags full of cucumbers, fat vine-ripened tomatoes, pole beans and purple-hulls, new potatoes and all sizes and colors of peppers she'd haggled away from the truck farmers and their wives down there. She was an absolute fiend for the fruits of the earth, carrying them into the kitchen like carnival prizes.

'No more than our just recompense for this damnable heat,' she'd say as L.A. pawed through the bags looking for the crook-neck squash she loved. Which was always there.

What little money Gramp had left her was pretty much gone, so Gram looked for deals everywhere. She'd stop every Friday at Cana-day's to buy what she called jit-burger for meat loaf when it was marked way down on the last day they could sell it. But it absolutely had to be fresh. Jit was short for 'just in time,' but the meat cutter knew her standards and never tried to put any blinky meat over on her. He'd set two pounds of ground chuck — which I was pretty sure he sometimes snuck from that day's tray — aside for her on Friday morning and when she came in he'd dip his scarce mustaches and say, '*Buenas tardes, señora, tengo su carne zheet,*' and hold it up for her to sniff.

He knew I was trying to learn Spanish and if I was along with Gram that day he'd wink solemnly at me and say something like, '*Que tal, compa?*' or '*Donde esta su caballo, hombre?*'

'*Bien,*' I'd answer. Or '*En el establo, capitán, y tuyo?*'

If the meat was okay, which it always was,

97

Gram would say, '*Mil gracias, Serafino,*' and watch as he wrapped it.

'*De nada, señora.*'

She found clothes for herself and sometimes L.A. and me at secondhand stores, and had bought some old books for me at a flea market. At the time it didn't occur to me that it was probably exactly what she intended, but lately I'd been getting lost for hours at a time in these stories about show collies and their owners, who were called only the Master and the Mistress. The dogs, who had names like Wolf and Lad, thought straighter and behaved better than most people I knew, including me, but I liked the stories anyway and would sometimes read through the whole day if L.A. left me alone.

She and I still went swimming a couple of times a week, but on Thursdays we had to get home early enough for her to change so Gram could drive her to her appointment with Dr. Ballard. This had become part of our household routine after L.A. punched me out and then started getting the drooling shakes every day or so and staring off into space, getting into a fight one morning with some guy at school who accidentally bumped up against her. She did everything but tear his gallbladder out, and after that the school counselor gave Gram Dr. Ballard's number — no options, no slack. Seeing Dr. Ballard was the only way L.A. could stay enrolled.

Sometimes when they came back from these visits L.A. would be driving, depending on Gram's level of confidence in heaven that day.

Then we'd go out and buy hamburgers, onion rings and milkshakes at the Sundown on Beckley and bring them home to eat at the kitchen table. L.A. always put big puky gobs of mayonnaise on her onion rings, even with me looking at her funny about it, which incidentally was how I learned what a waste of time it was trying to influence her with disapproval.

By this time, even though she'd never even set foot on a high board until last summer, she'd moved completely beyond what I'd taught her about diving, practicing until the final whistle at sundown almost every Adult Day, and at this point her skill was so unbelievable that people from the neighborhood would stop by the pool just to watch her. And Gram had finally let her get a bikini, hot-pink, a super color for her with her dark skin and eyes. I suppose her wearing it helped some when it came to attracting attention. It certainly attracted mine. When she climbed the ladder up to the high board I'd look around and see guys elbowing each other in the ribs and pointing and I'd enjoy the feeling of being her original coach, the one who got her started diving in the first place. Then she'd somersault through the air, come cleanly out of her tuck and slip into the water silent as an ice pick, and there'd be claps and whistles around the pool and even out on the sidewalk.

But as far as you could tell from looking at L.A. she never even noticed anybody was watching. Looking on, I felt a weird combination of pride, humiliation and envy, knowing the time when my diving was equal to hers, the time when there was anything I could teach her, was gone forever. She was now at a level of ability that I couldn't even truly understand, much less compete with.

I don't remember now why, but on the morning I'm thinking of we didn't go to the pool even though it was an Adult Day and the weather was clear. L.A. left the breakfast table as soon as she'd finished her coffee and milk — 'café-oh-lay,' Gram called it — and carried the cup and saucer to the sink, rinsed them off, then went out to the garage.

I could hear her thumping around out there as I was trying uselessly to get Jazzy to jump up for a leftover corner of my toast. She wouldn't jump, just kept trying to get the toast by turning around in circles on her hind legs, the way L.A. had taught her. I guess it was hard for her to let go of a skill that had always worked for her, with her mind shorted out by the smell of the food right there above her nose.

'Kitchen detail,' said Gram, pointing her finger at me as she stood up. She went into the laundry room and began sorting through a basket of clothes, throwing whites left, colors right. I gave Jazzy the toast and she took it straight to her box. Then I started clearing the table, not my favorite thing, but I had a rhythm for it: hot water on, soap in, grab the silverware and slip it into the water, then saucers, plates, cups and cereal bowls as the water level came up. Pitchers and serving bowls in last when the water was deep enough for them. Butter, milk, jam and juice back into the fridge, bread in the box.

100

Couple of passes with the rag over the table, then the dishes in reverse order, large to small, rinse in hot, into the rack and I was done. Even though Gram herself used a towel and made L.A. do the same, she let me rack-dry, a break I got for being the man of the family.

As I worked I watched L.A. in the doorway of the garage next to the loose black coils of Old Sparky, our thrill-a-minute outdoor extension cord, ferociously rug-shaking a burlap sack, dust clouds billowing around her in the morning sunlight. When she was satisfied, she dropped that sack and picked up the other one she'd brought out.

Gram, who had walked back into the kitchen, looked through the window at L.A. and said, 'Mercy! What's the girl doing, fighting off snakes?'

In a minute L.A. came in through the back door holding a sack in each hand. 'Let's go find bottles,' she said. This had been one of our routines for years. Now that L.A. lived here Gram gave us both a pretty okay allowance, but this was an angle we couldn't pass up, good bottles being easy to find if you knew where to look. You could rack up a few bucks in an afternoon if you showed a little energy, and then if we took the bottles to Beauchamp's there was Froggy's bonus on top of that. At the time I actually thought it was about the money, not realizing that projects like this were what Gram had meant by *lollygagging* and that she was encouraging them.

I pushed aside the thought that I had

outgrown this kind of stuff and said, 'Sure.'

Jazzy, hearing the word 'go,' watched L.A. with her eagerest expression, hoping to hear 'basket' too, which would have meant L.A. was taking her bike and Jazzy could ride along in the carrier behind her. But for us riding bikes was pretty much a thing of the past by now, and since Jazzy was too short-legged to walk very far with us, taking her along just wasn't something we worked into our plans much anymore.

When she figured out that she wasn't signed on for this expedition she trudged back to her box with her tail drooping, circled around three times counterclockwise and lay down with a sigh, gazing up at L.A. with piteous eyes.

We took off up Harlandale with the tow sacks over our shoulders. Both of us enjoyed walking, and for summertime this wasn't a bad day to be out, the air clean and bright, not too hot yet and with a nice breeze in our faces. We knew the dogs and cats, and one parrot, along this route and liked to check in with them if they were the sociable type, petting them or at least talking to them in the case of the dogs and cats, and whistling to the parrot, whose cage hung out on the front porch of his house in good weather.

I was thinking that lately L.A. had seemed a little stronger and more like her old self, and I considered asking her how she really felt and maybe testing the waters about bringing up my nighttime visitor. It was something I definitely wanted to know her thoughts about, but I couldn't mentally put the words together in a way that sounded right, so instead I got out the cigarette I'd swiped from Froggy the last time we were down there, lit it with a kitchen match and took a drag. I offered the smoke to L.A., but she shook her head.

At the overpass above the tracks I looked at the road and at the weedy downslope, visualizing the trajectories of the bottles as they flew through the air. People threw them out as their cars approached the railing, trying to get them as far down toward the tracks as possible. The traffic was fast along here, which gave the bottles a lot of added velocity, and I was amazed how far down some of them carried. We were headed for the general area down below where most of them ended up.

Green bottles were fairly dependable and would usually stay in one piece when they hit, but you couldn't say the same for the brown ones, which didn't bring refunds anyway. They were not only worthless but treacherous because of the way they'd sometimes break into long ugly spikes that stuck up like fangs in the weeds. The broken bottles worried me more than they did L.A., so she was in the lead as we headed down the slope, picking our way carefully through the grass.

Near the bottom of the main slope, L.A. had just come to the top of a small rise in the ground about fifteen feet ahead of me when she suddenly stopped. She turned around and bent over with one hand covering her mouth and her eyes shut tight. She stayed that way for a second or two, then opened her eyes, blinked a few times and took a couple of deep breaths.

'Hey,' I said as I came up to her. 'What's wrong?'

She swallowed and straightened up to put her hands on my shoulders, then walked me around past her so I could look down at what she'd seen.

'Jesus Christ!' I yelped, jumping back.

There was a bluish white dead girl lying on her back in the grass just down the slope. She was naked, lying with her legs spread wide apart and bent at the knees, her hands over her breasts and her eyes half closed. A few strands of hair straggled across her cheeks and between her lips, and her face had a peaceful, faraway expression, as if being here dead like this were no big problem for her.

But it was for me. I was having a hard time getting enough air.

'Oh, man!' I blurted. 'Oh, shit!' I turned around. 'Let's get out of here.'

L.A. was looking at the dead girl and still breathing pretty hard herself. But she said, 'Wait.'

I stopped.

'Come on,' she said. 'I want to see.'

Which was L.A. for you.

My hands were shaking and my heart was in my throat, but L.A. said, 'Come on' again, and we moved down to opposite sides of the body. L.A. sat on her heels with her elbows on her knees and her hands on her head, looking at the pale girl, her eyes going everywhere over the body without embarrassment or favoritism. The fact that the girl was about our age made the whole thing that much weirder.

But it wasn't the only thing that did.

'I've seen her somewhere,' said L.A. 'At the movies, I think. She must have lived around here.' She touched the dead arm on her side of the body.

I was too shaken up to say so, but I had most definitely seen this girl. In a way it seemed wrong not to tell L.A., but even if I could make my tongue work, what would I say? *I know where she lived — she lived in my dreams.*

She was the girl who'd been standing by my bed every night as I slept.

L.A. leaned forward and lightly took one of her fingers, lifting cautiously. The hand and arm came up a little, but not freely.

'She's a little bit stiff,' L.A. said.

Under the hand we could see a nickel-sized black circle where the girl's nipple had been cut off. I tried to swallow but my throat was too dry. L.A. put the first hand down and carefully lifted the other. That nipple was gone too.

This was getting too unnatural for me. I wanted to cover my eyes. I wanted to be somewhere else. I wanted time to reverse itself so this whole thing would be undone. And then, without any kind of warning at all, I had one of my flashes of knowing something other people didn't, something I didn't have any right to know. And didn't want to know.

'She was glad when he did that to her,' I said. Then when I heard myself I yelled, 'Damn!' and rapped my forehead with my knuckles, feeling like I'd just had my heart licked by a hyena.

'What?' said L.A., her eyes wide. These spells

105

of mine were nothing new to her, but the situation may have had her a little spooked too, even if she'd never admit it.

I looked at the body, then back at L.A., my head thumping. 'She tried to make herself believe that would be the last thing,' I said. 'That he'd be through with her then and let her go.' We both just breathed for a while, looking at each other, me thinking about how totally wrong the girl had been.

Finally L.A.'s eyes went back to the body. 'Look,' she said, pointing to a bruised line around the girl's neck. 'Choked.'

Her wrists and ankles were marked the same way. Looking at the girl's body, I realized her legs would have been pretty if she were alive and wondered if she'd shaved them. This wild thought, along with seeing the matted hair between her legs, made me sick with embarrassment, and for a second I wondered if I might be going crazy right here in the weeds.

'Wonder how she ended up down here,' I said.

Looking around at the grass, L.A. said, 'Somebody drug her from somewhere, maybe the road. Then he fixed her like this.'

'How do you know it was a *he?*' I asked stupidly.

L.A. confirmed that with the *you dumb shit* look.

Of course. Whoever had killed the girl was absolutely a man. Women didn't do things like this. And it came to me as an obvious fact that arranging the body just so, not hiding or burying it, meant something. It meant the man who'd killed her wanted her to be seen this way. I imagined him fussing around, arranging the body, getting everything just right, maybe talking to himself or even to the body as he worked, like little kids do when they play with dolls.

Maybe he wasn't gone yet. Maybe he was watching us right now, to see how we reacted.

I looked around us in every direction, up and down the slope, along the edge of the trees, down the double ribbon of the tracks. I checked to make sure my Case knife was in my pocket and experienced a rush of relief when I felt it, along with a flicker of amazement at how important a three-inch blade could suddenly seem.

'We've gotta get back and report this,' L.A. said. 'We shouldn't touch anything.'

'We touched her.'

'Well,' said L.A. She looked around until she found a piece of cardboard and brought it over to cover the girl's lower body and thighs. Then she stood looking at the marks on the wrists and ankles, frowning slightly and biting her lower lip. I saw that her eyes were starting to get that wild look you had to watch out for, and she was beginning to shake a little.

L.A. had this thing about people being tied up. For some reason the idea had an unraveling effect on her mind. If she saw somebody tying a person's hands in a movie or on TV she'd get up and leave, and later wouldn't talk about it. For no reason I could put my finger on, it seemed to me this had something to do with her other little problem, the one about being surprised, and

107

how you had to remember not to come up behind her or grab her as a joke or anything. Because it wouldn't be a joke to her, and you can believe me when I say she'd make it a fun-free occasion for you too. Just ask the poor guy at school.

'I gotta pee,' she said. 'Stay here.'

She ran behind the concrete piling. Watching her disappear, I thought of the time on one of our jaunts along the tracks a while back when I suddenly had to go, so I turned aside, unzipped and let fly. L.A. just stood there without saying anything for a minute, then dropped her jeans and panties to half mast, leaned back slightly as she pulled up on herself somehow and shot a golden arc down the other side of the embankment, getting about as much distance as any guy could have. All I could do was stare at her in disbelief, having had no idea any such thing was possible. To this day I didn't know what the hell her demonstration had been about, but it created in my mind the long-term question of whether this was a special talent only L.A. had or something girls in general could do if they really wanted to.

I waited, feeling awkward and trying not to look at the body in the wrong places. But I couldn't help myself, my eyes lingering on her breasts, and in spite of myself I wondered if she'd ever done it with anybody. Then suddenly I knew she had, with the guy who'd killed her, or rather he'd done it to her, not only in front but from the back too. And it had hurt. It had made her scream. Another thing I didn't want to know and didn't feel I had any right to know. Even here in the full sun a dark chill found me.

When L.A. came out she was slightly more like her usual self, and I relaxed a little. We stood and thought about the dead girl a while longer, then started back up the slope. On the way back we worked out how we were going to tell the story. Gram would be the first to hear it, and naturally L.A., being the actual finder, would lay out the main points. But I had clear standing too because I'd been there and checked out the body on an equal basis with L.A. I may not have actually touched it like her but I didn't see that as neutralizing my position, because seeing the dead girl naked was a bigger deal for me since I was a guy. This was a fairly subtle point but a significant one, and I knew it wouldn't get past L.A.

Gram was ironing when we came in. The way she did it was sort of a production, setting the board up, or more likely having me set it up if I was around, next to the window under the floor lamp with a big glass of iced tea on a coaster and a few windmill cookies on a small plate on the library table beside her. She had her own special braided rug that she stood on in her woolly slippers and the radio was always on a station that played old-people music, Gram humming along with the tunes she liked. There were baskets of clothes to be ironed on her left and a rack to her right where she hung the pieces when she was finished with them.

When Gram saw the look on our faces she said, 'What is it, you two?'

'We found a dead body,' said L.A. In situations like this she never wasted her breath on the small stuff.

Gram's mouth opened. She set the iron down on its end. Jazzy appeared and began carefully sniffing our ankles.

'It was a girl with no clothes on,' said L.A. 'She was choked, and somebody cut her here.' L.A. pointed to her own breasts.

'Oh, my Lord,' said Gram, taking off her glasses. 'Where was this, honey?' You had to give Gram credit, not coming back with any bullshit about whether we were fooling or whether we were sure the girl was dead or whether we had let our imaginations get the better of us.

'By the overpass,' I said.

'You couldn't see her from the road,' L.A. added.

Gram nodded. 'Yes,' she said. 'Yes, that's right, there was an article, last week sometime.' Gram read both newspapers every day and at any given moment knew pretty much everything there was to know. She moved to the side chair and sat down. 'Did you leave her as you found her?'

'Yes ma'am,' I said, seeing the girl again on her back in the weeds, her head over to the side, her half-closed eyes unfocused and vacant, the narrow bruise around her neck blue-gray in the sun.

Gram nodded again. 'We'll need to call the police,' she said, reaching for her small address book.

As she did this, I felt the flow of things beginning to change. There was going to be a lot of excitement, no doubt about it, but that could definitely be a two-edged sword. As we watched Gram dial and heard her say, 'Detective Chamfort, please,' I understood that this wasn't a story now, and it no longer belonged to us. It had turned into a case. It belonged to investigators and reporters and lawyers. By the time they were through it would all be about them, and about whoever did the murder, and the lost blue girl would gradually shrink away to nothing.

But not in my mind. I thought about her and knew I would never forget her. And I wondered what she could have been trying to tell me during those long nights when she had stood by my bed.

FORESTS OF THE NIGHT

1

Audience

L.A. and I both had to answer a lot of questions from the police and reporters about the girl — it turned out her name was Tricia Venables — and of course every kid we knew had to come by to hear the story firsthand. But most of the excitement had worn off by now and I was ready for a break from all the fuss.

'Going for a walk,' I said to L.A., grabbing my Red Sox cap and pushing through the front screen door, not even thinking about where I was going, just wanting solitude. L.A., grooming Jazzy's fur with a hairbrush, glanced up at me as I went by but didn't say anything.

Walking and thinking, mostly about Tricia Venables, I eventually found myself passing the church, dark and silent now on a weekday, and it deflected my thoughts into the hopeless mental thicket of godliness. Gram never used the word herself, but it was the only one I could think of to describe her sub-intense and inexact requirements for doing the right thing, which seemed to mean behaving at all times as if the Sunday school teacher were watching. The concept was easy enough to talk about but amazingly tricky to put into practice.

Church was an every-Sunday thing under Gram's rules, but she could be a little perverse about holiness. She had this thing about insisting on actual right conduct, almost like it mattered as much as going to services. Not to say the sermons had a reverse effect on me, but they did sharpen my awareness of how confusing and tiresome doing the right thing can be and caused me to have doubts about even being saved in the first place. I knew if it was something you could directly feel, like long underwear or a toothache, I wasn't.

I thought of all the times I'd sat in the polished oak pew between Gram, who was a believer, and L.A., who wasn't, and I wondered — had Tricia Venables been saved?

It sounded like a horrible joke to me.

Tricia had probably prayed herself cross-eyed, but there she was, dead just the same. I pictured her standing naked in front of God with her head swaying on her ruined neck and her arms and legs gangling around like a puppet on strings, trying to point to where her nipples were supposed to be and asking God what happened, was He off duty that day or just out for coffee or what, and could He please put her back together again, thank you very much.

What it came down to was that I had a hard time seeing prayer as a practical tool in the face of real danger.

On the other hand, I remembered when I was just a little kid back in Jacksboro, walking out between two parked cars into the street, a strong hand grabbing my sweater to yank me back, a second later a truck bombing right through the space I'd been about to step into. But when I

116

looked around there was no one behind me, nobody anywhere near me. Nobody on the whole block. I had no explanation for this, but for me it raised possibly the trickiest question of all: Why save me and not somebody else? There had to be thousands of candidates who were more deserving than me.

I had a new mental image of Tricia, in her damaged state, standing side by side with me while some ghostly hand pinned a blue ribbon on me instead of her. Which for the first time ever gave me a feeling I hadn't even known was possible — it made me angry at my own mind.

But then came another idea. Maybe the big plan didn't call for people being entitled to explanations. Maybe all you got was the chance to think about things and try to figure out for yourself what's true and what's not. Maybe not explaining everything, all the whys and why-nots, was a form of respect for human intelligence.

The thought almost made me laugh out loud.

I had once asked Gram about talking in tongues the way some people did in church, and she said, 'We do not scorn other communions.' Okay, but did that cover drinking poison and picking up snakes to dance with? And what kind of store would you go to for the poison, some kind of anti-pharmacy? Would you need a prescription to make sure it was safe and effective? What would it taste like? Did it come in small quantities like eyedrops or in bulk like Epsom salts, or some other way? And the snakes — either you'd have to catch fresh ones for each service or have them on hand all the time, like communion wafers, meaning somebody would have to clean their cages and keep them fed. Or if they came from some kind of supplier who stocked the poisonous ones, possibly as a specialty item, would it be a matter of buying them outright or just checking them out for the day? Maybe paying a fine for late returns or any damage to the snake? Did you get your money back if the snake bit somebody and they died, or was it if they didn't die?

Which was when it came to me that things like these probably weren't as important as they seemed. They were only ceremonies. They had about as much to do with God as lighting birthday candles did with the passage of time, and most of them were probably made up by people as confused and ignorant as I was.

Two days later we went to church, just like always.

To my surprise, Colossians Odell was standing by the white steps that led up to the heavy carved double doors of the sanctuary, holding an imaginary broom and sweeping the paths of certain worshippers as they came abreast of him, shouting, 'Hark! Hark!' in his huge voice as they passed.

His eyes were blood-red and he didn't seem to recognize me at first. But then suddenly he did, and for just a second he looked right into and through my eyes and all the way to the back of my skull. Then the recognition was gone and he went back to his sweeping. It had been at least a year since I'd seen him doing the mummy-shuffle that went with the medication I knew he was supposed to be taking, and at the moment it was obvious his mind was in the grip of some irresistible power that didn't affect the rest of us. I started to tell Gram this was the basso profundo we'd talked about, but she was already halfway up the steps, and after another glance at Colossians I decided to let it go.

The steps were made of white marble, smoothly worn down in the center from all the hopeful feet that had come this way, and they were my idea of the way into heaven. Except for the clouds that would probably be scattered around and the golden light playing across the scene, this must be what it would be like, with the saved people in their serious clothes climbing on up and filing in through the sacred gates with nods and smiles as they took their places in eternity, which at the time I thought of as being constructed primarily of varnished oak and stained glass.

Gram was wearing her white hat and blue Sunday dress with the small white dots, and L.A. had on her A outfit, the cream-colored dress with red circles and her black patent-leather pumps. Diana was with us today too, dressed in a light blue skirt and white blouse, looking so perfect it made my throat hurt. Both of the girls carried white Bibles with gold lettering on the covers. The transformation they went through in an hour or so on Sunday morning was amazing. But it wasn't just the clothes and hair — this was what Gram referred to as a sea change, the girls moving and talking differently and somehow altering the gravity and atmosphere around them, changing the significance of everything.

Shepherd Boy Shepherd greeted us at the top of the stairs, standing there by the doors in his black suit, with his hands and heels together like a mortician. As usual, and unlike Colossians, he didn't look anybody in the eye. Making him a greeter seemed like a strange idea to me, Shepherd Boy being about as welcoming as a muddy grave, but you could tell he took the job seriously by the deep sober way he tried to talk when he greeted you.

Shepherd Boy was his real given name, or names. Gram's theory was it might have been the result of some confusion with the birth certificate at the hospital, maybe because his parents didn't have a name thought up yet when it was filled out. He wasn't very old as adults go, but he was earnest. He was also soft and white and had big sleepy gray eyes with long lashes and one of those damp, super-limp handshakes. He never had any friends that I knew of and wasn't married, but he was youth and music director at the church, which as far as I could tell was the only job he ever had.

A girl we knew named Lisa Childress had told me that back when she went to Vacation Bible School, Shepherd Boy had offered her five dollars to let him spank her. His idea was to wait until the other kids had left and then he and Lisa would go into the bathroom and do it.

The five dollars was going to be for ten licks — seven if she'd lower her panties. He had the five dollars out and a Ping-Pong paddle ready and everything. She said he had clothespins too, but she didn't ask him what they were for.

Looking at her expression, I just had to ask. 'Did you let him?'

'Not that time,' she said.

Shepherd Boy had had himself crucified in the church basement for Good Friday last year. The worshippers all gathered down there for the 'special blessing,' and when they pulled the cotton sheeting aside, there he was in a white diaper, with ketchup on his hands, feet, forehead and side, standing on a little box in front of a cross cobbled together out of four-by-fours with his arms out wide like Jesus on Calvary. There were a couple of turns of dried grapevine around his head, and they'd rigged some fake nails for his hands and feet. His eyes were closed, but you could see that his eyeballs were moving around behind the lids.

Now Shepherd Boy said, 'Good morning, Miz Vickers,' looking at Gram's throat, bending slightly at the waist and letting her take his hand. 'It's so good to have you with us today.' He pushed his noodly black hair back up across his forehead with the other hand, showing us his zits.

'Good morning to you, Brother Shepherd,' said Gram, giving the limp hand one businesslike shake and then dropping it.

Then he offered his hand to me, L.A. and finally Diana, who looked up at him through her eyelashes as she took his hand. When we went on into the church she said something into L.A.'s ear that made both of them cover their mouths and snicker.

121

For a change Mom and Aunt Rachel were both here, and I looked around for Jack, feeling lighter in my chest when I didn't see him. Gram slid into the pew next to them, glancing down at Aunt Rachel's short red dress as Mom leaned over Rachel's lap to hand Gram a bulletin. Rachel wouldn't look at Gram. I noticed her eyes were puffy, but Mom looked fresh and pretty. It was easy to see they were sisters.

Diana, L.A. and I sat in the next row up and across the aisle, L.A. slipping in first, then Diana and me. Diana shifted around a little to get settled, my favorite part of the whole sitting-down process.

I liked the booky smell and royal feeling of the church almost as much as the singing. The hymns themselves were okay, with simple lyrics and easy chords, but what I really enjoyed was trying to hit harmonies with L.A. and Diana, whose voices went together perfectly.

We had even caught Shepherd Boy's attention with our singing, and he was always trying to get the three of us to join the choir. I could have gone either way on this myself, meaning I'd probably have been willing if the girls were interested, but they definitely weren't, possibly because of the way Shepherd Boy always looked at us. His eyes just never seemed to make it any higher than our necks, and with Diana and L.A. especially he'd sometimes just stare at their breasts while breathing through his mouth. It wasn't that I didn't understand his feelings on that point and, being fair, that was more or less the way he looked at everybody. Still, something about him froze us out, and the choir thing never happened.

As Brother Wells began his sermon I was enjoying Diana's occasional movements and the warm feeling of her body against mine. She was gripping her small white Bible and looking serious, the way you try to do when you're in trouble and getting a lecture. It was from past sermons that I knew too much talk about eternal damnation would scare her, and I was hoping for something more along the lines of brotherly love and Christian charity today.

I watched Brother Wells getting his momentum up. He was a big, hearty, pink man who looked as if he'd been squirted down into his clothes like drive-in ice cream, with a little overflow at the collar, the fancy ring on his little finger flashing impressively as he opened his Bible. As it turned out, his text this Sunday was Jesus in the desert and temptation, which meant the fright factor was going to be a toss-up, depending on the angle he took. I glanced at Diana to see how she was taking it, and to my relief she looked composed and unworried.

I looked up at the huge stained-glass window in the eastern wall, where Jesus seemed to be standing on a little puff of cloud and holding his punctured hands out with an expression of unbelievable forgiveness, and wondered why nothing like Noah's flood or the loaves and fishes ever happened anymore and why moments in history didn't light up like colored jewels the way they had in biblical times.

But then I gradually lost my awareness of

Brother Wells and started reviewing my plan, which involved some thorny issues. One of these was my inability to think of God as a three-man crew, which I usually dealt with by ignoring the concept of the Trinity altogether, at least in the privacy of my own mind. And because I had no new ideas on the subject, that's what I did today, settling on what seemed like the most practical approach based on Gram's notions about how things got done. In other words — meaning no disrespect to the Lamb of God or the Holy Ghost or anybody, just going straight to the top when the situation was serious, as Gram always recommended — it was God Almighty Himself I had business with today.

But approaching God directly took nerve. I felt like a dumb farm hand tracking mud into the parlor, and didn't know whether I could expect a fair and impartial hearing or not. But now that I thought about it, fair and impartial were not what I actually wanted. What I was looking for was a break.

Naturally I had the regular mental picture of God as an oversized, fierce old man in a hospital gown, with thick white hair and a flowing beard, seated behind a huge golden desk in a high-backed swivel chair upholstered in black leather. And sure enough, that's exactly how He did look in my imagination as I felt myself being surrounded by the holy air and perfect light of His presence.

A semitransparent shadow that I could only assume was the Holy Ghost drifted silently in and out of view in the corners. Based on what little I understood of scripture, I wasn't surprised not to find Jesus here, because I took it for granted he'd be at the jail or the Cowboys game or some other place where there'd be a concentration of needy souls.

But it was beginning to dawn on me how many pitfalls were involved in dealing with authority at this level. I had questions about whether Shepherd Boy really worked for God, for example, and I wanted to know what was the point of letting the girl at the overpass die the way she did. I also wanted God's holy word that nothing like that was going to happen to Gram or Diana or L.A. But asking those particular questions could be taken as criticism, and requesting favors for certain people might make it sound like I was willing to throw everybody else to the wolves. I decided to stick to the main topic.

But it wasn't actual conversation I was here for, because I pretty well grasped that God didn't speak to humans straight out, generally relying on methods like writing on stone and blasting cities to get his ideas across.

Thinking in complete sentences seemed like the best bet: *Sir, it's about my dad*, I thought as hard as I could. *I mean, I know You took him for Your own good reasons, and I swear I'm not trying to tell You how to do Your job, but that was really a terrible wreck —*

They'd said the troopers had had to shoot all four of the horses that had been in the trailer, but it was too late for Dad. He was burned, like they say, beyond recognition, like recognition would have helped somehow. I plowed on: *Anyway, Sir, I know Dad wasn't good all the time, maybe hardly ever, like Mom says, but I'd appreciate it very much if You could keep in mind that he was good to me. He let me go with him to the horse auctions all the time and promised he was going to teach me to ride his motorcycle someday. I don't think the fights he got into were all his fault, and even though Mom is fairly honest about some things, she's probably not Your best source when it comes to that woman she threw her scissors at him about. Anyway, he told me it was only a onetime thing and Mom was blowing it all out of proportion. At least I know he didn't mean any harm, because he hated having anyone mad at him.*

I realized I was starting to ramble, and edging toward dangerous ground to boot, but somehow couldn't stop myself: *So, I just hope You were able to see Your way clear to put Dad in, uh, heaven, Sir, because I think he made a pretty sincere effort to be good most of the time, and as far as I know he never did anything bad enough to belong in hell.*

Reminding God of the hell option may have been a reckless move, but living with Gram and L.A. this long had apparently weaned me away from half measures. Before I could think through the implications of that, though, Diana moved against me and I was back in the real world, just in time to pass the offering plate. I sucked in a deep breath and looked around at the ordinariness of everything, the high colorful windows, the sanctified spaces overhead, the dressed-up

126

people in their pews. Focusing my thoughts on Diana's clean peppery smell and the warmth of her body against mine, I decided to let myself believe I'd taken my best shot for Dad. This, along with the fact that the dead girl hadn't visited my bedside since I'd actually seen her lying naked in the grass, tempted me to hope that maybe things were going to turn out all right after all.

Outside, after the service, I saw Aunt Rachel talking to a man who had appeared from somewhere, a guy exactly the same color as Colossians but completely different in every other way, with close-cut hair, big knotty hands and edgy eyes. He looked quick, limber and hard all at the same time, like a riding whip. I wondered if maybe he was a friend of Colossians, but that idea made me uneasy. I looked around, half expecting Colossians to come at us out of the bushes with his red eyes and his broom, but he was nowhere in sight.

When the man turned and walked away, light as a dancer on his feet, I caught up with Aunt Rachel and asked her who the guy was.

'A middleweight, I think,' she said, her breath strong enough to take the paint off a lamppost. 'Does odd jobs.' She gave a little snort. 'Or maybe not so odd.' At that angle, in that light, she would have looked like an older version of L.A. if her hair had been wild enough.

I couldn't get anything else out of her about who the strange man was or why she was talking to him.

We drove Diana home, then headed for

Harlandale. When we got back to the house, I knew something was wrong. L.A. obviously felt it too; she went straight to her room, checked her pillows, looked under her bed and into her closet, then opened her underwear drawer. She stood there frowning for a minute, then looked at me. In that moment some decision was made between us, and we never told Gram or talked about what we both knew, but we went on knowing it just the same: somebody who didn't belong here had been in the house.

2

Contacts

We kept expecting to hear or read something new about the murder, some solution to the mystery that seemed to hang in the air around us like a dark humidity, but there was nothing. The papers were down to column heads like 'No New Leads' and 'Police Seek Witnesses,' and TV reporters had started collecting old unsolved murders to compare this one to, their tone opening the door just a crack to the possibility that the cops weren't doing their job.

Then we got the call about Jack. Somebody had beaten him up and left him lying in the street, where a cabbie found him. He was still unconscious when he arrived at Parkland by ambulance, but they got an address from his driver's license and notified Mom.

At that point it sounded to me like he was going to survive, but you never know.

When Gram hung up, she said, 'We'd better go on over there, you two. Leah's just beside herself.'

L.A. jammed her hands in the back pockets of her jeans and looked down at her sneakers without saying anything. It was clear to me that somebody lying unconscious in the street could very well get run over. Maybe even by a truck. Or a trolley.

Grabbing the keys, I headed for the door and held it as Gram and L.A. walked out, then locked it and double-checked the knob. As far as I knew it had never been locked before. Gram didn't say anything, but she gave me a curious look.

I suddenly remembered it was L.A.'s turn to drive, so I tossed her the keys and we loaded into the Roadmaster with her behind the wheel. Since Gram favored young ladies having practical skills, I had no choice but to share driving time with L.A., but the truth was I didn't mind riding while she drove. I know that sounds like disloyalty to guys, who are the true drivers of the world, but L.A. was a special case. Other people drove on the principle that all the bad things that are possible are equally likely to happen and had constant frights as a result. In fact, I had to admit that was more or less my style, because when you got behind the wheel of a car the streets turned into a jungle screaming with predators. But L.A. was basically a gunfighter by nature, about as bluffable as Doc Holliday, and didn't think survival had anything to do with traffic signs and lanes and stuff like that. Instead, she kept us out of wrecks by seeing absolutely everything and always knowing exactly who her enemies were and what they were going to do next. But I could tell Gram didn't understand this because she just kept stomping her imaginary brake pedal at every crisis point as we went along.

As much as it seemed to amaze her, we made

it to the hospital and got the Roadmaster parallel-parked without incident. With her feet on solid ground again, her nerve returned and she briskly got directions from the candy striper at the desk and marched us all straight back past a sign stating that these weren't visiting hours. She was very law-abiding in most ways, but once she laid her course she was unstoppable. We took the elevator to the third floor, got off, turned right and kept going until we saw Mom standing outside one of the rooms blowing her nose into a tissue.

'Well, how is he?' asked Gram.

Uninterested in secondhand reports, L.A. went to the door of the room and craned her neck to look in.

Mom snuffled, her eyes red and puffy. 'Goddamn nigger beat him up,' she said. 'He got a call and went out in the truck to pick up a car, and the guy just jumped out of the bushes or something and beat the livin' shit out of him. Jack said Murval Briscoe was out there too.'

I knew by now that Murval Briscoe was the name of the huge cop who'd talked to Jack at the hospital after the fight at Mom's house, but I couldn't imagine what he might have to do with this.

We all went into the room. L.A. stepped fearlessly up to the bedside for a clinical inspection of Jack, who was a little hard to recognize in this condition. His eyes were purple and black and swollen almost shut, and his nose was flattened and pushed off-center. His lips, which looked like raw meat, were kind of

131

ballooned out, like he was blowing the ceiling a kiss.

Gram stood over him. 'What exactly happened to you, Jack?'

'Guy bussid m' buckin teet,' he said. 'Swald two ub'm.'

I saw the truth of this; Jack no longer had any teeth at all in the front, a fact that in combination with his overall condition sent a wild surge of joy through me. But that didn't last, the pleasure almost immediately turning to constipated guilt. Mom honked into her tissue again and Gram patted her halfheartedly on the shoulder.

'I'm sure he'll be just fine,' Gram said.

L.A. was still examining Jack. 'Can you smell stuff?' she said, checking out both sides of the wrecked nose.

'Duh-uh,' said Jack.

A tired-looking little doctor with spiky blond hair came in the door. 'Hello, folks,' he said without looking up from his clipboard.

'Enter young Hippocrates,' said Gram.

The doctor glanced up at Gram with a professional smile. 'Are you the family?'

'Some of it,' she said. 'Can you tell us about the patient's condition, Doctor?'

'Well, we have multiple blunt-force traumata here, over most of the head, neck, upper torso and abdomen, but except for the neck apparently no internal injuries worthy of note. In terms of brain damage, which technically happens any- time someone is knocked out, whatever's there seems to be minimal in this case. A number of defensive bruises on the forearms. In a couple of places you can actually see what appear to be knuckle marks. It looks like he got beat up.'

The words *riding whip* appeared in my mind and then vanished without explanation.

'Remarkable,' said Gram. 'Are you a Harvard man?'

'A&M,' he said. 'But I studied real hard.'

'Ah. Well then, you seem to believe our Jack is going to recover?'

'I think so. There's some damage to a couple of disks in the neck, which may or may not produce sequelae . . . '

It was clear from Gram's expression that she understood perfectly well what this meant, which gave me a fantasy of college classes where the students did nothing but sit around and learn weird words.

The doctor went on, ' . . . and he's lost some dentition, as you can see, along with the broken nose. There may be a little residual laziness of the right eyelid due to superficial nerve and muscle damage.'

'Sumbidge caw me nod loogin,' said Jack.

'But that seems to be about it,' the doctor said. 'We'll probably discharge him tomorrow. I imagine he'll want to talk to an orthodontist.'

Mom indignantly piped up, 'Rachel was here, and you know what she said? She said, 'Well, hell, there goes the taffy apples.' Can you believe that?'

Gram looked at her for a long beat. Her nostrils quivered and she cleared her throat but gave no other sign. Finally she said, 'I suppose he

133

was lucky at that. It's just not much like our Jack to get into a fight with anyone who could do this to him.'

Behind her L.A. nodded.

'C'mon,' said Mom. 'Don't start up with that.' Her own nose was red and tender-looking by now.

'Well, since you mention it,' the doctor said, 'these injuries don't exactly look like the result of an ordinary fight to me, especially when you take into account the condition of the patient's hands. Or maybe we should say noncondition — '

'What do you mean?'

'I don't think he got many licks in.'

'You seem to have a forensic turn of mind,' said Gram, giving him the little lopsided smile she dispensed for dog tricks and clever children.

The doctor looked pleased. 'It is an interest of mine,' he said. He glanced at Jack. 'The damage we see here is quite a bit in excess of what it would've taken to simply win the fight, but on the other hand it doesn't look like the guy, who I think was left-handed, by the way, was trying to finish him off either.'

'What do you conclude?'

'I think it may have been a matter of prolonging the action. If I were Sherlock Holmes I might say this was done in a rather clinical fashion, not out of rage. In fact, as bad as this is, it looks to me as if the other guy could have hurt him a whole lot worse if he'd wanted to.'

'Well,' said Gram. 'That is intriguing. You know, Jack is a trained boxer.'

134

The doctor looked at Jack again. 'No, I didn't know,' he said. 'That does add an element of mystery, doesn't it? In that case you'd have to believe the other guy was very impressively skilled, though I don't know what his motives might have been.'

L.A. went back to take another look at Jack's face. She stood on her tiptoes and seemed to be comparing his eyes.

'Can you blink?' she said.

Jack blinked.

A long narrow nurse in silent shoes came in. The doctor talked up to her for a minute with a slightly annoyed expression, then shook hands with Gram and left. We all stood around watching Jack as the nurse leaned down and checked his pulse.

This was now a situation of expert routines and there didn't seem to be anything left for an ordinary person to do or say here. I kept having mental pictures of somebody beating Jack up and thinking about what it would have taken to accomplish that. I couldn't make myself believe anyone but a professional fighter could have done it, but that's where I ran out of ideas.

'Jack,' said Gram, handing Mom a fresh tissue. 'When you go out to repossess a car do you have to notify the police first?'

He nodded. 'Esh,' he said.

'Mm,' said Gram, as if that settled the matter for her. 'Well then, since it looks like you'll live, I think the youngsters and I will be on our way. Leah, let me know if there's anything I can do.'

'Sure, Mom.' She gave each of us a quick hug.

135

Now that I'd seen Jack, I wanted the hell out of there. I didn't like hospitals. The air in them was full of pain, and death skulked around every corner.

On my way out of Jack's room I ran smack into Shepherd Boy. He said, 'Oh!' like somebody who'd never taken a hit before. In fact he felt as soft as a girl.

I couldn't make sense of seeing him here, but he told us he was on a pastoral visit to see Jack. Then it didn't make sense in another way because Jack, not being what you'd call an active member of the congregation, usually just showed up at church for funerals and maybe Easter. A look passed between Jack and Shepherd Boy.

We finished our excuse-me's and I walked on down the hall. I never knew what this was all about but the next day I did hear Gram mention some shared literary tastes Jack and Shepherd Boy seemed to have, whatever that meant.

As we turned the corner at the end of the hall I glanced back at Mom in the doorway of Jack's room, knowing she'd stay here at the hospital with him until he was discharged. He always had to have her nearby if he was sick or hurt, that being one of the reasons she didn't have a job. This was in addition to his suspiciousness — like if he got the idea she'd been talking to some other man, for example, or wasn't telling him the truth about something — which would mean he'd beat her up. As a matter of fact, trying to help Mom during one of these fights had been pretty much my last act before getting sent to

Gram's. Afterward Mom told everybody she ran into a cabinet door, and said I'd fallen off my bicycle.

Thinking of this reminded me somehow of Hubert, who kept a notebook that he drew pictures of skulls and snakes in. I didn't know if there was any connection between the two facts, but he also drank beer or even hard liquor anytime he could get it. Even his music was edgy, full of rough chords and growling vocals, nothing like what you heard on the radio. For a second, for no apparent reason, I visualized him huddled over forbidden books with Jack and Shepherd Boy in some poorly lit, undefined place of shame.

'Now, James, I want you to drive us home,' said Gram when we were outside. 'And I want you to get us there safely and unfrightened.' She slid into the passenger's seat, set her purse on her lap and gripped it with both hands.

L.A. piled into the back and assumed her heckling position, elbows on the back of the front seat. 'Scare me if you can,' she said.

I started the Roadmaster, backed out and headed for the house by way of Hampton. It was an uneventful trip except for one moron in a white Chevy with chewed-up fenders who ran a stop sign and almost hit us, scaring the hell out of Gram and me.

'Lord-love-a-fool!' Gram shouted, giving the floorboard a mighty stomp. 'Curse and blast!' She glared at me as if I were to blame. 'Now, you see there, James?'

'I knew he was gonna do that,' said L.A.

I looked at her in the rearview mirror. 'Why didn't you say so?'

'How else are you gonna learn?' Then she put her lips against my ear to keep Gram from hearing and whispered sweetly, 'You dumb shit.'

We turned into the driveway and saw Diana sitting on the porch steps, her hair tousled up in the wind, twirling a dandelion in her fingers and watching the little parasols of fluff stream away. She wore tan cotton shorts, white low-top canvas shoes and a red golf shirt I happened to know Don had given her when it got too small for him. She dropped the dandelion stem, stood up in that unbelievably fine way of hers and walked across the grass to meet us as we got out of the car.

'I park,' said L.A. She enjoyed putting the Buick up in the garage, having absolutely no fear of the tight space.

'Guess what I heard,' said Diana.

'What?' I said, trying desperately not to stare at her legs.

'What?' said L.A.

'Pray tell,' said Gram.

'Some other girls got killed before the one Harpo and Biscuit found. Two of them. I heard Dad talking about it on the phone.'

3

Moving Day

You can focus on an idea, even an idea as big and momentous as other people dying, just so long before it numbs your mind and you run out of things to think and say about it.

The names of the other girls who had been killed were Mandie Peyser and Marybeth Nichols, Diana told us. Mandie's body had been found at the drive-in theater, behind the screen, and Beth's at the old lumberyard. Both of them had been naked, just like the girl L.A. and I found. I couldn't remember any news about either of the first two at the time, but a lot happens in a city as big as Dallas and not every murder makes the front page, which I had to admit was about all I usually read if you didn't count the comics and the sports section. And it was possible I had heard of the murders in a background kind of way, but because at that point I still hadn't really gotten it through my head how much death actually had to do with me, maybe they didn't get my attention above the general roar of school and everything else that was going on in my life.

None of us really knew either of the other girls, but Diana was pretty sure she'd seen Mandie around school back in sixth grade and thought maybe she'd moved over to the Catholic school the next year.

We talked about the two of them for a while, little by little letting go of the unspoken assumption that dying was for the old and infirm, not people our age. For a while we kept coming back to the things you say, like how rotten it was for them to die that way, and asking what kind of lunatic would do such a thing, but it wasn't long before the conversation began to lose steam.

I still couldn't bring myself to tell anyone about my night visitor, secretly suspecting she was a sign of insanity and, whether that was true or not, being sure nobody was going to have any answers for me anyway. When in doubt, saying nothing is nearly always the best policy. Silence can sometimes be repaired after the fact if need be, but not the wrong words. You can't unring a bell.

'It's just so ugly and sad,' said Diana. 'Who could do a thing like that?'

L.A. shrugged. Dee looked at her with an expression I couldn't read.

'Somebody who's nuts,' I ventured, still locked on to the idea of insanity.

'More like evil,' said Diana.

And that pretty much covered what we knew and thought. Gram, who had walked into the room during the conversation, *tsked* one last time, warned us against lurking fiends and strangers at the door, grabbed her purse and left to go sit with Dr. Kepler. Diana and Dee, who'd been hanging out with L.A. and me for the afternoon, stuck around to play gin rummy. The

140

murdered girls stayed in my mind, but not, as far as I could see, in Diana's, so here was another item on the long list of things that didn't worry her excessively.

Of course, there was never any telling what Dee or L.A. were thinking, but L.A. had now become the picture of deadly concentration. We were playing our third hand, and after my draw she carefully studied my eyes for a couple of seconds, discarded and said, 'I'm knocking.' She spread her cards, everything in runs and sets except a red deuce and the spade seven she knew I needed. Nine points.

I laid out my hand for Diana to count. There was no occasion for drama; as usual L.A. had looked straight into my defenseless brain, seen all the points I was holding and busted me. When she was on like this, she was insuperable. Generally my only hope against her was the fantastic lucky streaks I occasionally had, when for a while I'd somehow know with perfect clarity what to hold and what to toss and sometimes even what card was coming up. Fortunately I could usually feel these hot streaks coming and play them for all they were worth when they did, otherwise the opposition would've had no respect for me at all.

Of course, today L.A. had softened me up ahead of time, offering me a swig of peppermint schnapps from a half-pint bottle while Gram was in the bathroom and before Dee and Diana arrived.

'Where'd you get it?' I said.

'The schnapps bunny. Try it.'

I took a taste before handing the flask back to L.A., not liking it much. She tipped it up and swallowed, then recapped it.

Dee and Diana were usually pretty bored when we played gin and always won or lost according to the fall of the cards instead of by skill or concentration. And you couldn't really get them interested in competing with anybody, which pretty much ruled them out as spades partners too. But Diana was our scorer for everything because her head worked like a calculator, and Dee was our referee of choice because when he rendered a judgment it somehow settled the issue cleanly and conclusively, with no leftover doubt or malice.

'My deal,' I said. 'So watch out.'

I was on a losing streak, big surprise. I grabbed the cards and started shuffling. When Dee went to put some music on Diana yawned and took a sip from her Dr Pepper, then got up and wandered over to the cabinet where Gram kept the crackers and chips.

'Simon & Garfunkel or Diana Ross?' said Dee.

'Three Dog Night,' I said, ignoring the look Dee shot me.

Diana found a bag of corn chips and came back munching. When she sat down at the table L.A. reached across, took a chip from the bag and gave it to Jazzy. Diana gave her another one, saying, 'Here you go, Muttkin, have a party.'

As I dealt the cards the opening bars of 'I Can't Stop Loving You' by Ray Charles drifted in from the front room. When Dee came back into the kitchen Diana gave him a thumbs-up.

'Women and children take cover,' I said, squaring what was left of the deck and flipping the top card over to start a discard pile.

'You're already down a million points,' said L.A. 'You're gonna be doing my dishes for a year.'

'Make him do your algebra this fall,' said Dee.

'Too easy.'

'Does he do hair?' wondered Diana.

'Hey,' I said. 'Pick up your cards. I'm fixin' to get hot here.'

'Saints preserve,' said L.A.

Dee looked at his hand and gave a little sigh that told me he had nothing to work with, but I could tell by the way L.A. sorted her hand that she'd locked up six cards on the deal. Diana ate another chip and glanced out the window, instantly grabbing my attention.

'What'd you see?' I said.

She shrugged. 'Bird, maybe. I don't know.'

L.A.'s eyes caught mine for a second, which caused Dee to stare curiously at me, and suddenly it was a moment. I got up and went to look out the window. It wasn't quite dark yet and I could see down the driveway and across to the yard next door. There didn't seem to be anything there. I went out the door and looked around, feeling the hair on the back of my neck stand up, but I still didn't see anything. When I came back in I locked the door behind me, noticing that Jazzy was calm, her attention on where the next corn chip was going as Diana brought it out of the bag. I watched her for a while to be sure.

Okay, I finally decided, false alarm. I

rechecked all the locks and went back to the table.

'Good that we've got a scout,' said Diana as I sat down.

L.A. glanced at me and I shook my head slightly. I picked up my hand. 'Come on, play,' I said. Dee watched me for a second longer, then picked up his cards.

After two draws L.A. knocked again, this time for only three points. The situation was getting out of hand.

'Okay, here's what,' I said to L.A. 'Side bet: just you and me — first winner takes it.'

'What're you putting up?' said L.A.

Diana glanced at her, then tossed a chip to Jazzy.

'My room, against kitchen detail until football starts,' I said.

L.A. looked at me, fully understanding the weight of my words. The room was mine by right of seniority and it was definitely the best one next to Gram's, which actually had its own bathroom. Mine was at the front corner of the house and was a little bigger than L.A.'s, with an air conditioner in the window that worked most of the time. Hers was at the back, quite a bit farther from the hall bathroom.

The tricky part was, L.A. could get weird about her room and her stuff, and you couldn't always predict her reactions. There was her thing about pillows, for instance. Along with the one that Gram gave her when she came to live with us, she'd scrounged up several others around the house and even bought a few more at the

144

five-and-dime one time when we'd had a really good bottle day. Even on hot nights she'd pile them around and over herself until you could just see her eyes, or sometimes none of her at all. A lot of nights she still did. Then after making up her bed in the morning she'd stack all the pillows just so, always knowing the exact way she left them, so that when she went in to go to bed that night she could tell if they'd been tampered with. Next to sneaking up behind her or touching her when she wasn't looking, messing with L.A.'s pillows was the quickest way I knew to get in trouble with her.

She was skeptical about the bet. 'You're gonna cheat,' she said.

'Hell no,' I said. 'Nothing but the luck of the draw. That and my demonic skill. Not chickenshit, are you?' I clucked a couple of times.

'Hah! Deal the cards.'

We played to gin this time, L.A. slapping her hand down when I still needed another keeper, and just like that I'd lost my room.

'Ho-hum,' said Diana, finishing off her Dr Pepper.

Dee gave a crooked little smile.

'Chinaman's luck,' I said, folding my hand. 'Hey, why don't we do it all in one fool swoop right now? Move our stuff before Gram gets home and surprise her?'

But the way it worked out, Gram came home early. She caught Dee and me carrying L.A.'s fish tank with her six neon tetras down the hall past L.A. and Diana, who were coming the other way with my radio and the last of my shirts, the worried Jazzy hustling along right at L.A.'s heels. I'd left L.A. my second-best Louisville Slugger as a housewarming present, holding my breath until I was sure she didn't see anything suspicious about this.

'Goodness,' Gram said. 'Why are you imps burgling each other?'

'Biscuit gambled his room away,' said Diana helpfully.

We set the tank where L.A. wanted it and I came back to tell my story. I tried to keep my thoughts arranged correctly, for fear of Gram's mind-reading.

'No big deal,' I said. 'It's really L.A.'s turn in the good room anyway. This way I can play my radio a little louder.'

Gram walked into the kitchen and turned the fire on under her teakettle, then looked at me over the top of her reading glasses. 'Chivalry does begin at home, I suppose,' she said.

So that was okay.

But that night I couldn't sleep. I kept thinking about the morning of the day before. Jazzy had been at the vet's to get her dewclaws removed and L.A. and I had gone with Gram to pick her up. Arriving home, I carried Jazzy up the walk and opened the door as L.A. parked the Buick. With her front paws wrapped in cotton and gauze, Jazzy had seemed kind of limp and discouraged all the way home, but at the door she started trembling and growling in my arms and finally threw back her head and let loose a miniature howl. When I set her down she scooted away on three legs, holding one front paw and then the other up as she rounded the camellia bush toward the garage.

'Now, what on earth can that be about?' Gram said as she came up behind me.

In a minute L.A. came around the camellia from the garage, carrying Jazzy in her arms. After I told L.A. what had happened we went inside and looked in all the rooms and closets without finding anything.

But later that day, while L.A. was at Diana's house, I had seen Jazzy sniffing around the bottom of the window in L.A.'s bedroom, growling to herself. I looked all around the window myself without seeing anything, then walked outside and around back to where L.A.'s room was. The grass under her window was kind of flattened down, and there were marks on the windowsill.

I sat down on the gas meter to think, my stomach unsteady and my hands shaking, trying to think as clearly as possible. My first idea was to get Gram to call Don Chamfort and arrange for police protection. But then what would happen? All I could visualize was a couple of TV-style cops sitting in their car day and night in the alley behind the house, drinking bad coffee out of paper cups and watching L.A.'s window. Then for a second my thoughts went off on a crazy jag, the way they sometimes did in times of stress, and I had a mental picture of the cops sitting there day after day like zombies, their hair getting shaggier and their beards growing out, or possibly abandoning their car for a tent in the back yard, sleeping with their guns clutched in their hands, maybe eventually reverting to the wild, holding out here forever like Jap soldiers in their island caves.

But I didn't think police protection was going to help us at all, in spite of my confidence in Don. Most likely a couple of cops would come, look at the grass and at what I'd seen on the windowsill, scribble a line or two in their notebooks, tell us to be careful, tip their hats and leave, and that would be the end of it.

And the other possibilities I thought of were even worse: some social worker deciding L.A. should be in foster care where she would be safer, maybe even both of us having to go. Or Gram, old as she was, taking some kind of spell from all the worry and dying.

Then, without a single good idea to show for my efforts, I'd stood up and gone back to look at the marks on the sill of L.A.'s window again — a neat half circle of deep indentations in the painted wood. As I stared at them I could feel my heartbeat shaking my body. No matter how much I wanted to find one, there was no harmless explanation for what I was seeing, no way around what the marks were and what they meant.

They were the imprints of human teeth.

4

Hot Licks

Echoing space and cold, dead air surrounding me, my skin crawling with desperate horror. The naked girl who has kept watch by my bedside so many nights, her hands bound behind her back and a cord knotted around her neck, stands on a wooden box in the glare of a swinging bare lightbulb, shaking her head and crying, No-no-please-no. Blood trickles down from where her nipples should be. There is a blinding flash from a camera and the sound of a man's laughter. The box is kicked away and the cord tightens, instantly silencing the girl's voice. Suddenly I see that she is L.A. Urine flows down between her legs, drips from her feet and patters onto the concrete floor. I can't move, can't do anything to help her. I can't watch either, and I try to turn away but somehow the image stays in front of my face.

A cut of meat, still blood-wet and hot from the carcass, brushes against my mouth. L.A. struggles silently as she hangs twisting in the air, her eyes wide and wild, but my arms and legs still refuse to move. There is another flash. The meat slides up over my nose with a wet smacking sound, smelling like a dog's breath —

149

I opened my eyes and saw Jazzy's face three inches in front of mine, her whiskers quivering. Hubert Ferkin was holding her, aiming her at me, and when he saw I was awake he put her down and sat on the arm of the couch.

'Here comes them baby blues,' he said. Jazzy, who had never much liked Hubert, hustled back to her box.

'Jesus!' I gasped. I sat up. My T-shirt was wet and my heart was banging.

'Man, you are one rowdy sleeper,' said Hubert. 'Shoulda seen yourself thrashing and groaning down there.'

I shook my head hard and stood up, wanting to be all the way out of the dream. With Hubert behind me, I walked into the kitchen for a glass of water.

'Hey, man,' Hubert said. 'I heard you gave up your room.'

'Who told you that?'

'Heard it around. What's the deal?'

'No deal,' I said. 'I lost it in a card game.'

He looked at me in disbelief. 'You're weird, man.'

I didn't say anything, just grabbed a glass from the cabinet and filled it from the tap.

Hubert had never had much of an attention span. He lost interest in my room. 'I'm going over to the Jukebox for a set of strings,' he said. 'Wanta go?'

'Sure, why not?' I said. Gram and L.A. had left early to go shopping and then to visit Dr. Kepler, leaving me on my own for at least a couple of hours. I didn't want to stay in the house. I might go to sleep again.

I drank half the glass of water at the sink, then bent down and poured the rest over my head. I toweled myself off with a dishcloth, carried it into the laundry room and tossed it into the hamper. I peeled off my sweaty T-shirt and tossed it too, then found a clean one in the laundry basket by the washer and pulled it on.

By now feeling a little more together, I said, 'Let's go.'

Hubert was never anything but ready, and a couple of seconds later we were out the door. As we walked along he hocked up a goober and blew it away, the gob of spit spinning through the air like a little white dumbbell. Then he got a round Copenhagen can from his back pocket, where it had worn a pale circle in the denim, tucked a pinch behind his lip and threw his head back to clear the hair from his eyes.

Everybody wondered why I hung around with Hubert, who was as off-the-wall and unpredictable as L.A. but with almost no redeeming features. I knew having him with me didn't do much for my social standing, but we did have a few things in common. For example, he wasn't too welcome at his mom's house either, his stepfather being a drunk who kicked the living shit out of him for no known reason at least twice a month, the difference being that he had nowhere else to go. This had made him a little mean and caused him to talk like he didn't care much one way or the other about anything or anybody. Which, on my bad days, I admit made a certain kind of sense to me.

But I knew with Hubert the attitude was mostly smoke because of the way he acted at our house, where he was always polite and agreeable and helpful and well-behaved enough to give you diabetes. In fact you could tell he kind of wished he lived there with us, even though he had to know it would mean doing chores and always getting his homework in and giving up his freedom to run the streets at all hours even on school nights.

Not that he didn't have his tough side. At school, and everywhere else besides Gram's, he got into a lot more fights and trouble than the average kid. And he was extra dangerous in a fight because he tended to attack without warning and didn't know when to quit, a little like L.A. I'd once seen him cross the street after somebody he thought gave him the finger, a boy almost twice his size. Hubert broke his nose and a couple of his teeth and wouldn't stop punching until I dragged him off the guy, who was whimpering and trying to curl himself into a ball on the sidewalk.

But Hubert was one of those people who seem to have quite a bit of information, even if it tended to be kind of narrowly concentrated, and fairly often I asked him about various stuff I didn't understand. I don't mean he was book-smart or anything, because a lot of academic things I considered obvious were complete mysteries to him, like algebra, for instance. But he read a lot, if you count magazines, and he had hundreds of them. One rainy day he lifted up his mattress and got out

152

his special collection, which included bunches of true-crime periodicals depicting women with a lot of lipstick on getting murdered in their underwear. The articles had titles like 'Coed Bloodbath' and 'Lovers' Lane Horror.' Then there were his naturist journals, with photographs of adults, old people and kids of all ages doing regular things, running around, playing volleyball or just sitting in lawn chairs looking completely normal except for being naked. You knew which magazines and which pages were Hubert's favorites from the wear and tear on them. He'd look at a picture he liked and say something like, 'Ooh, sweet mama!' or maybe just grab his crotch and moan.

Hubert told a lot of stories about wild things he'd done with girls, but they were never girls I knew and you could never connect the stories to any particular time or place. I don't know why, but I got the feeling Hubert was more obsessed with girls than most guys just because he wasn't very good with them in real life, and when you got right down to it I didn't think he even really liked them all that much. But in spite of this kind of stuff, and as over-the-fence as he could be in some ways, he was my consultant for certain things I couldn't ask L.A. about.

Speaking of L.A., Hubert was hopelessly hung up on her, and I really think he'd have let an alligator eat his foot just to get in good with her. He'd talk constantly to me about how fine she was and how much he'd like to get together with her, like maybe I could help his case with her. Or would if I could. It was disgusting, like having a two-legged dog around, wagging his tail and grinning all the time. He always wanted to watch whatever she was watching on TV or go wherever she wanted to go or eat whatever she wanted to eat, which was practically nothing. He even smiled and complimented Gram's cooking, which actually was pretty superior but tended to feature a lot less frying and a lot more vegetables than Hubert was used to.

'The only things he seems to understand as food are salt, grease and ketchup,' Gram had once said.

But that wasn't the worst thing about him by a long shot.

'Oh, man,' he said once when it was just the two of us and the subject of L.A. came up. He moaned and held his crotch, saying, 'I just gotta do her.'

Somehow this caused me to become aware of the blood pulsing in my hands and booming in my head. I said, 'Get off it, asshole. You're not her type.' I looked at him. 'And don't talk that shit to me.'

I didn't know what L.A.'s type was or what I was feeling exactly, but when Hubert looked at me to see if I was serious, whatever he saw was enough to shut him up once and for all about doing L.A.

Now I slowed down to light the second half of the Chesterfield I had started the day before yesterday. I said, 'Why do you think anybody'd cut on a person and kill them like they did with those girls?'

He shrugged. 'Why's anybody do anything,

man? Because that's what they wanta do. Haven't you heard of people that like to hurt girls they're doing it with? Tie 'em up, whip 'em, stuff like that?'

I didn't answer, trying unsuccessfully to imagine what relationship there could be between wanting someone and wanting to hurt them.

'And then you got your snuff movies,' he said.

'What's a snuff movie?'

'It's like they're just making some porno movie, but then when they got the girl tied up and everything they go ahead and kill her.'

'That's bullshit,' I said, the thought generating a twisting sensation in my gut.

He gave me a look.

But, thinking it through, I decided he could be telling the truth. It had been my experience that nobody ever went broke overestimating how bad people could be.

'Damn, man,' I said, feeling like I needed to take a bath or brush my teeth or something.

'Then there's people that want to get hurt,' he said. 'Mosko-something-or-others. I guess they get together with the ones that like to hurt people. Match made in heaven.'

At this point I stopped even trying to track what he was saying because it seemed to have left reality too far behind. Or maybe because it hadn't.

We angled down across the grass to the edge of the freeway between Illinois and Saner. Hot booming air rocked us on our heels as the traffic slammed by, both of us watching back to our left

155

for a break to get across. Hubert started bouncing up and down on the balls of his feet with his jaw out and his hair flying in the diesel-flavored wind, and I knew he'd take the first excuse for an opening. All I wanted was to get to the other side alive, but for Hubert this crossing was always a grudge match. I took a last drag, dropped the butt and stepped on it.

Sure as hell, Hubert was off and running before I thought he had any kind of shot at all. Ignoring the horns and screaming tires, he made it across the inside lane about half an inch ahead of an eighteen-wheeler, then kept on going across the median and onto the concrete of the far lanes without even seeming to break stride or look at the traffic. Then he was all the way across, dancing around triumphantly with his arms above his head, both middle fingers up, giving a loud whistle through his teeth.

I waited for a real break and made the median, then a few seconds later got enough of a gap to cross the last two lanes. I caught up with Hubert and we headed on up the slope to hit Zang and turn down toward the Jukebox.

We hadn't been on Zang more than a minute when Uncle Cam pulled up beside us in his van. 'Where ya goin?' he hollered.

'Jukebox,' I said.

'Hey, I'm goin' that way,' he said. 'Jump in.'

Hubert leaned aside to spit, then we piled into the van and Cam pulled away. Hubert got out an emery board and started filing the ragged calluses on the ends of his chording fingers.

I glanced at Cam as we drove along, noticing

how his fine brown hair — which had always reminded me of baby hair — was getting farther back on his forehead. He was skinny, with arms that didn't look particularly strong, but had a soft little beer belly — a look I'd once heard Gram call 'dissipated.' His mind always seemed to be somewhere else, and his eyes didn't look exactly the same, like they were considering two different things at the same time. His expressions tended to change all of a sudden too, meaning you could lose track of his attitude if you weren't careful. In my thinking all this was connected in one way or another with the fact that he was a musician. That and him being drunk most of the time.

'How's it shakin', Hube?' he said. Hubert had known Cam a couple of years, actually a little longer than he'd known me. They'd riffed together a few times with the other two guys that Cam referred to as his band, the Nitecrawlers.

'Good, doin' good, Cam,' said Hubert, putting up the file and popping his hands on his legs like a bongo player. 'You workin'?'

'Fixin' to start a regular Friday and Saturday night gig at the Legion Hall over here. We need a front guy that can actually sing, though.'

I could almost see and hear how Rachel would have reacted to this if she'd been here. She'd have frowned, pooched out her mouth, crossed her arms and sent Cam one of those looks of hers, turning up the heat on him to get a real job and start bringing in some regular money so they could maybe get a little ahead for once instead of scratching by on what she made waiting tables

157

and cashiering at the Whistlin' Dixie and her always having to wrestle with the drunk owner trying to get his hand up her dress.

But Hubert saw it a different way. Regardless of how little money he made, Cam was a professional, in Hubert's eyes a wild man out walking the ragged edge, not answering to anybody, staying up all night and smoking pot and pulling off guitar licks Hubert couldn't even have a wet dream about. In other words, a god. There was nothing Hubert wouldn't have done to get into the group as an official member.

'You a celebrity now, Biscuit?' he said. 'Found that dead girl and all?'

'I guess,' I said. A lot of times I didn't know how to answer Cam's questions, and the subject of the dead girl gave me a cold feeling inside.

'Musta really been something. What'd the body look like?'

'Pretty blue and stiff.'

'Heard y'all were on TV and everything.'

Which was true. L.A. and I had talked to several reporters and even been interviewed on camera by a thin man wearing a wig and a bow tie who had a voice like the Lone Ranger, the lights burning down on us like a dozen suns.

'Yeah,' I said.

'Had to be a kick,' said Cam.

'Not really,' I said. 'I was mainly afraid of saying something dumb.' I didn't know why the hell I was telling Cam this, and in front of Hubert at that, but there it was.

Cam decided to let it go and I was glad to do the same. I looked around the inside of the van, which was royally cluttered from end to end with beat-up concert speakers and amps, duffel bags, toolboxes, an old guitar case and other odds and ends. Next to Cam's seat on the floor was a pump-up air pistol that he used to shoot at squirrels and cats he saw as he drove around, and on the dash there were two or three empty Raleigh packs, a can of lead pellets, half a roll of Life Savers, an old ballpoint and several matchbooks.

As a driver Cam never seemed to be in a hurry, but he stayed alert as he drove, kind of the opposite of Jack, who was one of those kill-or-be-killed drivers, always seeming to be on the verge of having some kind of seizure when he was behind the wheel, like he was flying a fighter in a sky full of bogeys and he was out of bullets. Everything that happened in traffic seemed to catch Jack off guard and make him yell. But riding with Cam you could actually relax a little.

Going on with his band problem, Cam said, 'Last guy we had on the mike, I swear it sounded like you was frying live chickens. Way the guy juked and strutted around out there making all those faces, musta thought we was at the bottom of Deep Ellum or something. Mighta made a halfway good show if you unplugged his mike.'

'What'd you do with him?' said Hubert, setting Cam up.

'Put him on the road with a red ass, whattaya think?'

Hubert laughed. Cam looked out the side windows and in his rearview mirror.

'Here we are,' he said, pulling up in front of the store.

The sign over the door had the outline of a jukebox in different colors of neon. Below that it said *FROM BEGINNER TO PRO*. There were no other cars in the parking lot. We got out and looked at the guitars, drums and horns in the window. Cam scratched under his chin as he stared at a pearl-inlaid bass guitar, a sure sign he wanted it, and I figured he was thinking of ways to sell Rachel on the idea.

Finally he went inside, Hubert trailing along behind him. For a while I stayed at the window inspecting the merchandise. One of the guitars hung straight down from a cord looped around its neck. Looking at it, I felt something twang inside me. I took a deep breath and went inside.

Cam was showing Hubert some tricky chord changes. I wandered around looking at the instruments until Cam and Hubert had worked their way through the display guitars and started a heavy conference with the clerk about various kinds of strings. The clerk kept pushing his thick glasses up on his nose with his finger, and when he turned to get something Cam had pointed at, I saw Hubert slip a couple of picks from the display into his back pocket. Then, when he saw he had the time, he grabbed a few more.

I didn't know anything about music, but I liked the exact artistic look of the different instruments. I visualized myself learning on the sly to play guitar and then springing it on Gram and L.A., ripping out some Slowhand or B. B. King for them. On optimistic days I thought it

160

might be possible; I wasn't tone deaf or anything, and L.A. and Diana even said I had a good sense of rhythm. But somehow I could never get the hang of making music. I figured maybe it was like Hubert's problem with algebra, just a locked door for me.

When Cam and Hubert finally settled on the right strings and Hubert paid the clerk from the tight wad of bills he brought out of his pocket, I was ready to get going. We climbed back into the van.

'So how's that girl of mine?' said Cam, glancing at me.

'Pretty good, really diving good. We go to the pool whenever we can.'

Cam looked up and down the streets and along the storefronts. We swung out into the traffic. 'I need to pick up some stuff,' he said. 'We'll go by the studio and then I'll drop y'all off.'

Hubert, looking as happy as he ever did, nodded. Cam glanced at me with some sort of expression.

'She still seeing that head doctor?' he said.

'Yes sir.'

He never said so but I had the impression Cam didn't much like the idea of L.A. seeing Dr. Ballard — because I figured he wouldn't want her talking about him and Rachel and their drinking, for one thing — but he said when Rachel and her mama got their heads together about something you could just forget about it, which was pretty much true.

'I just can't picture that place in my mind,' he

161

said, meaning the doctor's office.

As a matter of fact, I couldn't either. The best I could do was an image of L.A. walking into a room something like a principal's office but better furnished and without the sense of danger. All I really knew was that when she came out after an appointment she always had a little peppermint stick in her mouth. I shrugged.

Cam said, 'Wonder if them headshrinkers can get you to tell stuff you don't want to, like hypnotize you or something when you're not looking.'

I thought about it for a minute. 'Not L.A.,' I said.

No one said anything else until we stopped in front of the old Conoco station Cam's parents had owned before they died. It had been closed for years but you could still see some of the green and white paint on the brick. He called it his studio because he sometimes got the Nitecrawlers together there to practice new stuff they wanted to work into their act. Hubert had sat in on a couple of these jams and later said, 'Man, those guys are at light speed. No way I could keep up.' We waited in the van while Cam went in. Somebody had painted over the glass sometime in the past, but I didn't need to maintain visual contact to know Cam's last stop would be the little refrigerator he kept beer in. Sure enough, when he came back out with the old flight bag he carried his sheet music in, he was holding three opened bottles of Lone Star by their necks. He got in behind the wheel and offered one to each of us.

162

Hubert took one, but knowing I'd be coming up on Gram's radar pretty soon, I passed.

'More for me,' said Cam, tucking the extra bottle between his legs.

Cam and Hubert threw their heads back and their bottles up together like a drill team, and I saw their throats working. A pleasant malty smell filled the van, and Hubert belched as we turned toward the Illinois overpass. A minute later we drove past a blond girl in a red and yellow bathing suit washing a white Chevy Nova in her driveway, leaning over to reach a spot on the windshield.

'Hey-hey-HEY,' said Cam, slapping Hubert on the leg with the back of his hand. 'Is that choice or what?'

'Better know it,' said Hubert, taking another swig of beer. 'Like to get me some of that.'

By the time they dropped me off in front of Gram's, Cam and Hubert were talking about amplifiers. They hardly noticed when I slid out of the van and closed the door.

I went up the front steps, across the wide porch and into the house. It was quiet inside but I could feel that L.A. was here so I crossed the living room and went into the kitchen. She had the newspaper spread out on the table and was on her knees in a chair, leaning over the table with her elbows on the paper and her chin in her hands. There was a pencil stuck in her hair, just the way Gram did it, and her eyes were slitted with concentration. Her all-out crossword attack stance.

Reading over her shoulder, I had the feeling

zebra was the word she was looking for, but I didn't say anything. When L.A. wanted help she'd let you know, and I wouldn't advise anybody to hold their breath. She glanced at me, gathered up the paper and jumped to the floor.

'Guess what,' she said.

'Tell,' I said.

'We're cooking.'

From this I knew Gram had dropped L.A. off, left on some other errand and was going to be late getting back, leaving it to us to get supper together. Which under other circumstances would have been good news to me because I secretly liked cooking, but it was L.A. who'd received the assignment and that gave her absolute control of the operation. Gram required L.A. and me to be sea-cooks, which she said meant not starting anything you couldn't finish, always cooking enough food to go around and getting it on the table regardless of the weather. Also never leaving the galley while anything was still dirty. But the first, last and no-exceptions rule was that there's only one cook at a time in the galley. Anybody else passing through better be a helper, and if his tongue has been cut out ahead of time, so much the better.

Not needing to ask what L.A. wanted, I went to the cabinet for a box of macaroni and cheese while she got out a pan and filled it with water. She put the pan over a burner and turned on the flame, then shook some salt into the water. After considering for a second, she shook in a little more.

I was standing respectfully back, holding the

164

macaroni box for her and watching the blue flames curl up under the pan when Gram came in the front door. As she walked into the kitchen, I saw tears in her eyes and noticed she seemed a little more bent, and older somehow, the way she sometimes did after she had been downtown talking to Mrs. Bruhn, the social worker. And I was sure that was where she'd been this time. She stopped and looked at us, then said, 'Come here, you two,' and gathered both of us to her with trembling hands.

5

Telling

Gram coming home with tears in her eyes was trouble any way you cut it. It seemed to me the more trips she made downtown to see Mrs. Bruhn, the more dog-miserable each one made her, but this was way worse than usual. She cried about as often as L.A. did, in other words next to never, which made it clear we now had an out-and-out situation on our hands.

'What's wrong, Gram?' asked L.A.

'Come into the living room, both of you. I've got some things to tell you. Your mothers will be here in a few minutes.'

Now I knew we were in it up to our hocks. L.A. was no easy scare, but her expression told me she was thinking along the same lines. Which for me confirmed the worst: the women were now spooked, which removed my option to be afraid. As the only male on the scene, I had to think of something useful to do or say.

'I'll get you some tea,' I said firmly to Gram, heading for the refrigerator.

Gram said, 'I know we've always talked about both of you going back to your homes someday, but I'm afraid that's all changed now. It looks as if you two vagabonds are mine for good.'

Hearing it said right out loud this way stopped me in my tracks, but L.A. reacted

166

differently. She looked at Gram with a little frown line between her eyes, an almost visible question mark forming in the air above her head, not troubled or anything, just waiting for the punch line. And that was when it dawned on me for the first time that for L.A. the possibility of leaving Gram's had never been on the table. And I guess now that it came down to cases, something inside me had probably understood for a long time that I wasn't going anywhere either. I was past answering to anybody but Gram for my uncombed hair and unfinished homework.

'Okay, Gram,' we both said.

She looked at us and wiped the tears from her eyes. After a minute she said, 'Well, now, that wasn't so hard, was it?'

'No ma'am.'

Gram blew her nose in a tissue and motioned us into the front room, where we assumed our bad-news positions on the couch. She took the green chair.

'All right, then,' she said. 'What I'll start with is that I've made a decision about some things, and about the two of you, that Mrs. Bruhn has urged on me. And I agree with her — both of you have seen and heard more, been through more, than most adults . . . ' She looked hard at L.A. 'I believe you are strong enough for this.' She took a deep breath and let it out. 'A better question would be, *am I?*'

She stood and walked across the room and into the hall, and a second later we heard her bedroom door open. After a minute or so she

167

came back holding a letter that was old and yellowed, with creases from folding that were worn through in a couple of places. She handed it to me and said, 'Read this, both of you.'

It was written in pencil. I held it so L.A. could read with me:

Dear Miriam Leah and Rachel,

I hope this letter finds you all in good health and happiness and hope you all are going to be able to forgive me for this that I am fixing to do and maby go on and have some kind of normal life after I am gone to what ever their may be waighting for me on the other side God will have to decide that as I know he will in his wisdom and good custom. Their is just no other way to solve this and I am sure you will know I dont want to hurt nobody. I leave a pretty good business so with that and the burial policy and with what is in the bank it will keep the family at least for a while if it is managed half right and as you know the house is pade for. I wont blame the whisky for what I donn but it is a Demon and I was a different man with it and donn things I never would of or thought of otherwise I just hope the harm is not to great and in time to come I may be rembered for what good I donn in this world moreso than the bad. Lord knows how hard it is sometimes to see the right and then do it.

with best regards
Thomas Jefferson Vickers

I heard L.A.'s breath catch, and as I finished the letter a sharp-edged image of Gramp came to my mind — a big man, whiskey-soaked but impossibly strong, with a voice like rocks rolling down a wooden chute, always good to me but somehow crossways with Mom and Aunt Rachel for as long as I could remember.

Gram said, 'Silence has ruled us for too long. The time has come to put an end to that.' She honked into her tissue. 'I've lost track of the occasions when I argued with Mrs. Bruhn that what she seemed to be driving at couldn't be so, that so monstrous a thing wasn't possible, not in our family. But finally the weight of it became too much, too many things began to make sense to me at last — I simply couldn't deny it any longer.'

Just then Mom came in the front door, looking mad, confused and maybe scared all at once, but trying not to show any of it. Not so different from me, I realized. She was wearing blue jeans and sandals and a tight orange pullover top with no sleeves, not an outfit Gram would approve of, I knew, but to me she was as beautiful as ever, and at that moment I missed her so much I could hardly breathe. I wanted to hold her, to make this instant last, but I also wanted to turn away or shut my eyes or maybe even yell at her. At that point my thoughts bottle-necked, and I ended up not saying or doing anything.

Mom dropped her purse and car keys on the coffee table and flopped into the green easy chair. 'Hi, baby,' she said to me as she shook out a Kool and lit it with the thin lighter from the pocket on the side of her leather cigarette case. 'Hi, Lee Ann. You guys doin' all right? I'm about burned down myself.' She crossed her legs and blew out smoke. 'Rachel coming or not?' she asked the ceiling.

L.A. bit her thumbnail. Jazzy huddled in her lap, looking from Mom to Gram and back.

'You heard her say she'd be here, Leah,' Gram answered. 'This would be an excellent time for her to live up to her word.'

Mom looked at Gram. 'Yeah. Right. Well.' She fiddled with her cigarette and the ashtray.

Suddenly Aunt Rachel banged in through the front door, seeming not to notice L.A. looking away from her, then glanced around at all of us and sort of let her shoulders drop. 'Just the women and children, huh? Good.' She shot me a look and said, 'Sorry. No way we need to be calling y'all kids anymore, is there? My God, look at the size of you, Bis. Where'd you get those shoulders?' Even at this distance I smelled the alcohol on her breath. Just alcohol, no whiskey or gin smell, so it was vodka, probably straight from the bottle as usual.

Aunt Rachel was a little more hard-edged than Mom, with sharper movements and a more direct way of looking at you. Her hair, the same color as L.A.'s but not as out of control, was brushed back to show the little amethyst earrings she wore. In this light it was just barely possible to see that one of her eyes was green and the other brown. She was usually a boots and jeans kind of person but now was wearing her tan skirt with a light blue blouse. She set her purse on the end table and went into the kitchen. I heard the refrigerator door open and close, and a minute later she came back with a bottle of Dr Pepper.

'This stuff is an addiction all by itself,' she said and sat on the couch next to me, glancing first at Gram, then at L.A. L.A. met her eyes for the first time, and a look sizzled between them. 'So is it truth time, or what?'

Gram took off her glasses, looked down at them and pinched the bridge of her nose. 'In a way, I suppose that would be refreshing,' she said with a break in her voice. 'I can't say how it affected Leah, but Mrs. Bruhn has refreshed me with considerable truth lately. And dear Lord, I think today it was about all the refreshment I could've lived through. However, one goes on — if one can. And there are things we must deal with.'

She wiped away tears again and put her glasses back on.

'Mom,' said Mom tightly. 'Why can't you just leave it alone? What are you after here?'

Gram stared at her for several seconds, then said, 'Leave it alone, Leah?'

'Yeah, leave it alone. What's the point now, after all this time?'

Another hard look from Gram. 'Then it is true,' she said.

This was one of those exchanges that sometimes happened between women — especially when one of them was Gram — seeming to me to leave out whole paragraphs but still going straight to the next page with no loss of meaning or rhythm.

171

'I'm going home,' said Aunt Rachel. She didn't move.

Gram looked at all of us one at a time, even Jazzy. 'Leah, you and Rachel are my flesh and blood,' she said. 'So are these two youngsters. I love all of you with my whole heart, and what has happened to you hurts me more than I can express, more than I think you will ever know. But we are not going to live under this poisonous cloud of deceit any longer.'

'That's easy for you to say . . . ' said Aunt Rachel, drawing a line with her finger down through the beaded condensation on her Dr Pepper.

'No, dear, it isn't,' said Gram. 'Far from it. But I am through with willful ignorance, and so are we all if I have any say in the matter. I needed to hear Mrs. Bruhn today, like it or no. And I need for us all to face the truth right now.' She looked at each of her daughters.

'Good Christ,' said Aunt Rachel.

'Yes, I'd like to think so,' said Gram. 'But I do often wonder.' She closed her eyes for a second, then said, 'But I ask — no, I demand — that you tell me here and now, both of you, why I didn't know this terrible, terrible thing about you and your father. Why neither of you found a way to talk to me. Or to someone.'

There was a long silence. Finally Mom said, 'Oh, fuck,' and stabbed her cigarette out in the ashtray. 'That's totally unfair, Mom. Would you have even heard it back then? Could you have stood up to him?'

'Shut up,' said Aunt Rachel.

I noticed L.A.'s jaw was tight and her eyes full. Gram took a jerky breath and looked down at the tissue she was holding. 'I suppose that's a reasonable question,' she said. 'Evidently neither of you thought I could.' She looked up. 'Was I, for the love of God, the only one in Rains County who didn't know?'

'I was just so scared,' said Mom.

'Shut. The. Fuck. Up,' said Aunt Rachel through her teeth.

Mom looked at her sister, then at me, and down at her own hands. 'At first I didn't understand it,' she said. 'I didn't know things like that weren't supposed to happen. Then later when I did understand, he said if I told I'd be taken away and locked up and never see you or Rachel again.'

'Jesus, Leah,' said Aunt Rachel. 'Like you didn't follow him around. Like you didn't offer it to him.'

'Goddamn you, Ray!' Mom screamed. 'You are so full of shit! At least I never asked for it in the mouth! Asked for it, Ray! Down on my pretty little knees!' She thumped her knees with her fists.

Throwing her head back and baring her teeth, Aunt Rachel let out a strangled moan and grabbed a fistful of her own hair in each hand as if she were trying to tear it out.

'*No!*' Gram stood up suddenly and threw her glasses to the floor with both hands. 'By *God*, no! That's enough! This is not what I brought you all here for, and I won't have it!'

There was a crackling silence. Mom and Aunt

Rachel glared at each other, panting, as I bent down to pick up Gram's glasses. L.A. was holding Jazzy tightly and looking bleached out. Jazzy trembled all the way out to the ends of her whiskers.

'Your father was an alcoholic,' said Gram. 'I didn't fully comprehend that then and I probably don't even now. Thomas himself certainly didn't. I was raised to expect men to drink; it was simply the normal thing. Even if it hadn't been for the church and what people might have thought, I wouldn't have left him. Not just for that. Not with you two girls to support.' Gram slowly sat back down, accepting her glasses as I held them out to her. 'But dear God, if I'd only known about the rest of it,' she said. Glaring at her daughters one after the other, she said, 'How dare you not tell me!' She slammed her fist down on the chair arm, her voice breaking. 'How *dare* you!'

I saw Gramp again in my mind, this time on his tractor, dressed as he usually was at home in overalls and a railroad shirt, muddy brown boots on his feet and a straw hat on his head, his veined hands big as catcher's mitts and hard as hickory knots. Because I was so good at eavesdropping, I knew most of what had happened to him: it had been late in the year, on a clear, cold, windy day. Coming home from her Eastern Star meeting, Gram had found him dead in the gazebo behind the house under the big willow that stood by the lily pond where he'd hung a swing for the kids. After buying a new box of Federal shells at the Western Auto store in town he'd taken the old .32 revolver that he kept in his sock drawer out to the gazebo along with his whiskey bottle, a glass, a green Scripto pencil and Gram's stationery tablet, and sat in the wooden glider he himself had built for Gram. Before putting the muzzle of the pistol to his temple and pulling the trigger, he'd used the Scripto pencil to write the letter L.A. and I had just read.

Aunt Rachel had arrived just after it happened, and she and Gram had come up with a story about a gun-cleaning accident that satisfied the sheriff, but they knew the truth then and we all knew it now, even if none of us had ever spoken it.

And now it was obvious why Mom and Aunt Rachel had never seemed to want to go out to Rains County, where Gram and Gramp lived then. Thinking about all of it, I became aware that I couldn't look at Mom. I had an image of Hubert saying, 'Ooh, sweet mama!' and grabbing himself as he grinned at her, and I clenched my teeth against the nausea that boiled up in my throat.

Gram said, 'May God forgive me for my failures. I've been weak and I've been blind and I am sorry, but there is more than enough blame to go around. Except for these two youngsters here, none of us is innocent.'

She looked at me and then at Mom, who concentrated on her fingernail. I didn't know what was in L.A.'s mind, but I didn't consider myself the least bit innocent. Maybe words like that had different meanings at different stages of life.

'I realize that Jack may not face any legal consequences for what he's done to James,' Gram went on. 'But at least we're going to function as a family this time.' Her fierce gaze went around the room. 'Aren't we?'

Aunt Rachel had crossed one leg over the other and was waggling her foot up and down. She frowned at her Dr Pepper.

'And it's not just what happened to you girls and to James,' said Gram. 'Someone *will* tell me right now about Lee Ann and Camden.'

'What do you mean?' said Rachel.

'I want to know what has happened to this girl.'

L.A. and Jazzy looked at Gram. So did Mom.

Without meeting Gram's eyes, Aunt Rachel said, 'You mean why her and Cam couldn't get along?'

'What little intelligence I have is battered enough, dear — please don't insult it further.'

'Then what the hell *are* you trying to say?' Aunt Rachel asked, setting the Dr Pepper bottle on the floor. 'Make sense, Mom.' Looking at her expression, I had the feeling she knew as well as the rest of us how dumb and hopeless this sounded.

Gram ignored her. L.A.'s face was whiter than ever, and I saw that she and Gram were now looking at each other as if no one else were in the room — a full female eyelock. Large, dangerous things were being decided.

'Your father used you sexually, didn't he, Lee Ann?'

176

'Whoa, *HEY*!' Aunt Rachel yelped.

L.A. kept her eyes on Gram's, breathing like she'd just run up a flight of stairs. Jazzy's whiskers went on trembling and she glanced at Aunt Rachel, then up at L.A., then put her chin down on L.A.'s knee.

'Is this what you got me over here for?' Aunt Rachel gritted out. 'I'm getting sick and damn tired of this shit, Mom.'

But nobody paid any attention to her. Finally L.A. looked down at her own hand as it ruffled Jazzy's fur and then looked back up at Gram. The silence was almost impossible to endure. After a second or two Gram drew in a deep breath through her nose. The answer had passed between L.A. and her, and I knew nothing could ever be the same with us after this. Looking at L.A., seeing her in a way I never had before, I remembered her curled up asleep in her clothes under all those pillows on the bed with the light still on and my Swiss army knife clutched in her fist.

Gram hung her head, weakly twisting the used-up tissue in her hand. Finally she said, 'My God in heaven — the sins of the mothers.' She wiped at the corner of her eye with what was left of the tissue.

Aunt Rachel said, 'Goddamnit, Mom! How can you be *doing* this? Haven't we got enough trouble as it is?'

Mom had been staring at Rachel, her mouth half open. She said, 'So that's why she — '

'Don't you start up again, Leah!' yelled Rachel.

There was a strange kind of settled, broken look on Gram's face as she watched L.A., the two of them totally disregarding the noise Aunt Rachel was making.

Gram put her hand on L.A.'s knee. 'Have you told Dr. Ballard?'

L.A. gave one quick shake of her head.

'I think I can imagine why not,' Gram said in a shaky voice, trying without much luck to control her tears. 'But at some point it's going to be necessary, isn't it?'

Aunt Rachel paced around the room, running her hands desperately through her hair, as if there were things in it that had to be clawed out. She turned to Gram. 'Mom, for God's sake, they'll lock him up, don't you know that? Is that what you want?' She faced L.A. 'Is that what *you* want? Your own father in jail?'

L.A. gazed at her mother as the seconds went by. Finally she said, 'I don't have a father.'

'Oh, shit!' Rachel screamed. 'Shit shit *SHIT*!' She held up her arms as if praying for rain.

For a while now Mom had been watching her with a funny expression. Then she said quietly, 'Ray, you're trying to act like you didn't know, but you did. You had to.'

'What? What the hell's wrong with you, Leah?' Aunt Rachel stopped pacing and glared at Mom. 'Hell, no, I didn't know. I *don't* know. It's not true, goddamn it!'

'You knew,' said Mom.

'Jesus H. Christ!' Rachel yelled. 'Can you please just shut the fuck up, Leah? For once in your goddamn life?'

178

'When you quit sleeping with Cam and moved into the other bedroom, Ray. Or didn't come home at all. That's when you gave Cam your daughter.'

L.A. turned her face away. I could see she was going to cry. I already was.

'You're all goddamn NUTS!' Aunt Rachel screamed.

'You knew,' said Mom. 'There's no way you didn't.'

'Shut up! *Shut up!*'

'All those books and magazines full of naked kids stashed everywhere — I bet he whacks off a dozen times a day.'

'*No-no-no-no!*' yelled Rachel, covering her ears. She bent forward as if she were going to throw up.

Gram got to her feet. All of us but Aunt Rachel watched her walk unsteadily across to the telephone.

6

Casualties

I don't want to tell Dee Campion's story, at least not this part, the part about how it ended, but I have to. And I won't disrespect him, or Gram, by saying this is what *happened* to him. Gram taught me better than that. I have to tell what Dee and his dad and I did. What it all means is probably not for me to say, but it made me wonder for the first time in my life if it's actually possible to sell your soul.

One of the most important things to know about Dee is that he was an artist, and the way I'll always see him in my mind is standing at the easel in his room, painting some arrangement he's set up on a little card table in the light of the north-facing window. I see the same light surrounding Dee, making him glow like a religious painting himself as he moves the tip of his brush around in the paint and water and then touches it to the paper to create a curled root hair or almost-transparent seed. As he works, his face becomes still and neutral and he seems to lose track of the world.

I never spoke to Dee or made any unnecessary noise when he was like that, knowing he was in a place that wasn't mine to enter or disturb. In that way he was like a placekicker or a diamond cutter, impossible for regular people to really understand.

But Mr. Campion didn't see Dee or his paintings the way I did. Sometimes he'd stand for a minute watching Dee at the easel and his face would go red, or he'd hitch up his pants and march into his study, where everything was leathery and solid. On the study walls were what seemed like dozens of photographs of Mr. Campion smiling at the camera from between the horns of downed game, or shaking hands with some ballplayer, or sitting on a horse, and at the center of everything, a rosewood-framed gold putter he'd won the year before last in the pro-am at Cedar Crest. He'd rock back in the chair at his desk and twiddle a pencil or play with the letter opener as he looked up at the stuff on the walls.

Some days he'd take me out to the driving range to hit a bucket of balls, Dee not saying anything as we left, just standing there with a brush or paint rag in his hand. Sometimes I'd look back at him as we walked out to the car, trying to understand his expression, half wanting him to object. Other times Mr. Campion and I would go into the den, find a game on TV and talk defensive alignments and quarter-back tendencies while Mrs. Campion did something in the kitchen and Dee painted in his room.

One day Mr. Campion came into the den with two Pearls from the fridge — Dee's mom fussing along behind him about what Gram would say — then popped the caps and handed me one. After calculating that there was no way I'd be seeing Gram in less than a couple of hours, I took it. It was cold and delicious, going down smoothly and warming me inside.

'Fuckhead,' Mr. Campion said to the wide receiver on the screen. 'Third and six, guy runs a five-yard hook. See that, Jim?'

'Yes sir. It looked like he could've picked up ten, easy, with the corner playing that loose.' I burped. It was late in the second quarter, the Cowboys down 17–3 against the Cards, no letup in sight.

'That's the trouble with these assholes anymore,' Mr. Campion said. 'Their mind's on their contract and their endorsement money, they forget to play the goddamn game.'

'I heard the other wideout had a groin pull,' I said.

'Yeah, delicate bastard. But he walks on out there and lines up just like everybody else, so I guess he earns his pay. Just too bad about them wooden hands.'

It was different when Dee and I talked. For instance, after he found out about Tricia Venables he fretted over how L.A. and I felt about it and whether it was going to continue to bother us, and he worried himself sick about how Tricia's friends and family were taking the loss. He even speculated about the right way to dress a girl her age for burial. That's how he was, always thinking about other people and always putting their feelings ahead of his own.

It was around this time that Mr. Campion decided to send Dee down to Halberd Academy, a military school outside Austin. It must have come up suddenly because one day Dee told me about it, and the next thing I knew I was riding down to the bus station in the rain with Dee and his parents to see him off. Mrs. Campion was crying and so was Dee. At the station he got me aside and told me he didn't want to go, could I talk to his dad and maybe get him to change his mind?

'You know he's not gonna listen to me, Dee,' I said.

'But I want to stay here — I just want to be with you, James, please . . . '

I told him I'd try, but when I spoke to Mr. Campion a little later I didn't. I couldn't think of a way to bring it up. A few minutes after that the bus hissed and rumbled as it pulled out carrying Dee, his white face framed in the dark window, sliced into wavy sections by the rain streaking down the glass.

The call came while Gram and L.A. were out, and the second I heard the ring I knew what it was about. I had to force myself to touch the phone. When I picked up, all I could hear at first was a man crying. I wouldn't have been able to tell who it was from the sound, but of course I knew, and it sounded like the sobs were tearing his chest apart.

He said, 'Jim, this — this is Joe Campion. It — oh, Jesus — it's Dee, my God, he's dead, Jim — '

Then nothing but more sobbing.

I slowly hung up the phone and stood for a long time looking at it. It didn't seem to be an electrical or mechanical thing. It was like a creature from some unnatural place, alive and dead at the same time, poison to the touch.

Later I learned that Dee's squad leader had gone into the mess hall early that morning ahead of everybody else and found him slumped against a table, thinking at first glance that somebody had left a duffel bag or something behind. But then he saw the blood. The dress sword Dee had stolen from the sergeant major's quarters was rammed completely through his chest. I knew where the idea for that had come from: Dee had once shown me a book about ancient Romans with an illustration of a general in a little dress falling on his sword.

'We lost him, Jim,' Mr. Campion said the next day, wiping at his eyes with a folded handkerchief. 'How'd we do that?' He'd sent Dee to Halberd to make him different, not to have to leave Mrs. Campion sobbing helplessly on the porch and drive two hundred miles down there on a normal-looking day to claim his son's body.

He told me later that the flags were still at half-mast when he got there. The cadet corps had turned out in full dress on the parade ground and a four-man honor guard met him in the quad and escorted him to the commandant's office.

Later Mr. Campion, looking across at me from inside some other reality, said, 'Military's got good ceremonies for death.' Wiping at his nose with the handkerchief, he circled back to the center of his pain as if being pulled by some irresistible gravity, saying, 'Sergeant major told me Dee had to've made at least a couple of runs at it. Didn't think he could've gotten that much penetration in one try.'

Mr. Campion was never the same after that. When he hugged me at the funeral I could feel that he was old and broken now, his voice thin and his hands shaking. I knew he could never really believe in himself again, his courage lost forever.

As for me, I kept wondering about odd things, like whether they'd given Dee's painting stuff back to Mr. Campion along with the body, and why it seemed like such a strange joke that the funeral home had fixed Dee up to make it look like nothing was wrong with him. And how Mrs. Campion had won the battle over how to dress Dee; he was in the shiny blue suit he wore for church instead of his Halberd uniform.

In the chapel Mr. Campion brought me up to sit with him and Mrs. Campion in the section reserved for the family, leaving Gram and L.A. and Diana in their pew two rows back. As I sat beside her, Mrs. Campion gave my hand a squeeze and touched a tissue to the corners of her eyes. I tried to get my tie straight and concentrate on the service, but all I could really think about was how things had worked out, and how I didn't belong up here with Dee's parents. I thought about losing Dee this way and about having no father of my own. I thought about how it must feel when your only son dies.

Now Dee had stopped everything. Set it in stone. Now nothing could ever be repaired.

'*What's it like to be an orphan?*' he had once asked me. *He is sitting in the swing next to me at*

185

the park looking off into the distance where a bunch of small kids are kicking a soccer ball around on the open green.

'I'm not really an orphan,' I say, a little irritated for no reason I can understand. I eat a couple of animal crackers from the box we bought at the 7-Eleven on our way here.

'I know. But in another way you are. Do you ever dream your dad's alive?'

'Once in a while.'

'Like everything's okay again? Like him being dead was a bad dream, and you woke up from it?'

I look at him. 'How do you know about stuff like that?' I say.

He shrugs. 'No reason.' He bites his thumbnail.

'C'mon, there's always a reason.'

'I dream sometimes.'

'That your dad's dead or something?'

'Not exactly.'

'Then what?'

He stares at his thumb. 'Me,' he finally says. 'I dream that I'm the dream.'

'You? What do you mean?'

'I'm the dream everybody wakes up from.'

That was what I was thinking about as I looked for the last time at Dee in his casket, understanding clearly now that his story and mine could never be separate again, that he would live forever in my mind, and die there forever too.

7

In & Out

The day after Dee's funeral I was sitting with L.A. in the living room, pretending to be interested in the Cubs-Giants game on TV, but it was really L.A. who had my attention. She was sitting in the green chair reading *The Long Walk* by Slavomir Rawicz, so I knew her mind was in Siberia. The family showdown at Gram's was still echoing in my mind, and I wondered how L.A. had gotten herself back together like this already, having no understanding yet of such things or even of how little I knew about them.

The frizzed ends of her cutoff jeans were fluffy blue bands around her brown thighs, and her hair, which looked wilder than usual, was fringed with a halo of sunlight from the window behind her. Hundreds of hot-looking little specks of dust drifted slowly in the air between us. She turned a page, and the flecks floating in front of her moved around a little faster for a while. But they still weren't going anywhere.

On the television screen the center fielder came trotting in and took an easy fly to end the inning. As I looked at L.A.'s smooth skin I thought about Cam's white fingers and how they moved like spiders over the strings of his guitar when he practiced, usually in his bare feet as he sat on his living room couch, his toes spreading and curling in sympathy with the fingers. I remembered how skillful his hands were and how the nails on his picking hand were long and slightly bent, orange with nicotine, grooved like horn. I imagined those hands on L.A.'s skin, everything Mom and Aunt Rachel had said coming back to me in a choking rush, and I began to wonder if going crazy worked on the same principle as burning out a fuse by plugging in too many appliances at once. It occurred to me that if you were smart enough, maybe you could somehow learn to turn off your thoughts temporarily when the circuits got overloaded, which could be a big help to me in some situations.

Like right now.

I got up, turned off the set and walked into the kitchen. I looked in the fridge and the cabinets without finding anything I could get interested in. Then I suddenly understood for the first time that the emptiness I felt had nothing to do with actual hunger, that it wasn't in my stomach but somewhere in space behind me, just out of sight. I went back into the living room and switched on the stereo without looking to see what was in the slot. It turned out to be an old Johnny Mathis *Greatest Hits* collection, and his light, smooth voice started in about 'The Twelfth of Never,' a number that somehow always caused a tightening in my throat. I walked over to the couch and sat down.

'Hey,' I said. 'You're gonna use up your brain with all that reading.'

L.A. looked up at me. 'Still be ahead of you,' she said.

'No shit.'

'You tired of baseball?'

'I'm thinking about Dee.'

'What about him?'

'I just keep remembering how he was.'

'You mean about liking guys?'

'Yeah. I can't even imagine what it would be like to feel that way.'

'So ask a girl.'

Johnny Mathis sang about the poets running out of rhyme, and the end of time.

'Wouldn't help,' I said. I took a deep breath. 'What's really on my mind is, it's like all those times when Dee was with me it was one thing for me and something else for him. Like the world was completely different for the two of us.'

Until the twelfth of never, sang Johnny.

'Okay,' said L.A., tilting her head to the side and watching me. She put a folded Baby Ruth wrapper in the book as a marker and laid the book on the end table beside her.

'What I mean is, what the hell difference does it make what he thought, right?' Tears were coming up in my eyes again, and I tried angrily to stop them.

L.A. waited.

'Like if he put his hand on my knee the way he did that time, it didn't really have anything to do with me. Because he was still in his world, not mine.'

I guess L.A. had given up on my sanity by this time because she didn't say anything, just stared

189

at me like you might at some foreigner who won't stop yakking at you even though it's obvious you don't understand a word he's saying.

'It didn't change anything about me at all,' I said. 'It didn't matter who Dee was seeing when he looked at me. It wasn't really me he was touching.'

At least this seemed to make some kind of sense to L.A. 'Yeah,' she said. 'So?'

'So everything about you that really counts is still okay.' I caught a flash of her *back off* expression, and swallowed dryly. 'No matter what happened,' I said.

There was something different in L.A.'s face now. Today was her day to see Dr. Ballard, and I hoped I wasn't somehow setting her back in her treatment. But I just couldn't shut myself up. I brushed at my eyes.

'Some things they can't touch,' I said, and swallowed again.

For a long time it was so quiet I could hear the small whirring between the ticks of the clock on the mantel across the room. I looked down at my hands, then back up at L.A.

I'm not sure, but I think she nodded.

8

Night Things

We had finished the supper dishes and L.A. and Gram were in the living room watching TV. After wiping the table down I dug around in the junk drawer at the end of the counter by the back door until I found the stump of a citronella candle and two wooden matches. Then I cracked ice cubes from one of the metal freezer trays into a big glass, filled it with sweetened sun tea from the pitcher in the fridge and walked out to where the wrought-iron chairs were arranged around the patio table beside the garden. It was almost full dark. I set the candle in the little dish on the table and scratched a match on the flag-stones to light the bent black wick.

As the candle pointed its short yellow flame straight up and filled the still air with a soapy smell a couple of birds woke up and flittered around for a minute in the pecan branches above me. I looked carefully around the yard for any sign of an intruder, and when I saw nothing out of place decided it must have been my arrival, and maybe the lighting of the candle, that had awakened the birds. I sat down to watch the lightning bugs as they circled and glided over the grass I'd cut with the old Sears push mower that morning. I breathed in the watermelon smell of the St. Augustine, thinking about Dee, the girl

L.A. and I had found and the other two, and wondered what it felt like to die. What it would be like to have a sword through your chest or to choke to death.

The green lines and loops of the fireflies in the air gave the impression that some slow invisible hand was trying to write an important message on the darkness but kept getting puzzled and stopping in the middle of letters. I remembered the days when L.A. and I had chased lightning bugs together and filled jars with them to carry through the darkness like magical lanterns, but that time seemed as long ago to me as the Mesozoic right now. I thought about how the world had looked and smelled and sounded then, wondering if this was what it was like to be old.

The sky in the west wasn't completely black yet but the night was already so thick with the sound of crickets and tree frogs and cicadas that the air seemed almost solid, and I could hear a mockingbird singing its night songs in the top of the cedar elm behind Mrs. McReady's house. The candle flame cast a wavery circle of light on the flagstones and carpet grass around me, and beyond that I could just see the silvered redwood fence covered with frangipani and white jasmine at the back and along the south side of the yard. At the other edge of the garden was a mossy concrete birdbath with a bronze figure of a round-bellied little boy standing on goat feet and playing a funny-looking harmonica. Looking out from the candlelight, I could make out the shapes of some of the plants, the showy blue irises, pink and yellow verbenas and lantanas, gladiolus in a dozen colors, the sentinel hollyhocks at the back of the garden, some of them taller than the fence, their pale blooms like ghosts against the darkness behind them. Along the fence to my right were the big hydrangeas that Gram sometimes dosed with coffee grounds or old nails or baking soda to adjust the color of the blooms.

But no matter how hard I tried to keep my mind on thoughts like these, I kept coming back to the subject of dying. I pushed against my throat with my fingers until I couldn't breathe in, then took the pressure off. It didn't take much of a push at all to stop the flow of air. For years I'd been unable to get the idea of burning to death out of my mind, and now this.

I'd once managed to hold my breath for over sixty seconds without even getting mentally fuzzy, which taught me something about how long a minute could be. When the man had first taken Tricia, I knew, without understanding how I knew, that she'd tried to tell herself she was only being raped, and thought, *This is what it's like*. But she'd really known better. Later, when she'd realized what he was about to do to her breasts, she'd hoped and prayed that would be enough for him, even felt a little bit relieved, and said in her mind, *Okay, do that if you have to and then please be satisfied, please let me live, let me go home*, because she'd wanted to believe that surely he wouldn't have to do anything more awful to her than that. But then it couldn't have been long before she'd understood that doing

193

that to her wasn't going to be nearly enough for him, and she must have wondered why this man she'd probably never seen before hated her so much.

I remembered her dead, sleepy-looking eyes and peaceful expression. I'd heard that when the policeman told her mother what had happened she'd shaken her head like the deal wasn't necessarily done yet and gotten down on her knees on her living room floor, taken the officer's hand in hers, kissed it front and back and asked him to please stop saying her only child was dead.

How someone like the killer could just walk around in the common world in the middle of everybody and not be noticed, I still couldn't imagine. It seemed unbelievable, like having a tiger in your bathtub without knowing it. This thought reminded me of something Gram had once read to L.A. and me, a poem about a burning tiger in the forests of the night and an immortal eye.

Were there beasts that could only be seen in darkness? Or by an immortal eye?

One thing that never got far from the center of my thoughts was the image of Hot Earl with his gap-toothed grin, like a human jack-o'-lantern. Not a pretty picture, but at least Earl was no tiger.

But I couldn't completely shake the idea that there really was something out there. I gathered my courage and tried to open myself, to extend my senses out into the night, to feel the tiger as it burned. It was nearby, I could tell, breathing softly, waiting. Somehow knowing me, knowing all of us, hungrily accepting the touch of my thoughts, purring like distant thunder with anticipation.

I heard the back screen door open and close behind me, and L.A. and Jazzy came out. L.A. was carrying a plate of roasted shelled pecans and the small guitar we'd found last month next to the trash barrel behind a house where the people were moving out. She was wearing Levi's and an old short-sleeved white button-down of mine that had a big lopsided ink stain at the edge of the pocket, right over her heart. She put the plate on the table and sat in the chair beside me, Jazzy circling herself down into a ball by her feet. The pecans were from the trees we were sitting under, and Gram had roasted them with butter and salt and a little red pepper. They were still warm from the oven, and I crunched down a few, then took a drink of tea from the sweating glass.

'How come you're not watching the show?' I said.

'Jugglers,' said L.A. She started chording on the guitar strings and then picked out a sweet little optimistic-sounding melody. She stopped playing and adjusted one of the tuning keys.

'What's that?' I said.

'Nothing. I made it up.'

'The hell.'

She shrugged.

'Gimme,' I said, and reached for the guitar. I fingered the strings and got nothing but plunks and plonks. I tried again but it sounded the

195

same. 'Damn,' I said.

'Well, see there,' said L.A. She bit the end off a pecan half.

I handed the guitar back to her. So I wasn't a music maker. You've got it or you don't.

Whole 'nother kind of quick, Hubert had said once when we were talking about it. *Fingers gotta work on their own. With you it's not in your fingers; all your speed and control is in your arms and fists. You're a natural boxer. That's how come Asshole Jack's afraid of you.*

Bullshit.

Hey, believe it, man. He's scared of what you're gonna be like in a year or two. If you didn't have nothing, he wouldn't be wanting to get the gloves on with you all the time to prove himself. He wouldn't give a shit.

Now I fished out the Chesterfield I'd been saving, glanced back at the house and leaned forward to light it from the candle flame. As I smoked, a toad hopped out from under the hydrangeas into the light and squatted in the grass like a flat goblin, waiting for bugs. It made me think of pictures of gargoyles I'd seen in one of Gram's books. I found part of a gum wrapper in my pocket, wadded it into a tight ball and tossed it in front of the toad. Quick as a speargun, the toad's tongue shot out and caught it.

I knew there was a tarantula somewhere in the garden too, because I'd seen it this morning when Jazzy barked at it in the lantanas. It had been as big as my hand, black and hairy and apparently not the least bit afraid of Jazzy or me.

I wondered whether tarantulas came out at night, and if so, whether their eyes shone like other arachnids. The word I'd heard somewhere for this red pinprick was *spiderspark*, and to me it seemed to condense and focus the mysteries of the night the way a magnifying glass focuses the sun.

I offered the smoke to L.A. She took a quick puff and handed it back. I got out the blue stone the old woman had left me and rolled it in my hand. It seemed warmer than it should have been from just being in my pocket. 'What do you think it feels like to choke?' I said.

She thought about this for a while, leaning back in the chair and hugging herself. 'I don't know,' she said. There was something odd in her voice.

I said, 'I've heard fear can make you numb.'

She stared at the candle, saying nothing, two little repetitions of the flame shining in her eyes.

I felt a chill even in the dense heat of the night, seeing Tricia Venables's dead body and the marks on her neck and wrists. I rubbed my eyes, then finished the cigarette and kicked up a divot in the grass, dropped the butt under it and pressed the sod back down with the toe of my sneaker.

'D'you think maybe that's how it could've been with those girls?' I said. 'They stopped feeling anything?'

L.A. looked out across the dark garden with the candlelight moving on her face, seeing into distances that existed only for her. After a long time she said, 'They felt it.'

197

I took a deep breath and blew it out, trying to organize my thoughts. I knew I understood almost nothing about evil, but once again I had a sense of it, or something like it, waiting out there, its mighty heart beating in the night.

But thinking of it as a tiger wasn't really right. It was something much worse. Remembering the teeth marks in L.A.'s window frame, I was suddenly certain that whatever was out there was no obvious monster at all. It didn't need the darkness. It wasn't afraid of the sun. And I was sure I had seen it face-to-face.

No. More than that.

It had touched me, skin to skin.

9

Skills

Rachel had been right to worry about Cam going to jail. When the cops arrived they had found her in the front room wailing and sniffling, but no Cam. A radio alert, what Don called a BOLO, was sent out, but then before anything else could happen Cam pulled up in his van. They handcuffed him, searched him, perp-jerked him around and threw him in the back of the patrol car. As I heard the story, he had a dopey smile on his face the whole time, which I knew from experience signified that he was royally pissed off but couldn't do a damn thing about it.

Knowing now what he'd done to L.A., I had no sympathy for him. So naturally I didn't have any argument with him getting arrested either, but when the next news about him came I was on the couch with Diana in the den at the back of the Chamforts' house, with several other things on my mind. We were babysitting her little brother Andy and had the house to ourselves for a while because he was asleep and her parents were at work. It was L.A.'s day to see Dr. Ballard, so she wasn't around either.

I was sitting on the couch with one of Don's *Outdoor Life* magazines open to a story about trout fishing, but I was mostly still trying to sort out my thinking about Mom and L.A., the murdered girls and everything else that had happened. For one thing, I wasn't sure what to say or how to act around L.A. anymore, and my uncertainty was beginning to generalize to other girls and women. I guess it was starting to dawn on me what a different world they live in.

A vodka ad on the page across from the article showed a tall couple dancing on a wide balcony, which seemed strange for this kind of magazine, but it got me thinking about L.A. and Diana and how they had taken a serious interest lately in my dancing abilities. In fact, it had become one of their programs for the summer to bring me up to specifications in that respect.

That's girls for you; they look at a guy and they see raw material.

Sometimes, before the lessons, the three of us would go up to Diana's room and I'd fool around with the Chinese checkers or a deck of cards or something while the girls messed with their hair or jewelry and kind of forgot about me. It was during these times, and on account of my ability to keep my mouth shut, that I learned things about girls that I wouldn't have known any other way.

Not that I understood everything. Once, when Diana and L.A. were trying on necklaces in front of the mirror, Diana said, 'Jason Mackey's going out with Melinda. I told her he was cute.'

L.A. said, 'Like a rat's ass.'

'I know, but I still owed her for history last semester.'

It wasn't just eavesdropping, though. Another time I was leaning back on the bed halfway

200

watching L.A. and Diana doing something with hairbrushes, thinking about the pillow under my elbow, about how that was where Diana laid her head every night, and wondering whether she slept on her back or her side or her stomach. I visualized where her shoulders went on the bed, and her hips and legs too, and I wondered whether she wore pajamas at night, or maybe a big T-shirt like L.A. Or maybe nothing at all.

Then I suddenly sat up, my salivary glands and other things threatening to get out of control. This kind of stuff was happening to me a lot lately — girls beginning to figure into every part of my life and gradually establishing control over my mind. But at the same time, and as contradictory as it might sound, it came to me that getting along with them wasn't the impossibility most of the guys I knew thought it was. What I realized was that almost all it takes to stay in good with girls is keeping yourself at least semi-clean, being polite and actually paying attention when they're talking. It may sound too simple to work, but I swear it does.

Then when it was time for my lesson, we'd usually start with the fast stuff I enjoyed, like Santana or the Doors or maybe Mungo Jerry, then work our way from there up through the music they liked — James Taylor, slow numbers by the Supremes and other stuff Diana had, plus records from her parents' collection.

It's important to realize that when you're in training with girls you can't pass off the moves you make to a fast rock beat as real dancing. Guys tend to favor that stuff because it's sort of freestyle and more a matter of action than grace. And they like the music better too. But in general, girls can take fast dancing or leave it. One of the things I knew because I had the skill of silence was that they like slow dancing because it's more romantic and shows them off to better advantage.

I was a fairly quick study with all kinds of steps, though, for a couple of reasons. In the first place, I didn't like being disciplined for screwing up, which generally came in the form of some nasty comment on my intelligence from L.A. or a knuckle rap on the head from Diana. But really I think what motivated me most was how much I liked the feeling of these two slender, absolutely different girls moving against me, taking my lead and talking softly into my ear about what we were going to do next. And another thing that helped me was realizing how dancing well isn't just about the steps or the music, it's also a matter of understanding that when you're dancing, the real center of a guy's movement is his shoulders and arms, and everything else has to coordinate, whereas the center of a girl's movement is her hips and her legs.

But today was not for dancing. Diana, wearing green shorts, a white T-shirt and leather moccasins, had just come from taking a shower and turned on the stereo as she walked into the room. Jay and the Americans came low and soft from the speakers — 'This Magic Moment.' As Diana leaned on the back of the couch, reading over my shoulder and humming quietly along with the music, I could feel her hair touching my neck and her breath on the side of my face.

'What's a Coachman?' she said.

'A lure he's gonna use. Looks like a bug.'

'How's it work?'

'Just lays on the water until the fish grabs it.'

'Oh,' she said doubtfully.

It sounded a little odd to me too. We were both more accustomed to bass fishing.

'You use a long rod that's got a funny-looking reel at the back end,' I said. 'The fishing line is really what you cast, because it's kind of heavy, and the fly just gets pulled along for the ride.'

'Then what?'

'When the fly lands on the water, it floats. The fish thinks it's a real bug, and *bam*.'

'Do they fish that way in Minnesota?'

'I don't know. I'm not even sure if they have trout up there.'

I noticed the light pressure of Diana's crossed arms against my shoulder and the smell of soap and shampoo on her, and I began losing my focus on the idea of fishing. I could even smell her Gleem toothpaste as she looked over my shoulder at the picture of a man in waders standing in a mountain stream. Visualizing her stepping out of the shower wet and naked, the way I'd seen L.A. that time, I looked up at her face and saw the window reflected in her eyes and saw how the individual eyelashes curved away from her lids. Thinking back to what L.A. had shown me, and hoping I wasn't being in any way like Hubert or Cam or Jack, I reached up with both hands, carefully turned her head toward me and pressed my mouth to hers.

'Mmm,' she said.

I pushed my tongue between her teeth exactly as L.A. had done with me, and Diana invited it in. She put her hand behind my head and held my mouth to hers. The feeling was unbelievable, much more powerful than L.A.'s demonstration because it meant something so different. When we finally broke the kiss, we were both breathing hard. Diana looked at me with a serious expression, and I wondered for a second if she was going to hit me. Then she came around the end of the couch and knelt on the cushion beside me. She held my cheeks with her hands and leaned down to kiss me the way I had just kissed her. I turned farther toward her and slid my hand up from her hip toward her breast.

'Mmmm,' she said again.

At the other end of the house the front door opened, and in my guilty mind it was nothing less than the crack of doom. Diana jumped back from me as if I'd suddenly turned red-hot, and Andy started yelling in his crib.

'It's Porkchop!' Diana hissed, a rabbit in the spotlight.

'Oh, goddamn,' I said. I took a couple of deep breaths, aching, feeling like an overinflated balloon.

'C'mon,' said Diana, and we went into the other room to get Andy. 'Hey, Fubb,' she said as she gathered him up. 'You're wet.' We heard Don go into the kitchen.

While Diana started changing Andy, I looked down at myself to make sure I was safe to be seen, then walked into the kitchen. I was feeling remorseful over what I'd just been doing and wanting to do with Don's daughter, but I'd lived with worse. At least with Don I never got the feeling he could hear what I was thinking the way Gram and L.A. sometimes could.

'Hiya, Jimbo,' he said.

He turned from the refrigerator with a bottle of root beer in his hand and held it out to me as he reached for another one. His jacket was hanging over the back of a chair and he was wearing a short-sleeved white shirt and tie. His short-barreled Smith & Wesson .38 in its dark leather holster was still clipped to his belt. His hands were wide and clean, with short nails, and his strong arms were lightly covered with hair the same color as Diana's. What hair was left on his head was a little darker and lay more or less as it pleased instead of how he'd tried to comb it, with a few gray loners salted in along the sides. He got a bottle opener from the drawer and popped both caps off. We sat at the table.

'Where's the rest of us?' he said.

'Andy's getting a retread.'

'Yeah, the little late arrival — he does go through those diapers. By the way, we got that uncle of yours booked in. I dropped by lockup right after they got through taking his mug shots and prints, and I gotta say he didn't look too amused. You pretty sure he did what they said?'

'L.A. says he did.'

Don drank root beer and thought about this. 'Then he did,' he finally said. 'But I can tell you it beats the hell out of me how a guy does a thing like that. How'd we find out, exactly?'

205

'Gram did. She called the police.'

'Do you know who it was caught the call?'

'A tall serious-looking guy with a big ring, and a sort of chubby one who took off his hat in the house.'

Don nodded. 'I know who they are. I'll make a chance to talk to 'em, see what they can tell me.'

'L.A. had to tell them what Cam did to her.'

'Poor kid. Too bad there wasn't some other way. We need more female officers.' He shook his head. 'And it's not over yet. But Lee Ann's tough, isn't she?'

'Yes sir.'

'Well, Cam'll probably bond out pretty quick now, if he hasn't already — not a damn thing we can do about that. But with these judges we've got up there now, this is gonna go hard on him if it sticks. I'd hate to be him or his lawyer.'

'What's going to happen to him?'

'If he's convicted, which it looks like he probably will be, he'll go to prison. The judges have guidelines on the sentencing, but they don't have to follow them, and this is the kind of case where they're likely to go the max.'

This caused me to imagine Cam sprawled in some forgotten cell with a long gray beard and spiderwebs strung out from his knees and elbows to the walls around him.

'He may be your uncle and all,' said Don, 'but if it was up to me I'd throw away the key on a guy like him myself. But hey, you looking forward to the big trip?'

I nodded. 'Sure am,' I said. 'It's gonna be the farthest I've ever traveled. Gram says my folks took me to Ruidoso for the races when I was little, but I don't remember it.'

'Yeah, this's a little farther. North country's way different too — gets cold up there even in the summer sometimes. Marge's daddy told me he saw it snow on the Fourth of July one year. I remember the mosquitoes being pretty bad last time I was up, what was it, five years ago I guess it's been. But you can put stuff on for that. Old-timers up there get so they don't even pay attention to 'em anymore. What I'm wanting is for Diana to get to see the place, and that country. It was her granddaddy built the cabin, but she's never been there the whole time we've had it.'

I tried to imagine what the place looked like but got only a mental picture of a little log house half hidden in the woods, which didn't seem to fit at all with the way Don was talking.

He pushed his root beer bottle a couple of inches to one side, then back, thinking. 'We're gonna try something new on these damn killings when I get back,' he said. 'Ferguson's gonna be setting it all up while I'm gone.'

'What is it?'

He picked up the root beer, saying, 'I've got this crazy theory that if you add up one and one and one the right way, you just might get more than three.' He smiled at me and took a drink from the bottle. 'Anyway, as long as Marge's little sister doesn't back out on keeping Andy, I guess we're about set. Ought to be a real field day for you, Jimbo,' he said. 'Maybe you'll get lucky and hang a muskie.'

'What's that?'

'Muskellunge. Like a pike, only bigger. Mean-lookin' fish. Always been talk about eighty-pounders coming out of that lake, but the Indians say there are some in there a whole lot bigger than that. They even tell stories about them — or something — grabbing off kids and dogs.'

'Have you ever caught one?'

'No. Well, I mean yeah, but nothing like that size. I caught one on the last trip that went eleven pounds, but it was just a fluke. I was after walleyes.'

'How come?'

'They're the good eating. None of those pikes, pickerels and pick-handles are much good on the table, too many bones. Natives call some of 'em snakes — shows you right there how much use they've got for 'em.'

I could have listened to this all day. As Don took a long swallow from his bottle, I tried to think of ways to keep the conversation going, which as usual made my mind go blank.

'Daddy,' said Diana, coming into the kitchen with Andy on her arm and closing a cabinet door with her free hand. 'He's dry now but I need to feed him. Are you home for the day?'

Looking at her, I was dumbfounded. How could this possibly be the same girl I'd been kissing just a few minutes ago? She seemed older, purified somehow, and her expression, the completely natural way she stood there with Andy on her hip, made my chest tight. I wondered if what I was seeing and feeling had anything to do with the special energy between girls and their fathers.

'Yeah, babe, I think so,' said Don, setting his root beer down. 'Want me to take him?'

She passed Andy to him and started getting the pan ready to heat his milk. She expertly took a clean bottle from the sterilizer and set it on the counter, then got out the formula. I watched Don grinning and jigging Andy on his knee. They looked like a picture in a magazine. I tried to swallow the strange sadness that rose in my throat.

'I got one other thing, Jimbo,' Don said, shifting Andy and picking up his root beer again. He swallowed the last of it and leaned over to toss the bottle in the trash. 'Lee Ann's got to come down to headquarters pretty soon anyway to talk to the stenographer, but I want you and her to come in with me before we get started on that. I need a little help on something.'

Suddenly I felt much better. Don had my entire attention now.

'Yes sir?' I said.

'You and her are both pretty sharp, and you seem to get all over this end of town. Located us one dead body already this month.' He smiled, gave his head a small shake.

'Yes sir.'

'I want you both to look at some pictures for me, see if you recognize anybody, maybe tell me a few things I don't know.' He kissed Andy on the cheek and then scratched his own chin.

Andy began to fret.

'Here, Fubbit,' said Diana, bringing the bottle

of formula over to Don, who took it and touched the nipple to Andy's lips. Andy turned his head a little from side to side for a second before he located the nipple and locked onto it. He sighed and sucked.

'There you go,' said Don. 'Get after it, fullback.'

'Sure,' I said, my heart filling with the desire to help Don. 'Anything you want.'

10

Lessons

When I opened the unlocked screen and knocked on the door of Dr. Kepler's neat little pink-brick house on Fernwood, Miz M, the nurse, let me in. As always the house seemed bigger on the inside, with hardwood floors and foreign-looking furniture in light colors. The air in here was cool and medicinal, and the whole place had that quiet, suspended feeling that terrible sickness brings to a house.

'She's asleep,' said Miz M. She looked at the dish I was carrying, which was filled to the top with half the apricot cobbler Gram had baked this morning. Jiggling her round cheeks over it, Miz M took me back through the arched doorway of the deep sunny kitchen, her thick legs whisking as she walked.

'Gram says there's enough for us to have some too,' I said.

But Miz M was already into the dish cabinet. She set out small plates along with forks, napkins and glasses for milk.

'She had her morning morphine at ten,' said Miz M. 'She'll sleep for a while yet.'

As she talked, Miz M was dishing up cobbler and pouring milk for both of us. I sat down at the maplewood table. She took a bite of cobbler and said, 'Hmm-mmm, Lord, this is iniquitous!

Are you going to stay awhile?'

'Yes ma'am, till Gram and L.A. get back this afternoon.'

'Good. She does love having you. Sometimes she'll say, 'Where's that listening-boy of mine? I've got talking to do!''

'Yes ma'am.'

'I hear you're going on a trip to Canada or someplace like that.'

'Minnesota. With the Chamforts.'

'Good for you,' she said, taking another bite. 'Isn't it awful about those poor girls? My friends could hardly believe I knew the young man who found one of them.'

'Yes ma'am.'

I had no appetite for food or talk, so I drank some milk as I looked out through the window above the sink at the mimosa in the back yard. Its powderpuff blooms were mouth-colored, and the clusters of seedpods looked like snow peas. I wondered how long it had been there and how long it would live after this house and all of us were gone. Then, I thought, it would die too.

Thoughts and images of death kept coming — Dee's funeral, naked and strangled girls lying in the grass, and finally Dr. Kepler herself, not dead yet but not really living either. Gram had told me her mother, father and all three sisters had died in the war in Europe, and explained that Dr. Kepler was an atheist who believed in a strictly mechanistic universe.

This had been a new idea for me; hearing it, I imagined a huge noisy factory with gears and levers and drive belts everywhere, turning out some unknown but essential product. Then I was off into speculation about how all the devices got there, how they knew what to do, who'd turn them on and off and keep them oiled and in repair.

But I knew speculating about it was a waste of time, because my mind wasn't organized to deal with questions like that. And not only was I too ignorant to figure anything out on my own, there was no one I could conveniently get answers from, because generally people already had their minds made up and couldn't discuss this kind of question sanely. Of course, that didn't include L.A. — not that she was necessarily sane in the strictest sense, just that she wasn't the type to have any do-or-die opinions about mystical subjects. The problem was that she would consider it all a matter of guesswork and foolishness. She only really believed in what she could see or hear or touch, so if I asked her about the mechanistic universe thing she'd probably just look at me and say something like, 'That's dumb, Biscuit,' or 'Pass the ketchup, sprocket-head.'

For all I really knew, though, Dr. Kepler didn't actually believe in all the gears and machinery. I did know she was extremely intelligent and had taught things like relativity and something called particle physics at SMU. She was too sick now to come to the book club meetings anymore, but she was still Gram's friend, and I came to see her every Friday because Gram asked me to. And because I wanted to.

'She's not long for this old vale,' Gram had

said. 'And since she doesn't think she's going anywhere when she leaves it, you should try to give her what comfort you may in the meantime, James. It'll be a star in your crown, whether Joan thinks so or not.'

Actually it was me who did most of the talking when I was with Dr. Kepler, because that was what seemed to make her happy.

'Speak to me a little, dear boy,' she'd say. 'All my words are old and tired, and I've had enough of them.'

But from time to time she did explain some interesting things to me, like who Max Planck was and what quantum mechanics was about and why a full moon can only rise around the time the sun is setting. She said people of normal intelligence who considered things like this too complicated to understand were just mentally slothful — they'd never gotten in the habit of curiosity about how things work, or of thinking clearly about cause and effect. It was a pleasure to listen to her, her words creating new ideas and bright, clean-edged images in my mind.

But mainly she wanted to listen to me, especially when the stories included Diana and L.A. And nothing was trivial to her. She wanted every detail about where we went and what we did and thought, what we were wearing or how the sky looked the day something happened. It was like she was hungry and the stories I brought her were gifts of food. She'd listen and nod and smile in the right places even when she was very tired or in a lot of pain. She particularly wanted to know L.A.'s reaction to things,

214

chuckling or shaking her head at the stories, sometimes even laughing until she made herself cough.

'Ah, she is *schelmisch*, that one. *Und so klug.* What did she say then?'

So I tried to remember everything for Dr. Kepler. Of course, I couldn't, but it amazed me how much I did remember. And it amazed me even more how much better I understood things when I kept them in mind to talk about later, as if ideas could somehow germinate and grow in the dark like mushrooms while you were thinking about something else.

I trusted Dr. Kepler with my thoughts, eventually even some of the ones I had about Diana and me, because Dr. Kepler was different from other adults in that nothing I said to her ever came back to bite me on the ass. And there wasn't much point in trying to be sly with her anyway, since she was almost Gram's equal in her ability to read my mind.

One of the things she took a special interest in was what I was going to do about Diana. Of course, this sounded a little strange to me, because I hadn't thought that was up to me. I'd thought it was more a matter of what Diana was going to do about me. Or rather what she was going to let me do.

'Don't obfuscate, James,' Dr. Kepler said. 'You want to have sex with her, of course. I'd be worried if you didn't. And soon enough, you will.'

Suddenly I didn't know whether to smile or not, or what to do with my hands and feet. I coughed.

215

'But responsibility to each other is all we really have in this world, dear, and you've got some serious responsibilities where our Miss Diana is concerned.'

Seeing that I was blushing, she said, 'That is precious, James! You didn't expect an old lady to talk about such things, did you?'

I had to admit she was right, and the longer I thought about that the dumber I felt. This was sort of a turning point for me, because after that day I quit worrying about what I told Dr. Kepler and just more or less let everything come out when it was ready. And she seemed to understand it all, hardly ever being critical or trying to talk me into or out of anything.

But she was damn strict on certain points.

'You absolutely must keep condoms with you at all times,' she said. 'Here, let me have your billfold.' When I handed it to her, she opened it and said, 'Yes, this will be fine. Leave the wrappers on and keep them right in here. That way you'll always have them with you.'

'Yes ma'am.'

Later I looked Hubert up and asked, 'What's a condom?'

'Same thing as a rubber, man,' he said. 'Don't you know nothing?' He pulled out his own billfold, and damn if he didn't have two rubbers in the secret compartment. I could see the circles they'd made in the leather, so I knew they'd been there awhile. A day or two later he brought me three of my own in individual foil packages. He wasted one by unrolling it and trying unsuccessfully to pull it down over his fist, playing with it, snapping it and blowing it up like a balloon. 'Make a hell of a water bomb,' he pronounced. He watched as I stuffed the remaining two into my billfold. 'Now you're all set,' he said.

It felt weird at first, like carrying concealed weapons, but eventually I got used to it. I tried to adjust my thinking around the need to keep my billfold from falling into Gram's or L.A.'s hands, which was going to be tricky because of the mysterious way their curiosity and powers of detection were always amplified by me having something to hide. But I was determined. For all I knew this was something else L.A. would punch me for if she found out, and I didn't even want to imagine what Gram's reaction would be.

Another time, Dr. Kepler and I talked about boxing. She seemed to know a lot about the sport for a woman, and it sounded like Gram had told her about Jack and me and the lessons. We talked about different champions and styles of fighting for a while, then she sighed and closed her eyes, saying, 'You never wanted to learn any of this in the first place, did you, James?'

Nobody had ever asked me that before. I thought about it for a few seconds. 'No ma'am,' I said.

'And yet I'll bet now you wish you knew even more than you do. Enough to turn the tables on him.'

I rubbed my eyes, remembering how the universe had turned blood-red that day with Jack. 'No,' I said. 'I mean yes. I don't know. I wish somebody would tell me what's right to feel.'

'I can tell you it's not wrong to hate a true enemy, James, no matter what you may hear in Sunday school. Any other feeling would be a violation of nature. But you must take care to maintain the distinction between thought and deed. Ideas and emotions are not good or bad. They come like birds in the air, beyond our control. But our words and actions are a matter of choice, and they will always have consequences.' She put her hand on mine. 'Do you see?'

I nodded. This I understood perfectly, because of the huge gap that had always existed between what I felt about Jack and what I'd ever been able to do about it.

'Tell me about your father, James.'

'My father?' I said, surprised by the sudden change of gears and unsure how to answer.

'Who was he really? Was he a good man? Did you love him?'

Hearing this, I saw myself once again in our kitchen in Jacksboro: *Our last breakfast as a family — Mom in her yellow bathrobe setting out cereal, orange juice and coffee, Dad in his jeans, boots and a red plaid snapfront shirt, smelling leathery and smoky, headed for the auction barn with the horse trailer, everything okay between him and Mom, the orange sun just coming up beyond the live oaks outside the kitchen window. Dad pulling away in his old Ford longbed, the trailer bouncing and rattling along behind. That night a state trooper appearing at the door, speaking briefly to Mom as I watch from the hall in my pajamas, Mom swinging back from the door as if she has been hit, her arm out for support that isn't there, falling on her butt next to the easy chair.*

'He was real good with horses,' I said. 'I think he drank too much, and I know he got into fights sometimes, but he loved us. He took good care of us.'

'All was well, then?'

I looked down at the floor, wondering if I had any right to answer.

'He and Mom yelled at each other a lot,' I said. 'She says he ran around with other women. Sometimes she talked about leaving him.'

'Do you think she would have?'

'No.'

'Why not?'

'I don't know. Maybe she loved him too much.'

'And after that?'

'It took a long time for her to get over him dying.'

'What about you?'

'Me too,' I said, thinking how after Dad was gone it seemed like just Mom and me against the world. The emptiness in my chest never really left me, but in another way being with Mom and having all her attention, without the fights between her and Dad, was the best time of my life. 'But then she found Jack,' I said.

'What a shock that must have been for you.'

I shrugged.

'What were your thoughts then?'

219

'I couldn't understand why she would want him. He's nothing like Dad. But she said she loved him, he was there to stay and I'd just have to get used to it.'

'And you tried, didn't you — tried very hard?'

I nodded miserably.

'If I believed in such things, James, I would call you both cursed and blessed,' Dr. Kepler said. 'What others understand with ease and never question, you cannot fathom, and that is your blessing. Your curse is that you grasp without effort so many things that most people will never comprehend.'

Deciding after a little thought that this pronouncement must fall in the category of a blessing, I said, 'Are you really an existentialist?'

'Ho! That grandmother of yours has been talking about me, I see. Do you actually know what the word means?'

'No ma'am, not really. I guess it means you don't believe in God.'

'What I believe, dear, is that perhaps God is beside the point. We are not given reliable instructions, we are not rescued from our troubles, and our obligations in the world remain the same whether a supernatural being is watching us and keeping score or not. Do you understand?'

'Yes ma'am, I think I do.'

'But that isn't what you believe.'

'I'm not sure. I don't think I know enough to have beliefs.'

'Ah, there you have put your finger on it, dear boy. Never accept that you must believe in order that you may know.' She looked at me for a long while. 'Do you mind if I take this off?' she said, touching the purple scarf that covered her head.

'No ma'am.'

She unwound the scarf and laid it on the nightstand. Her head was smooth as an egg.

'Are you offended?'

'No ma'am,' I said truthfully. To me she looked like a gentle alien.

She took my hand, laid it on her head and closed her eyes. Her scalp was warm and dry, and I could feel the blue veins under the surface. I looked at her tired face, wishing I was like one of those tent preachers, my touch powerful enough to make her well. I actually tried it, mentally shouting for God to heal her, but I didn't feel anything, and as far as I could tell she didn't either. When I finally drew my hand back she opened her eyes and looked at me.

'Perhaps there is yet some little hope for this race of perfumed baboons,' she said. 'My dear boy.'

One day I asked her about the killings. She looked at me with an expression I couldn't figure out, sadness maybe, then said, 'Unfortunately nature does make mistakes, James. Sometimes very bad ones. There will always be monsters among us, but we cannot let that take from us our courage. There is still much that is good in the world.'

'What kind of monster do you think it is?'

'A man, if we may call him that, who takes pleasure in the pain and fear of others, who kills human beings for his own enjoyment, it is right to call him a monster. Hitler found many such men to do his mad work. In other times a creature so misshapen inside might have been destroyed in childhood. Or perhaps made a shaman.'

'Do you think they'll catch him?'

'I think he will catch himself, *mein lieber*. He will see to his own destruction.'

She sighed, her eyes fluttering and closing.

It was hell watching Dr. Kepler die, but there came a day when she made it much harder for me. It was a Friday afternoon, and it had been raining all day. In Dr. Kepler's room time had slowed almost to a standstill, the air around us seeming to listen for something. She lay still on her bed, her breathing barely noticeable.

'James,' she whispered, 'have you ever given any thought to what life really is?' Her voice making me think of the wind in winter grass.

'No ma'am,' I said, unsure what she meant.

'The thing itself, life — what is it? Is it more than just having a pulse and curiosity and lust?'

I tried to think this through fully, because Dr. Kepler would never settle for less. I'd heard life called different things, like a gift or a trial, but those seemed like religious ideas that wouldn't satisfy anyone with a mind like Dr. Kepler's. Finally an inspiration came to me. 'It's a responsibility,' I said. 'Like a job.'

'Bravo,' she answered in a faint voice. I thought of the changes the doctor had made in her medications yesterday, wondering if that was why she seemed so used up today. Her face was sort of carved away like desert rock, and her legs were like sticks under the covers. When she looked at me, I felt a kind of unreal heat from her eyes. She said, 'And when our job is accomplished, what then?'

Having no real idea how to answer, I said, 'I guess we're done.' Feeling goose bumps on the backs of my arms. Fighting off an image of myself turning in some cosmic resignation letter at an unmanned desk on my way out the door and disappearing into endless darkness and silence.

Dr. Kepler pressed her head farther back into the pillow and stared up at the ceiling with a daydreaming look. She said, 'I loved Sol Kepler almost every day for twenty-six years and eight months, James. He was a solid, honest house of a man, and, like you, noble without knowing it. When the storms blew him away, nothing was left but worthless ground that could never be built on again. Our two daughters dead before us, two amputations of the heart without anesthesia. I taught other people's children all I could about how to think clearly and how to love nature. Now I've said goodbye to that and to all of them, and I believe I am finished. Do you understand that, James?'

'Yes ma'am,' I lied.

'You know,' she said softly, 'I lived forty-seven of my years before you were born. Almost half of this monstrous century. Nevertheless, I consider you my compeer and true friend. I'm going to ask you to do something for me, a little thing to help me finish with my assignment.'

'Anything you need,' I said.

She took a deep breath. 'All right, then, James, here is what I want you to do. Go into the kitchen and open the cabinet to the right of the sink. Find the bottle with the large round white tablets, the ones with grooves on the side. Take at least a dozen of them and crush them into a powder in one of those little blue bowls that I use for desserts, and mix the powder with some applesauce from the top shelf in the refrigerator. Bring the bowl to me with a spoon, then get the brandy from the pantry and pour me a glass of it. Can you do that?'

I stared at her and swallowed, my heart banging against my ribs. The room was so quiet it hurt my ears. I thought of all the things I'd messed up in my life, of how I hadn't been able to help Gramp, or stop Dad from dying or Jack from moving in with Mom and beating her up. There'd been nothing I could do to help L.A., and Dee was dead because of me. What the hell was my life but a junkyard of failures? The word *responsibility* glowed in my mind as if spelled out in buzzing red neon. I stood up slowly from the cane chair beside Dr. Kepler's bed, setting aside the book I'd been reading to her earlier. 'Yes ma'am,' I said. 'I can.'

I went into the kitchen and opened the cabinet. The tablets were at the front of the shelf. I counted out twelve of them and put them in a bowl I found in the next cabinet. I took a heavy bread knife from the silverware drawer and used its thick handle to smash the pills into a coarse powder, visualizing Tricia Venables's dead face in the grass as I worked. Rain tapped against the window and trailed its weak fingers down the glass as I got the applesauce from the fridge. I carried the jar to the counter and spooned some of the applesauce into the small bowl, then mixed the powder into it with shaking hands. I took a water glass from the cabinet, set it by the sink and went over to get the brandy bottle. I unscrewed the cap and took a long swallow, coughed and took another, the liquor burning all the way down to the center of me. I poured some into the glass and carried it and the applesauce back to the bedroom.

Dr. Kepler's eyes were closed, and I thought she might be asleep. I stood by her bed and held the bowl. 'Ma'am,' I said, my tongue a clumsy paddle in my mouth.

She slowly opened her eyes. She seemed to be coming back from some far place, and she took a long time to recognize me, looking almost surprised to find me there beside her bed. Her eyes went to the bowl, then came back to my face. Her lips moved slightly, as if she were going back over the words we'd spoken earlier. After what seemed like a long time, she suddenly said, 'Oh, NO, no no *no*! What could I have been thinking? Where is my mind? Oh, James, forgive me, please! I was so wrong to have asked this of you.'

I set the brandy and applesauce on the table, sat down in my chair at her bedside and hung my head.

'I was so mistaken,' she said. 'I ask — I beg — your pardon.' Her hand was thin and cool as a bird's foot as she reached across to touch my fingers and then my knee.

Long minutes ticked away.

'I'm sorry,' I finally said, not even trying to stop the hot tears falling down onto my stupid useless hands.

11

Police Work

Gram and L.A. seemed unimpressed, but to me the outside of the municipal building downtown on Harwood looked kind of monumental and dangerous at close range, with its huge white columns and curlicued ledges and squadrons of pigeons clattering around the top. On the other hand, the interior, at least downstairs, was ho-hum, like a collection of assistant principals' offices. The squad room upstairs was more interesting, with a few lazily rotating ceiling fans above maybe two dozen desks placed in pairs back to back, and the smell of cigar smoke, leather and old coffee in the air. There was a business-like, slightly menacing feel to the place, but the walls looked like they hadn't been painted since Cochise was a kid.

Don met us as we got off the elevator, his sleeves rolled up and a gold badge clipped to his belt. He looked very different here, as if the surroundings had chemically transformed him from just Diana's father to the guy in charge. The change wasn't in his actual appearance, being more a matter of things like people unobtrusively keeping track of what he was doing and saying, and men older than he was addressing him as 'sir.' When he asked Gram if she'd like coffee or anything, two detectives were moving toward the break room to get it before she even finished saying, 'Yes, thank you.'

A chunky, busy-looking red-haired cop named Sperry took Gram into a deskless office where there was an old tan leather couch and a coffee table. Coffee and fixings were brought for both of them and Gram, being her usual self, had Detective Sperry filling her in on the policing business in no time: how many men worked here, how many secretaries were there, where did they keep their records and what sort of filing system did they use, where were the criminals brought in and on and on.

L.A. wanted to see the interrogation rooms, and Don showed us one with a dinged-up little table, three folding chairs and nothing else in it. The room was smaller than I would have expected, with no windows, dirty-looking light green walls and brown worn-out linoleum on the floor. I looked for the bright light hanging low over the suspect's chair, but there were only the buzzing fluorescents overhead. The air in the room seemed to hum with desperation, and it occurred to me that I might confess to pretty much anything to get out of a place like this. But then that raised the question of where I'd go from here, which was not an encouraging thought either.

Don showed us how the two-way mirror worked. L.A. checked out both sides, then put her face to the glass and shaded her eyes with her hands. 'You can see through it a little bit this way,' she said. 'Do something, Biscuit.'

I stuck my finger in my nose.

She laughed. A rare occurrence.

Don and another man brought us Cokes and sat us at a long metal table stacked with several big books full of pictures of different men's faces. I couldn't see the words 'Mug Book' on any of them, but there was no doubt that's what they were. It was the first time I'd ever seen any in person, and unlike the interrogation room, these looked exactly the same as the movie versions. The only difference I noticed was that in the movies and on TV they never brought out more than one.

'What I'm interested in,' said Don, 'is if either of you might have seen any of these players anywhere, maybe looking out of place somehow, cruising the street or trying to start a conversation with you or your friends. Or trying to follow somebody or just generally giving you a funny feeling.'

L.A. plunged right into this, and she was the perfect witness because she absolutely never forgot anybody's face. She looked at each man for a second, photographed him mentally, then moved on to the next one. Every so often she'd stop to take a sip of her drink, then go back to the photographs. I knew that if she ever met one of these men, even years later, she'd recognize him instantly.

But I didn't have an orderly bone in my body. I was a browser, and I caught myself getting interested in these people, wondering about their histories and making up stories in my mind about them. Some of them looked so sad and broken down that it made my heart hurt. But there were others who seemed to have invisible fire spiking from their eyes, and their expressions told you they could never possibly hurt you enough to be satisfied.

Don sat at the end of the table, occasionally taking sips of coffee from a tan mug that had his name painted on it in red fingernail polish. His left hand, with its wide gold wedding band, lay on the table without moving. He'd watch L.A.'s eyes for a while, then glance off across the room, or sometimes just look at the clouds outside the window. It was hard to say exactly how, but he gave a clear impression that it would be no problem for him if this took all night.

Once in a while somebody would come to ask him a question or get him to sign something, but the typewriters and all the other action around us seemed to pull back and go on without us so that it felt like we were closed into our own private bubble of time and space. I had started concentrating on a picture of a young dark-haired shirtless guy who reminded me of Hubert a little, except for the long whelp of scar tissue under his chin. I was wondering if somebody had cut his throat, and if so why that hadn't worked, since I'd always understood throat-cutting to be lethal, when I heard L.A.'s Coke can bang on the table.

'Here!' she said, jabbing her finger down on one of the faces.

Don snapped his own fingers once and pointed at one of the men across the room, who grabbed a tablet as he came over to stand behind L.A. and look down over her shoulder at the book. I moved around the table to get a better look myself, Don and another man joining me, all of us focused on the tip of L.A.'s finger and the picture under it.

'We know this one,' she said.

I stared at the face and saw that she was right. It was Hot Earl.

'Okay!' Don said, slapping one hand down onto the table. 'This could be Break One. Tell us about him, hon.'

While L.A. gave Don the story about how we met Earl — leaving out the parts about the five-dollar bills and me smoking pot with him — the other detectives were getting organized to catch him. 'Earl Vester Wiggins, also known as Earl Williams or Vester Peoples,' someone said.

'Priors for theft, forgery, indecency with a minor — guest of the governor for two and a half at Huntsville,' said another voice.

'Jerry, what've we got for a last known address?'

Phones were dialed and notes were scribbled. It was terrific, like a huge engine cranking up. Gram came out with Detective Sperry, sniffing the excitement in the air.

'We identified Hot Earl,' L.A. reported with satisfaction.

'Who?' said Gram.

'Hot Earl. He's a murderer, and we met him. He's in the book.'

'Well, he's somebody for us to talk to anyway,' said Don. 'But we're proud of our investigative consultants here.' He put his arm around L.A.'s shoulders.

This is when I would have seen it if I had been half as smart as I wanted to believe I was. But I wasn't and I didn't.

Just then Dr. Ballard and Mrs. Bruhn walked into the squad room. Mrs. Bruhn was wearing a dress suit like the one I'd seen her in at the hospital, except this one was light brown. Dr. Ballard wore a gray skirt and a peach-colored blouse with the sleeves pushed up. Her hair was light brown and kind of rolled at the back of her head, her little glasses hanging in front of her on a thin gold chain. She took L.A.'s hands in hers and smiled at her. There was another female eyelock, this one softer and not quite as loaded as the one at Gram's.

Dr. Ballard said, 'Ready?'

L.A. nodded.

'Hi, Dr. Ballard, Miz Bruhn,' said Don, shaking hands with both women. 'We've got a room ready, and the steno and policewoman are on their way up. Let me know if there's anything I can get you.'

A stiff-looking skinny woman about Mom's age carrying an armful of notebooks, and a short friendly blond policewoman with DEWBERRY engraved in white on her blue name tag, walked up to us. Don introduced everybody, and then all the women trooped off down a hall.

Reading the wanted posters on a bulletin board in the waiting area, I learned that crooks were generally referred to by all three of their names, like a kid who's in trouble with his mother, that they tended to go by a lot of aliases that were usually kind of alike, and that they always had tattoos. Also a lot of scars, which gave the impression that being a criminal must be a pretty rocky business. These characters were called Fugitives from Justice, the words making me think for a second of desperate men crouching in ditches as hounds bayed in the distance.

A lot of these guys were to be considered Armed and Dangerous, which I visualized as having large pistols on your hips, ammunition belts across your chest and a fierce expression on your face. But in real life I had never seen an ammunition belt like the ones I was picturing, which got me thinking about where crooks got their equipment in the first place. They used specialized gear like lockpicks and blunt instruments, and they bludgeoned people, which meant there must be places where you could get this kind of stuff. I wondered how much a bludgeon would cost and whether they came in different weights and sizes, or maybe in light, regular and heavy-duty models. There was also the question of how you'd choose the right lockpick, or know a good-quality blunt instrument from a shoddy one. But then the whole concept of blunt instruments sounded contradictory to me; I imagined bins full of them, shiny and looking something like surgical tools, but heavier and without sharp edges or points.

Did all this come from a specialized hardware store, maybe with dirty old windows painted up past eye level like a pool hall and a hand-painted sign reading CRIME SUPPLIES over the door, suspicious characters looking furtively back over their shoulders as they came and went? I assumed clerks who worked there would have to be experienced criminals themselves to be able to answer the customers' questions intelligently.

On the other hand, I wasn't sure how the idea of intelligence applied to crooks, because the guys in these pictures didn't look very sharp to me. Mostly they seemed dazed, with their hair sprigged up like they had just that minute been jerked out of bed and stood in front of the camera. It made me tired just thinking of all the trouble and effort it must take to be a criminal, and I wondered if it wouldn't be easier to just go ahead and clean up and find a regular job.

Gram would never expect them to do that, though. 'Never try to teach a pig to sing,' was how she put it.

Don looked at it pretty much the same way. 'Takes three or four perps to make a halfwit,' was his philosophy.

I walked over to a corner where there was a green plastic-covered couch, a shaky-looking coffee table and four or five chairs that looked like they'd been chucked out in the alley behind some school cafeteria in the poor end of town. In one of the police magazines I found on the table there was an article about the killing power of different bullets, something I'd never thought about until that minute, assuming bullets killed you according to where they hit you rather than on account of differences in the bullets themselves.

My eyes were getting tired, and I thought about putting the magazine down and leaning my head back just for a minute —

— *Hot Earl stood in the middle of the street in Dodge City, not far from Marshal Dillon's office, where there was a wanted poster on the bulletin board beside the door with a drawing of L.A. on it. Where her mouth should have been, there was a big black X. Hot Earl was wearing heavy six-guns on his cartridge belt and had a snow-white bandanna with bright drops of blood on it around his neck. On his chest hung a placard reading, 'Making them wait is the best part.' Then his face lost focus so that I couldn't make out his features.*

An armed posse was riding up the street, but the faceless man couldn't run because of the smelly old mattress he was chained to. He dragged it desperately through the dust, his pants unzipped, his hair scragged up in every possible direction. As the riders closed in all around him, he drew his guns one after another to shoot at them, but each time the barrels fell off when he pulled the trigger. The deputies all had nooses in their hands.

As they grabbed him, he turned to me and in a girl's voice said —

'Hey, Biscuit.'

I opened my eyes and saw L.A. looking down at me. Gram and Dr. Ballard were at Don's desk talking with him and another detective.

'We're going home,' L.A. said. She looked white and tired.

'I want to wait and see Earl,' I said, imagining him being dragged across the squad room swearing and struggling and having to be subdued by force, losing a shoe, his shirt torn half off, maybe a little blood running down from one ear.

'Don's not gonna let us do that,' said L.A. 'Anyway, Gram wants to go home. She says we've all had more than enough criminal justice for one day, and she wants to be in her own kitchen again and know we're safe at the pool, swimming.'

I could see there was no arguing with this. I rubbed my eyes with my knuckles. 'Did you have to tell everything again?'

She just looked at me.

'I'm sorry,' I said.

Tired as she was, there was something hard and dangerous in her eyes. I didn't say anything else. I stood up and we all walked toward the exit, my thoughts a million miles from where they should have been.

RECKONING

1

Mental Powers

Late in the afternoon of the day before the Minnesota trip L.A., Diana and I leaned back in the kind of folding lawn chairs that people who didn't have to answer to Gram called 'chase lounges,' lined up on the back patio at Diana's house like old tourists on a cruise. Six sneakers in a row, four tidy and clean, two big and shabby and at least a year past white. Nobody saying anything.

Diana and L.A. were doing that feline thing girls do where their eyes are closed but they're nowhere close to being asleep, just listening to everything and thinking their own thoughts, but I was trying to figure out how I was supposed to feel.

Don had said Cam's trial would be set for sometime in the fall, and everybody expected him to eventually end up in Huntsville for what he did to L.A. Hot Earl wouldn't go to death row, because there was no death penalty now, but he was behind bars for good. The danger was past.

But apparently some things left part of their energy behind after they were gone, like an odor, because I didn't feel one damn bit safe. Or maybe it was just that I understood the world better now than I used to.

239

Diana had done her best to talk L.A. into coming to Minnesota with us, but L.A. was sticking to her guns. I banged it into my head that Gram and L.A. were going to be all right, that it was practically impossible to fool or sneak up on either of them, that they were both probably tougher than me anyway.

Then something else occurred to me.

I said, 'Maybe we could dedicate the trip to Dee. Have a little ceremony or something.'

L.A. glanced at me, then closed her eyes again without saying anything.

Diana said, 'I think we should just let him rest in peace. That's what he wanted.'

The silence tried to come back, but I wasn't ready for it yet. 'Hard to believe it's all over,' I said.

'Don't start,' said Diana.

'Just saying.'

'Shut up,' said L.A.

So that's where we left that.

★　★　★

By some unknown method Don had been able to get Diana and Marge organized and loaded up early enough to pick me up at Gram's before six in the morning with the eastern sky still hanging halfway between gray and pink. L.A. came out of her room wearing an old robe of Gram's, her hair sticking out in dimensions Einstein never thought of, opened one eye about a sixteenth of an inch, said, ''Bye,' and went back to bed. On the front porch Gram hugged me fiercely and pressed two twenty-dollar bills into my hand.

When I threw my duffel in the rear of the wagon and piled in next to Diana in the back seat, she held out a slice of toast with a fried sausage patty folded into it, saying, 'Travelin' rations.'

Cities are cocoons, and after a while they can make you forget they're not the real world. As we headed out through Richardson and Plano and on into the misty countryside, making it all the way to McKinney while the morning light was still low and coppery, the open sky wide and clean, the whole concept of living in the middle of miles and miles of buildings jammed together, surrounded by the endless honking roar of traffic, made less and less sense to me.

Don was what Gram called a *jehu*, not mean or reckless behind the wheel, just a fast, focused driver who was like L.A. in knowing exactly what to expect from the other traffic and having absolutely no fear. He drove the big Impala wagon on the principle that he owned all the space around him, we had places to go and we weren't out here to homestead the damn highway. I recognized this as an extension of his being a cop and a boss and knew that as long as everybody else respected his thinking we'd all be okay.

Diana, having no fear either, slept most of the time. She was like a cat, able to conk out anywhere, anytime, in any position. I liked watching her sleep, I think because of the soft way she breathed and the peaceful look on her

241

face, the peacefulness being something I admired and envied. She woke up like a cat too, stretching the way a cat does, even down to crossing her eyes and showing the tip of her tongue, and she'd be wide awake in a couple of seconds.

As we drove, the countryside changed gradually, evolving away from hills, trees and forty-acre farms toward corn, cotton, soybean and sorghum fields that stretched away to the horizon. Double-winged crop dusters dropped in over the telephone lines to skim along the vegetable rows like big yellow dragonflies, and here and there the black walking beams of oil wells rocked like huge mechanical woodpeckers in the endless landscape.

We saw what was left of a rabbit completely flattened on the pavement except for one big ear sticking straight up and looking as good as new. Like he was listening down the empty highway with that one sad ear. A quotation I'd heard from Gram came into my mind:

What dies in summer never knows
Summer's death nor bitter snows

'That was a jackrabbit,' said Don. 'I think technically they're hares. Bigger than cottontails, and all legs and ears to help them keep away from the coyotes. Hares and rabbits have got to be fast; they're the Big Macs of the animal kingdom.'

Diana said, '*Daddy!*'

He glanced in the rearview mirror. 'I've never

seen it myself, but I hear the coyotes use a tag-team system to hunt them. A jack-rabbit can outrun just about anything that gets after it except a greyhound.'

This mystified Diana. 'How'd you know it was a bus that got him?' she said.

Don laughed. 'I guess they didn't evolve to compete with the internal combustion engine, at that,' he said. 'You can bet something chased that guy out into the traffic if it was daytime. Otherwise he'd have slept all day. But more likely it was night, and he got blinded by somebody's headlights.'

'Poor old hopper,' Diana said.

Don decided to let Diana and me do some of the driving, and I drew the first shift.

Marge was okay about it, but I could tell Diana was worried that my driving time would cut into hers. She was no pouter, though.

'Me next,' she said as I slid in behind the wheel.

I won't say I was fearless, but the only thing that really worried me was messing up in front of Don. When I eventually managed to get some control over that, I actually started taking some pleasure in driving, maintaining a kind of steady wide-angle attention and feeling like an airline captain, all the lives aboard safe in my capable hands. We cruised on like this until Marge and Diana started talking about restrooms, and I pulled into the driveway of a Texaco station that had a café next door.

All of us but Don had cheeseburgers with french fries and Cokes. He ordered coffee and eggs with corned beef hash, which I thought looked and smelled like fried dog food.

'Yankee habit I picked up,' he said, shoveling the stuff into his mouth.

Watching him, Marge gave a little shiver.

Then it was Diana's turn to drive. I shut out of my mind all the lethal possibilities this involved and gradually lost myself in fantasies of what it must have been like to live in frontier days when there were hostile Indians looking to scalp you on a moment's notice, and no police or telephones or electricity. People must have had to be ready for trouble at all times, carrying their rifles out to the fields with them and scanning the horizon constantly as they plowed.

But I'd noticed that in the movies it seemed to be mainly young to middle-aged guys who got scalped, and I wasn't sure why. Don had said fifty was pretty old back in the eighteenth and nineteenth centuries, which gave me the idea that it must have been in your best interest to age fast out here, at least if you wanted to keep your hair. I tried picturing Don and Marge as fifty and old, with white hair and no teeth, shuffling along their porch or rocking side by side in chairs. Obviously there was no way they could run from Indians in that condition, and I doubted they'd be able to see well enough to shoot straight either, so they'd have to rely on the fact that savages had less interest in old people's scalps for some reason, possibly because of the white color. Or maybe it was just that the old people got sly about not letting the Indians know where they were.

Old people could certainly be like that. Gram was a good example. She was unbelievably crafty at times, which I assumed was on account of her age as much as her intelligence and education. But I remembered her pronouncement about the difference between intelligent and smart, which definitely held true for me and most of the kids I was acquainted with. Of course, in my case I preferred to believe the underlying problem was mostly ignorance, which can always be fixed. Dumb, on the other hand, is there for the duration.

Of course there are a lot of different ways of being smart. Don had this quality of seeming to need help and wanting to listen that made people talk their heads off to him, and you could end up thinking you'd had a conversation with him when he hadn't said anything at all. And sometimes he had a way of being slow to catch on, of just not getting it. For example, after Jack got beat up he did his best to interest Don in the idea that he'd been set up by Murval Briscoe and that Murval ought to get in trouble about it. But somehow Don had a hard time catching his drift.

'A *police officer* in on it, you're thinkin'?' he said. 'Geez, that's a hell of a thought.' He pulled on his lip and looked at Jack.

'Hey, I'b ju tayin dah how it loogs,' said Jack.

'Y'know,' said Don, 'we did talk to Murval and that fella that put your lights out, what was his name, Arthron Weed I think it was — a lefty — used to be a middleweight fighting out of Beaumont or someplace like that — '

'Basser tugger-bunch me,' said Jack.

'And the way it lays out, looks like it was just a nasty coincidence him and Officer Briscoe being in that area talking about some thefts people were having down there. Right when you happened to show up.'

'Goddab butchwhagger,' said Jack.

'I heard you kinda mouthed off to Arthron, but I'm sure that can't be right. Called him a burr-head and whatnot?'

Jack shook his head half an inch from side to side.

'Guy happened to be a pro and just took you off the clock right then and there. That was a shit break, Jack. Lucky Murval was able to settle the guy down before it got any worse.'

'Hey, g'mon,' said Jack.

'It's perplexing,' said Don.

'I'b *terious*!' said Jack.

'Now that we're talking police conspiracy here, I can't tell you how bad that confuses me.'

'*Looga* me!'

'Been over the whole case personally, jot by tittle, and still not a clue in sight.'

'Buh hey!'

'Wouldn't surprise me too much if we never do solve the damn thing.'

Knowing Don, I wasn't holding my breath either. But none of this really did much to remedy my feelings of ignorance about the whole concept of smartness, which for me still seemed slippery as a fish. Like a lot of other things. I settled for hoping the increasing distance from home and Gram and L.A. would somehow scatter my confusions and neutralize my fears and endless nagging thoughts about everything I didn't know.

Maybe it did, a little.

2

Starry, Starry Night

We stopped for the night at a place off the highway named the Mille Lacs, in the farm country of northern Iowa. Marge referred to it as a tourist court, a half circle of little houses, bungalows she called them, built around a graveled parking lot with a huge cottonwood at the center.

I lugged my duffel down to eleven, a yard-dog of a bungalow with a small television set on a folding table and a little bathroom with peeling paint in the shower. Above the bed hung a faded cardboard picture of a moose standing in the water at the edge of a lake with mountains in the background.

By the time I'd put my toothbrush and toothpaste in the bathroom and figured out the television channels, it was getting dark outside. I looked at the sagging bed with its two flat pillows, hoping everything was all right with L.A. and Gram and wondering what I'd dream about tonight and sort of wishing I didn't have to sleep. Hearing a knock at the door, I opened it, and there stood Diana, bright as a candle flame under the yellow bug light over the door. Her snug jeans demonstrated her body in a way that almost vapor-locked my mind.

'Wanta go for a walk?' she said.

'What'd your mom say?'

'Don't be too late.'

I grabbed my sweater. 'Let's go.'

Beyond the lights of the court a soft darkness surrounded us, the moon not up yet, the sky glowing faintly along the western horizon but black and full of stars overhead. Somewhere in the distance, a coyote yipped a few times and howled, and a few seconds later a dozen more chimed in.

We walked along the shoulder of the road for a while, listening to the crunch of our steps in the gravel. I could smell the wild cherry Life Saver Diana was sucking on.

'How about if we went over into that field?' she said. On the other side of a barbed-wire fence we could make out the slope of a pasture and a few trees blacking out the stars along the skyline.

'You okay for the fence?'

'Sure.' She did a quick skip and hop in her sneakers. 'I'm an old cowhand from the Rio Grande.'

I spread the top two strands of wire to let her step through, then she did the same for me. We walked through the short grass toward the top of the low rise, Diana humming 'Happy Trails' under her breath. At the crest we stopped. All around us the stars burned thicker and deeper and brighter than I'd ever seen them, than I'd ever dreamed they could be. We sat on the grass.

Diana said, 'It looks like forever.'

'There's no such thing,' I said.

'What do you think's really out there?'

'I don't know. Everything, I guess.'

'Maybe people like us?'

'Not like you.'

She considered this for a while, gazing at the sky. 'All that space,' she finally said. 'I bet there's at least four.'

I saw a sudden pinprick of new light among the stars that immediately grew into a greenish white fireball, elongating itself across the sky, brightening by the second. It flared and dimmed and flared again, leaving a glowing trail as it tracked straight through the constellations above us. There was no sound, but the thing was so bright I could see our shadows on the grass. The meteor continued overhead and on beyond us until it dwindled and finally disappeared at the other end of the sky.

Diana had scrambled around to watch and was now on all fours looking in the direction the fireball had gone. '*Damn!*' she said. 'What *was* that?'

'Chunk of rock burning up in the atmosphere, I guess.' Dr. Kepler had actually taught me quite a bit about meteors, but I took so much time weighing out whether saying more would impress Diana or make me sound like a smart-ass that I lost the moment. I stared at the sky, wondering how anything so big and bright and obviously full of energy could be so silent.

Diana turned back around to sit beside me. 'My heart's thumping,' she said.

I leaned my head down and put my ear against her chest, feeling the valentine-shaped locket she wore under her sweatshirt and smelling the soap she'd bathed with and her Life Saver breath. I heard the *lub-dub, lub-dub* of her heart, a soft faraway thunder that actually did seem pretty fast. It got faster as I listened. So did her breathing.

'Don't breathe,' I said. 'I want to hear.'

'Schmuck.'

I lifted my head and put my mouth on hers, tasting her sweetness and instantly feeling lost in her. She held my shoulders as we kissed. After a minute, I drew back and looked at her. I tried to tell her how beautiful she was, but I don't think anything came out but a whimper. I grabbed her to pull her to me and kiss her again, but she put her hands on my chest.

'We've gotta go back,' she said, breathing hard.

I released her and sat back, listening to her breathing and mine. I looked down at the Mille Lacs a million miles away, imagining Marge and Don in their bungalow watching television and not thinking about us at all. The infinite sky just kept hanging there all around us. After a while I said, 'I don't want to go.'

'I know, Bis,' she said, giving my forehead a little rap with her knuckles. 'But we just gotta.'

Finally I nodded, got to my feet and gave her a hand up. She moved ahead of me along a path I was now beginning to see more clearly in the dark field as we walked back down through the stars toward the road.

In my bungalow I sat on the side of the bed and waited for my heart to settle down. After saying a silent prayer for L.A. and Gram and everyone else who had to make it through the night, I turned off the light and was asleep in a few minutes.

3

What Goes Up

When I woke in the morning the only dream I could remember featured Jazzy, sitting up to beg for a corn chip I was holding out to her. No cold sweat, no sensation of my heart trying to kick its way out of my chest, no hangover of danger or dread, and best of all, no memory of dead girls watching me sleep.

After loading all our stuff into the wagon we sat down for waffles with maple syrup and sausages at the Mille Lacs Café, then took 69 north past the turnoff to Clear Lake, where Buddy Holly's plane had gone down.

'Gee,' said Diana. 'S'pose we should say a little prayer or something?'

Marge glanced at her.

'I think it's too late,' I said.

Bemidji was the last real town we passed through.

'And so we bid fond farewell to city lights,' Don said happily.

A few hours later we made it to the turnoff to Duck Lake, where there was a little store called the Duck-In, with a small, neat house next to it and an old green International pickup parked in the driveway. Marge went inside to pick up a few things for the cabin and Don walked over to the house to roust Mr. Gundersen, who took care of the cabin in the off season. The old man came out blinking and scratching his head, saw Don and went back inside. A minute later he reappeared wearing a red wool duck hunter's cap with earflaps hanging down on each side. Marge came out carrying two bags of groceries, which we stashed in the wagon as Mr. Gundersen was climbing stiffly into his pickup.

It was a twenty-minute drive through the woods and along the lakeshore. When the vehicles finally rolled to a stop in front of the cabin everybody climbed out, Mr. Gundersen walking up to join Don in a way that told you the ride had been hard on his hip.

The cabin, looking nothing like I had imagined, sat about forty yards up from the water on the easy slope under the pines, with a wide screened deck looking out over the water. It was house-sized, with three stories counting the loft, the look of the walls and roof making it obvious the place had been built in stages. Wooden stairs led up to the deck and front door in two flights, and there was a stone chimney up one wall and firewood stacked on the deck and along the back of the cabin under the deck next to where the picnic table had been set on end and leaned up against the wall.

From the water's edge below the cabin a narrow wooden dock ran about forty feet out into the lake, and halfway along it a wooden boat was tied to one of the pilings. An old Evinrude motor was tilted up out of the water at the transom, a red gas tank stowed below it behind the rear seat. A hundred yards away along the shore, a motionless heron held its spear of a head aimed at the water.

'Got the electric turned on yesterday,' said Mr. Gundersen. 'Well pump's okay. Made sure the chimney's clear, so yez can have your fire if you want. With the weather you're used to, you might find it cool enough for that tonight. Far as your provisions, I made sure the canned goods, dry beans and whatnot are stocked up. Linens all fresh. Bailed the boat yesterday and got the motor back on. Had Ernie change out the gas and oil and check the plug, so she should start okay. Nothin' in the mousetraps the last couple days.'

Diana looked at me and mouthed, *Mice?*

Mr. Gundersen filled Don in on where the fish were and what they were hitting.

'Walleye, stay with your shiners,' he said. 'Pike, Dardevle's always good. Want muskie, I'd try them big red and white plugs they use. There's monsters out there, take your leg off that quick.' He sliced the air horizontally with his hand and grinned at Diana and Marge, who looked a little stricken.

Don took a couple of bills out of his wallet and handed them to the old man, saying, 'Thanks, Einar.'

Mr. Gundersen stuffed the bills in the pocket of his khaki work shirt and pushed back his hat. 'I'd say yez'll be all right for the week,' he said as he climbed back into his truck. 'Need anythin', you know where to find me. Have a good visit, eh?'

Don and I unstrapped the cartop carrier and

grabbed the luggage. Inside, he flipped on the lights with his elbow, giving us a view back into the bedrooms and up the stairs to the loft.

'You're bunking up there, Jim,' he said. 'Put the blue clothes bag and that smaller case in the front bedroom for Diana.'

When we had everything squared away, Don grabbed a couple of the fishing rods and clapped me on the shoulder, saying, 'Let's go take a look at the boat.' The lake was still and clear, the boat lying against the sections of tire tread that had been nailed to the sides of the dock as bumpers. Don checked the boat over and said, 'Looks like we're gonna be ready to sail, Popeye.'

We tied on a couple of lead weights and practiced casting off the dock for a while to get used to the bait-casting reels, then Don laid his rod in the boat and went back up to the cabin to lay in firewood for the night.

A few minutes later I felt footsteps on the dock and looked back in time to see a bright flash. Diana had taken a picture of me with her miniature camera.

'Sorry, didn't mean to sneak up on you,' she said.

'You can sneak up on me anytime,' I said.

'Whatcha gonna catch with that piece of lead?'

'Just trying to get the hang of it,' I said. 'It's not as easy as it looks.'

'Porkchop asked me if I wanted to fish. I don't think so, but I want to go with you on the boat.'

The air was getting much cooler, and Marge came down to the dock wearing a jacket. 'Aren't you two feeling the chill down here?' she said.

Diana decided she was, and headed up to the cabin to find a sweater.

'How are you really doing, James?' Marge asked when Diana was halfway up the slope.

'Pretty good, I think,' I said.

'Any trouble sleeping, bad dreams, anything like that?'

I shook my head, wondering if a silent lie carried the same moral weight as one you spoke aloud. Her question had made me think of L.A. and Gram back home, and suddenly I felt like a deserter. In particular, I was visualizing the layout of Gram's house and yard, which I now realized was all dark corners and ambush points. For a second I felt a jagged-edged certainty that I needed to be there, needed to just leave right now and somehow get back where I belonged.

But I reminded myself that Earl was locked up, and that I was stupid to think it was up to me to protect everybody and fix everything. I could barely take care of myself.

A deranged cackle of laughter echoed across the water, and I jumped.

Marge smiled at me. 'That's a loon,' she said, gazing off in the direction of the call. 'It's a waterbird.'

Marge smiled at me again and gave my arm a squeeze. 'Let me know if there's anything I can help with.'

Later that evening we arranged the small couch and a couple of chairs and some big pillows in front of the fireplace so we could watch the fire. Don and Marge sat together, and she laid her head on his shoulder. Diana lay back on the pillows with her ankles crossed over mine.

'This is nice,' she said.

'Mmm,' said Marge.

Every so often Don got up to put on another log or poke into the fire with one of the iron tools that stood beside the fireplace. The flames swayed and pulsed, and sparks went swirling up the chimney like orange fireflies. There didn't seem to be any need for talk. I thought about loons, and then I thought about Diana.

'Bedtime, James,' said Marge, touching my arm.

I opened my eyes. There was nothing left of the fire but glowing ashes, and Diana had already gone to bed. I climbed up to the loft, kicked off my shoes and crawled into the bag without undressing.

I dreamed of Tricia Venables, naked and trying to warm herself at our fire. But she couldn't, she was too cold, cold as granite, cold as eternity. When I tried to speak to her my tongue froze.

Then she was L.A., hurt and freezing, her naked skin bitten and torn. She was lost in some high, hopeless place above icy rivers that twined like silver veins through the dark canyons thousands of feet below. Her hands covered her bloodied breasts and she cried out to me, but the booming wind stole her voice, left her as silent and broken as a doll in the endless, terrible emptiness. Hubert and Shepherd Boy struggled toward her through hip-deep snow from different directions, their hands and grinning mouths red with blood.

4

Lines

Gram had made me promise to write, so I got up before Diana and Don the next morning and borrowed a ballpoint pen and a sheet of stationery from Marge. Then I sat at the table staring at the peach-colored paper while she started breakfast, my mind blanker than the page. Finally I decided the only way to start was to just start. I wrote:

Dear Gram,
I promised I would write so here goes. The trip was really long but there was a lot to see, especially corn. I got to drive some of the time which probably would have scared you but at least I didn't hit anything. Ha ha. The cabin is great. We had a fire in the fireplace last night and I went to sleep on the floor in front of it. Marge is scrambling eggs for breakfast and she does it just like you with a little milk and everything. After breakfast we are going fishing. Diana says she doesn't want to fish but she wants to ride in the boat. I have been thinking alot about you and L.A. back there and I miss you both. You know the skillet you scramble eggs in the big heavy one, well I was thinking maybe you could start keeping

258

it in that cabinet over by the kitchen door
where it would be handy if you needed it.

I was trying to think of a way to make this part seem important without sounding sinister or stupid when Don walked into the kitchen, and a minute later Diana followed. Marge said, 'Okay, guys, get the plates and silverware on the table. Breakfast in five minutes, James, so you'll need to wash up. You can finish your letter tonight.'

But I never did. I'll get to the reason a little later.

After we had eaten and cleared the table, Don and Diana packed lunch while I helped Marge with the dishes. I listened to Don and Diana as I worked, and it was the usual standoff. Don's idea was that with a hunk of jerky and a bottle of water you're good for the day, but Diana took anything that had to do with food way more seriously than that. In her mind they were outfitting for an expedition, and she wanted all the possibilities covered, like maybe we'd have to share our lunch with Asia.

When they finally got it all haggled out we lugged the food and fishing gear down to the boat. The sun wasn't all the way up yet. Our movements on the dock started ripples from the pilings that radiated smoothly away in interlocking circles, and I could see pale genies of mist drifting above the surface of the water in the oystery light. The sky shaded from the color of pale primroses in the east to turquoise overhead to smoky iron in the west, the tips of the tallest firs and spruces touched with coppery pink.

Don got the motor started, and it burbled and smoked in the water as we stowed everything in the boat and got our life jackets on. Then we pulled away from the dock and Don gradually throttled up until the boat was on plane and cruising smoothly. The world began to wake up, with lines of birds flying low over the water and the sun climbing above the treetops in the east.

We circled in toward a small island and Don cut the throttle, our wake swaying the reeds in the shallow water and sloshing up along the shore. Diana watched as Don showed me how to rig my rod for bottom-fishing, then got out her little camera and snapped a few pictures, saying, 'How far are we from Canada?'

Don looked around to get his bearings and said, 'Probably a mile or two.' He cast along the shore and watched the line until it went slack as the weight hit bottom. 'Hope we don't look like invaders. They might attack us with their hockey sticks.'

I caught the first fish, a green-gold walleye with a spined fin on its back and milky eyes. Don twisted the hook free of its mouth, hefted it and said, 'Pound and a half at least.' He clipped it onto the stringer and let the stringer down into the water. A few minutes later he caught one a little smaller, put it on the stringer with the first and held them up in the sunlight while Diana took a picture. 'Starting to look like supper,' he said.

My rod pulled strongly down, and I hauled back on it to set the hook, feeling the fish run for deeper water. It was bigger than the first one, and when I finally got it alongside and Don netted it, he said, 'Five, maybe six pounds.' Diana took another picture as he put it on the stringer.

The sun got higher in the sky, and Don decided we'd troll across the lake to a cove he knew on the south shore and have lunch there. We rigged a couple of lines with spinners and let them out about twenty yards behind the boat as we cruised slowly south, making just enough headway to keep the lures' blades turning.

I was daydreaming about Diana when suddenly I felt a sharp jolt, as if the boat had hit something. Don quickly cut the throttle and tilted the motor up out of the water. There was another jolt, then another.

'What *happened?*' Diana asked shakily.

Don looked over the side, then reached down and brought up the stringer. The two smaller fish that had been clipped to it were gone, and the biggest one had been bitten off just behind the gills, leaving nothing but the head and a dangling string of gray gut.

'What was it?' I asked Don, my mouth dry.

He unsnapped the head from the stringer and tossed it away. 'No telling,' he said. 'Muskie, maybe.' He tilted the motor back down into the water. 'Had to be a hell of a fish, if that's what it was.'

'They don't have alligators up here, do they?' I said.

'Not that I ever heard of,' Don said. 'No gar either, as far as I know.'

As we got under way again I could see from

his expression that he was still thinking about what it could have been, but if he had any theories he kept them to himself.

I looked at Diana. She swallowed hard, watching the water as if she expected something to rise up out of it and grab her.

A few minutes later we reached the south shore and Don killed the motor as we glided into the cove. The boat's bow crunched up onto the gravel, and Diana climbed out to tie the bowline off to a snag a few feet up the beach. She looked around, stretched and wandered off to inspect the rocks and chunks of white driftwood along the edge of the water. Thick, dark woods surrounded the cove and seemed to isolate us from the rest of the world, as if this were a huge theater and we were the only audience, waiting for the curtain to rise.

Don reached back to grab the cooler, saying, 'Good a place as any for some lunch.'

Diana walked up in the direction of an old windfall lying at an angle from the brush line down across the rocks toward the water.

Don said, 'Even cold baloney tastes like steak to me out in the open air like this.' He took off his jacket and laid it over the seat.

I opened the tackle box, pawed around a little, then looked into the eye of a green Lazy Ike in the top tray and saw that something terrible was about to happen.

'Don — ' I began, knowing everything depended on what he did next.

'Wow,' said Diana, looking down on the other side of the log. 'They're like fat puppies! Hey,

Biscuit, Daddy, come look!' She was about to climb over the log.

Don looked from me to her. 'Honey, *STOP!*' he screamed.

Diana froze. There was a bleating sound, and two black bear cubs about the size of coons scampered up a bare pine snag on the other side of the windfall. At the same time, I saw something much bigger running toward us along the beach, looking like a huge shimmying black cannonball, moving faster than I would have believed any animal could. In one movement Don grabbed the fillet knife from the tackle box and vaulted over the bow, stripping off the knife's leather sheath as he ran.

'Back up!' he yelled at Diana. 'Get behind me!' He was facing the charging bear in a crouch, holding the knife out in front of him, its thin blade maybe as long as his hand. As Diana scrambled behind him Don threw back his head and roared, *'GOODNESS GRA-CIOUS, GREAT BALLS OF FIRE!'* with so much force that his face turned red and the veins stood out in his neck. The sound echoed off the trees and out across the lake, and the animal skidded to a stop with its hair standing up along its back, huffing and glaring from Don to the dead tree and back.

'Please excuse the tone, Miz Bear and forgive me if you're not a Jerry Lee Lewis fan but I know you'll understand I got a lot on my mind here,' Don said in a reasonable tone, keeping the knife pointed at her and looking down at the ground in front of her, not meeting her eyes.

'We'll just go on back to the boat now move with me honey but nothing sudden don't look directly at her and whatever you do don't even turn your head toward the cubs so you don't have to worry about us ma'am we're on our way out of here God knows I wouldn't want to have to try and stick this little chickenshit knife in your ear while you're biting my head off and now that we're on that subject you can bet your sweet bear ass we're never comin' back out here without a gun.'

They inched toward me. I gripped one of the oars in both hands, trying to keep my movements invisible as I adjusted my grip toward the right balance point to swing it if I had to, imagining it coming around at the bear's head in ultra-slow motion, getting there too late, wishing to God boat oars were shorter and lighter. And had ax heads on them.

The bear gave a deep woof and made a quick fake at Don, and Diana clapped her hands over her mouth and said, 'Nnk,' but kept moving slowly with him.

'Yeah I know ma'am,' said Don, sounding sensible and friendly. 'If they were my kids I'd feel exactly the same way and as you can see I've got my own to think about so I do understand your reasoning you get into the boat first honey get low and curl up tight as you can facedown and cover your head and Jim you ease that oar over toward me.'

Trying to keep my hands from shaking, I slowly swung the oar far enough forward for Don to reach it. As Diana climbed into the boat and got down behind the front seat, Don carefully set the knife down on the bow and took the oar with one hand. He brought it around and held it crosswise in front of him as he backed slowly into the water beside the boat. 'You're gonna use the other oar to push off, Jim,' he said. 'What I'm gonna do in a second is roll over the gunnel, and you need to have us moving straight out as soon as I do.'

The bear's head swung from side to side, her muzzle lifting as she tested the air, watching Don with a nearsighted expression.

'One-two-three,' Don said softly, and swung over into the boat as I pushed as hard as I could against the gravelly bottom with the other oar. We scraped off the beach and glided silently away from the shore. Don dug his oar into the water on the other side of the boat to straighten us out and gain some more distance, then looked back at the bear, which whuffed again and turned to waddle away toward the fallen tree. The cubs clung to opposite sides of the trunk they'd climbed, one a little above the other about twenty feet up, watching everything.

Diana peeked up over the bow, then looked back over her shoulder at me. Her eyes were huge and her knuckles were white as she gripped the gunnels. 'Bears!' she squeaked. She turned to Don. 'The bears almost got us, Daddy!' She took a shaky breath and swallowed.

Don was still trying to get his own breathing under control. He rubbed his hand over his nose and mouth. 'Got caught a little out of position there, I guess,' he said. He turned to look at me. 'Scare you, Jimbo?'

'Naw,' I said, noticing that even my feet and toes seemed to be trembling.

'Scared me,' said Diana, nodding to herself.

'Really ought to go heeled out here this time of year,' said Don. 'Should've brought my weapon.' He yanked on the Evinrude to start it and we backed out of the cove.

'I know what,' said Diana. 'Let's eat lunch in the boat.'

5

Casts

After the bears Diana had no more interest in fishing, and Don decided he wanted to get the charcoal going for tonight, so I was on my own.

'How about if I go back out by myself?' I asked Don. 'I wanted to try that rocky point next to that last little creek we saw.'

'For muskie?' He grabbed the bag of charcoal. 'Yes sir.'

He thought about it as he slit open the top of the bag with his pocketknife. 'Might work, at that,' he said. 'Think you can run the boat okay?'

'Yes sir.'

'Then you got a deal,' he said. 'Just don't put in anywhere along that south shore, and get back by dark.'

I anchored thirty yards off the point where the creek drained into the lake between the high dark firs and spruces. Across the creek mouth was a wide flat with a few big rocks and stickups in the water.

I tied on an eighteen-inch steel leader and a red and white muskie lure, and cast as hard as I could, watching the huge plug carry up and out a surprising distance before splashing down onto the water. I slowly retrieved it and cast again, then again and again, with no results. I kept casting, becoming so engrossed that several times I forgot to worry about L.A. and Gram back in Dallas. I even forgot to ask myself why I was still worried.

Then something stopped me. I looked around at the water and the trees on the shore and up at the sky, but nothing had changed. I thought about bears, and dug the blue stone out of my pocket. I sat looking at it for a minute, wondering if it had been born in the earth or had fallen from the sky, and then, taking a deep breath, I threw it as far as I could out toward the center of the lake. It plinked into the water, and in a couple of seconds the ripples disappeared.

I cast again, and was about to start the retrieve when I felt the hair on the back of my neck stand up. Out to my right beyond the creek channel a table-sized region of the surface swirled into a fast-moving arrow of water driving across the open flat, straight for the lure, leaving a wake like a submarine. A dome of water boiled up under the lure, and an unbelievably huge fish reared its long-jawed head clear of the water, shook once with the lure in its mouth and then blasted a white wall of spray into the air as it slammed back down through the surface and disappeared.

The fish went for the center of the channel cut where the water was deepest, taking line from the drag without effort, the rod bent almost double as the line sliced through the water. I planted my feet on the gunnel and leaned back against the pull, feeling the boat come around to the end of the anchor line as it tried to follow the fish's run.

But I knew better than to think I was going to

turn this fish. Nothing was going to do that.

And then it stopped. I couldn't feel anything now but the thing's massive weight, so immovable that I wondered for a second if I had snagged a rock or stump. But then the fish gave three slow shakes of its mighty head and came directly at the boat, and before I could take back the slack line it drifted up alongside, a yard under the surface — tremendous jaws jagged with teeth and a soulless yellow eye the size of a clock face looking through my own eyes and brain and into the exact center of my soul, then the gray-green armored gills and the fish's barred side passing like a slow train in the fog. The creature looked as long as the boat, and when it was gone the water suddenly seemed as empty as space.

In the next instant the fish hit the end of the slack, emptied the reel in one straight run out the channel, and the line snapped. The surface gradually settled back to stillness.

I sat and breathed for a while, waiting for my heart to stop banging in my throat, feeling the small rocking motion of the boat and hearing the light lapping of the water against its side. The sun was dropping lower in the sky, looking bigger and redder and softer. Finally I pulled up the anchor, stowed the rod inside the gunnel and started the motor.

As I brought the boat around I saw something floating on the water out near the spot where I'd thrown the stone. I eased the boat alongside it and leaned down to pick it up. It was the lure, or what was left of it, the steel leader and a short length of line hanging from the front eye hook. The plug was made of cedar, thick as a shovel handle, but the back half was gone, treble hooks and all, the wood marked by the fish's teeth where they had sheared through it.

Looking at it, I could feel that something wasn't right, but I couldn't figure out what. I stared at the ruined plug a while longer, then dropped it into the tackle box and snapped the lid down. Bringing the boat's bow around, I gradually opened the throttle and headed back toward the cabin.

6

Magic Moments

I never told anyone the whole story of the muskie, just said I hooked one but lost him when my lure came apart. It was probably selfishness on my part, and I don't really know if I was afraid of making what happened smaller by talking about it or if there was some other reason, but I ended up keeping most of it for myself, like a miser hoarding his coins.

In the morning Don let Diana and me take the boat out again for a picnic. Marge looked worried, and for a second I was uneasy over how much she knew about my thoughts.

'Are these two going to be all right, Don?' she said.

Don was busy at the end of the dock shaking ashes out of the grill into the water. 'Long as they leave the bears alone,' he said without looking up.

'Bears,' said Diana, swallowing. Reconsidering, maybe.

'Islands only, Jimbo,' Don said, shooting me a look for emphasis. 'It's a really bad time of year, with the cubs as young as they are.'

I nodded and pushed the boat away from the dock with an oar, thinking there might be a lot of things for Don to worry about, but us messing with any more bears wasn't one of them. I pulled on the starter rope a couple of times and the motor growled and blubbed smokily in the water. I eased the boat backward out into open water and brought the bow around to head us out toward the far end of the lake.

We cruised along like old people, with Diana leaning over to trail her hand in the water, until we were out of sight behind the point, then I gradually opened the throttle to get us up to speed. Diana took off her sweatshirt, and I saw she had on a light green swimsuit under it. She threw back her head and held her arms out wide, her hair flying in the wind. The sun was already warm on my face.

When we got to the little island where we had caught the walleyes I cut the motor and we coasted in to the beach side. The island was partly covered with trees and had a long tail of beach on one side and some kind of dark green grass growing here and there in the water around it. When Diana jumped ashore with the bowline, half a dozen goldfinches spilled away from the high branches of a poplar at the water's edge and scattered across the sky above us like chips of sun. She tied us up to a limb on a big piece of driftwood as I tilted the motor up out of the water, and we carried our stuff up to a dry flat spot under a couple of pine trees. I set the cooler down as she spread the two big blue and white towels on the pine needles.

Diana took off her sandals and slipped out of her blue jeans, then got out two small bottles and poured mosquito repellent and sun lotion into her hand, rubbed her palms together and started spreading the oily stuff over her skin. I stripped down to my own trunks and picked up the fishing rod. I opened the tackle box, pushing aside the damaged muskie lure and finding a perch-colored River-Runt. I tied it on, then walked over to the other shore to cast into the deeper water on that side. I cast a few times, got a backlash, picked it out and cast again. Then, realizing I didn't care whether I caught anything or not, I carried the rod back to where Diana was sitting on one of the beach towels.

'Wanta go swimming?' she said.

I was a little doubtful. The water seemed pretty cold, but then I couldn't afford to show cowardice either.

'Okay,' I said. 'You go first. If you survive, I'll come in too.'

'You are my hero,' she said. She walked to the edge of the water and stood looking across the sparkling lake for a few seconds. She tested the water with her toe and instantly jerked it back out. She considered for a while. 'I'll have to wash my hair again; but I don't care,' she said, and ran splashing out into the lake until she was deep enough to dive in. When she came back up she shook her head and said, 'It's not too bad once you're in. But there's a few weeds under the water. Feels like feathers.'

Having no alternative now, I charged out and dove in too, surprised by how bearable the water turned out to be. I swam out along the spit a little way and then back to where Diana was putting her face under the water trying to see fish. She raised her head and said, 'There's not anything down there that bites, is there?'

'I don't think so,' I said, remembering the muskie and the lost fish from our stringer. I was semi-sure whatever was in the lake didn't attack people. Except possibly little kids. And dogs. I looked at Diana standing waist-deep in the water in her wet bathing suit. The small valley of her navel showed through the fabric just at the waterline, and all my thoughts about water monsters melted away to nothing.

Diana bent down to look under the surface again, but almost instantly jerked her head up and screamed. She ran splashing back up to the beach, slapping at her legs. I caught up to her, mental images of dog- and walleye-eating muskies coming back to me in a blood-freezing rush.

'It's got me!' she yelled, yanking at a slippery black leech that was attached to the inside of her thigh. 'Help me, Biscuit!'

I pulled at the rubbery leech, but it was stuck tight. Diana's teeth chattered with fear and cold. I said, 'Come on over here, maybe we can get it off.' I remembered Don saying something about leeches in the lake but I hadn't realized how tough they could be. While I went over to the tackle box, Diana sat on her towel, still trying to get a grip on the leech with her fingers. In the bottom of the box I found the metal tube filled with waterproof matches next to a little jar of red salmon eggs. I grabbed it and came back to kneel beside her. She lay back with her eyes shut and her arms at her sides, looking like a pagan sacrifice. Her teeth were clenched and she had goose bumps on her arms and legs. I struck a match and stretched the leech out from her skin. When I held the flame under it, it let go, and I tossed it away into the grass. Then I sat back and looked at Diana until she opened her eyes.

'Is it off?' she asked, shivering.

I nodded. I couldn't stop staring at her. I saw that her nipples were pushing up under the fabric of her suit. Her legs were smooth and tanned except for the small pink circle where the leech had been. There were sparkling drops of water all over her. I was beginning to get a strangled feeling in my chest. I bent down and kissed her, tasting the lake on her lips. She held my shoulders and kissed me back, groaning under her breath, then pulled me against her, and I felt her whole body tremble. I moved to lie beside her and we kissed again, longer this time, the world seeming to stop its turning as we held each other. After a while I pulled back and lay on my side looking at her, at her wet hair and the way her swimsuit followed the shape of her body.

Diana watched me for a minute, just breathing. She said, 'What are you thinking, Bis?'

I could barely speak. 'All I can think about is how much I wish I could see you without your bathing suit,' I said.

She looked at me without saying anything or showing any expression for so long I thought maybe she hadn't heard me, or I hadn't really said it out loud. Or maybe she was just deciding whether to smack me or not. I couldn't believe what I'd said, myself. I heard the air moving through the trees above us and birds calling somewhere.

Finally she said, 'You can.'

She didn't ask me to turn around or anything, just stood up, unhooked the top straps and worked the swimsuit down until she could step out of it, then lay down again on the towel. She was white where the suit had covered her, and the hair between her legs was almost exactly the same sandy color as the hair on her head. The sun caught the golden fuzz on her arms and stomach and the perfect curves of her breasts.

'You too,' she said.

I got out of my trunks, found my billfold and tore a condom from its package, remembering what Hubert had told me about how to put it on.

Watching me, Diana said, 'Doesn't that tickle?'

I shook my head and lay back down beside her. We kissed again and I cupped her small soft breast in my hand. The nipple felt firm and warm, exactly as I'd imagined it would. She spread her legs a little to let me touch her. It was all so much easier and so much better than my daydreams that I felt dizzy. She accepted me between her legs as I moved over her, her breath hot on my neck.

When I entered her, she yelled, 'Yikes!' sucking in her breath and grabbing the hair on the sides of my head, her eyes squinched shut. '*Yikes!*' she said again, this time her voice only a squeak.

I'd never actually heard anyone say that before and had thought it was only a cartoon word. It scared me a little. 'Should I stop?' I said.

'No, dummy!' she hissed through her teeth. 'Don't stop. *Never* stop.'

In a little while I began to feel as if I was drifting, slowly at first but then faster and faster, on a river of pleasure deeper and wider than the Amazon, toward a tremendous waterfall rumbling over the edge of the universe, with no control over anything and no awareness of anything but the irresistible river. There were colored spots in my eyes and everything sounded far off, like the time I got knocked out, and then I didn't hear anything at all. Diana's skin and hair smelled like the water and the pine needles and the lotion she'd put on, and her breath was sweet on my face and neck. She opened her mouth wide and wrapped her legs around mine. And then I did go over the edge of the world, because I couldn't possibly stop myself, and I fell and fell and fell through soundless white thunder until I knew I'd never breathe again, never even want to breathe again — just keep on falling like this forever.

And then it was over. For what seemed like a long time I just lay next to Diana and tried to catch my breath. The sounds of the birds and the light wind in the tops of the pines came back. I felt the sun on my skin. I couldn't believe a feeling like that could happen, or, once it happened, that it could ever end.

Diana lay with her arm over her eyes, breathing a little slower now. Finally she lowered her arm, looked at me for a minute and said,

'Wow.' She halfway sat up and looked down at herself. 'There's just a little blood,' she said without sounding too concerned, as if maybe she'd expected this.

'Does it hurt?' I said.

'Not enough to worry about,' she said.

'I'm sorry.'

'Don't be sorry. That makes it sound like you did something bad. Or we did.' She looked at me and then down at herself again. 'I'm not exactly sure what bad is, but I don't think this is it.'

'Okay,' I said, not completely convinced. It had never occurred to me until this moment that what we'd done might actually be dangerous, that it might involve bloodshed.

She didn't say anything for a while, both of us floating along on the feeling. Eventually I started wondering how long we could just lie out here naked as babies like this, nothing over us but the trees and the sky. Surely there had to be some kind of rule against it. On the other hand, I supposed we were in so deep on account of what we'd just done that there was no point in worrying about secondary misbehaviors like simple nudity.

Then Diana said, 'I don't think Mom'll be able to tell.' She drew in a deep breath. 'But Harpo's gonna know.'

'How's she going to know?'

Diana just looked at me.

I nodded miserably. In a way it was the story of my whole life — always saying something stupid before I thought, then hearing myself and realizing what an idiot I was. 'You're right, she'll know,' I said unnecessarily, the dread possibilities inherent in this fact beginning to circle like vultures in my mind.

Diana pulled the towel from under herself to use as a blanket, covering her body from her shoulders to her ankles. Thinking it over, calming down a little, I told myself Diana had it exactly right, we could probably keep our secret from the adults and most, or even with a little luck all, of the other kids except L.A. This limited the problem considerably, but I also understood that what we'd just done wasn't over, couldn't be over until all the consequences were in, and I had no idea yet what they were going to be or when they were coming. Sitting up, I took a long breath.

'It feels like she already knows,' I said. 'It feels like everybody knows.'

I looked off across the water, understanding that now another divide had been crossed, and there was no way back. It was a different lake now. It was a different world.

$\star$ $\star$ $\star$

When we got back to the cabin I felt almost as naked walking up to Marge and Don as I actually had been on the island, but to my surprise and relief neither of them seemed to sense anything different about Diana or me. By the time we had finished the steaks, yams and buttered onions Don cooked on the grill for supper that evening, I had myself convinced we were completely in the clear as far as Diana's parents were concerned. This didn't solve the L.A. problem, but she was still over a thousand miles away, so at least for the moment we had some breathing room.

Later we fell asleep in front of the fire again, and of course I dreamed of the — or maybe I should say *a* — dead girl, not necessarily Tricia Venables or anyone in particular this time, but still as real as ever and still wanting something from me: *She stares at me in silence for a long time, her skin blue-gray, the whites of her eyes not really white, I notice for the first time, but pink from the small hemorrhages caused by strangulation. She looks down at the big red and white fishing lure in her hand, and then her eyes come back to mine. She lifts the lure to her mouth, tears off a chunk of it with her teeth and chews slowly, the wood crunching, hooks tearing the bloodless flesh of her lips and tongue, her eyes never leaving mine.*

I sat up suddenly, gasping, my T-shirt drenched with sweat, the fading echoes of a scream ricocheting through my mind. I threw the sheet aside, pulled on my jeans and took the stairs four at a time, grabbing the flashlight from the kitchen counter on my way out the back door and running as hard as I could down the slope to the dock and out its length to the boat. I tore open the tackle box, scrabbled around in the bottom until I found the muskie lure and shone the flashlight's beam on its sheared-off end and the grooves cut by the gigantic fish's teeth, my hands shaking.

I felt footsteps on the dock behind me, too

heavy to be anyone's but Don's. 'Jim, what's going on?' he said.

I turned to him, my mouth almost too dry to speak. 'It wasn't Hot Earl,' I said.

7

Findings

There are a lot of ways a thing can become real, especially if you have no defense against it. How it affects you depends on things like who you are, what you already know, and how strong you are. Sometimes you're a player in what's happening, which has its own risks and consequences. But other times, without being any less powerful, it can be like watching a movie, only with real people: Don Chamfort — looking like what he is, a man who in the last thirty-six hours has driven more than a thousand miles without stopping for anything but gas and hasn't slept at all — walking into his kitchen through the door from the garage with three other men, setting the crate of files he's carrying on the end of the Formica dinette table and taking off his jacket. Hanging it over the back of one of the kitchen chairs, saying, 'Will, Vern, Fergo, y'all want anything to drink? Beer or something?'

Vern saying, 'Beer'd be good,' grabbing a chair, loosening his tie and unbuttoning his collar, blowing out a huge breath.

None of them having any idea they are being watched.

Now Will: 'Got any coffee?' He wasn't a drinking man anymore but he was hell on the

Luckies and Joe, a long-legged brick-red guy with a twinkle in his eye, the kind who wore cowboy boots every day. His face was long too, and on the rough side, and there was next to no hair on the top of his head. What hair he did have was trimmed close and rust-colored except for the white sidewalls above his ears. *Semper fi* never wears off, Don had said in that tone of special connection one Marine has with another.

Ferguson pulled on his nose as he looked into the fridge, deliberating, wanting to be sure he got this exactly right. He squatted down and peered around among the pickles and leftovers. Then he stood back up, finally grabbing a can of tomato juice from one of the door shelves, shaking it and opening it to take a hit.

More coats came off. It wasn't jacket weather; the coats were to cover the handguns holstered on the men's hips or at the small of the back, and the badges on their belts. There was the sound of shoe leather on linoleum, chairs being moved, an ashtray and cigarette lighter sliding across the tabletop. There was Aqua Velva in the air. Don laid his weapon in its holster on the counter, placed his hands on his lower back and pushed, groaning. His back chattered out a half dozen pops.

The men were into the cabinets and breadbox, bringing out pretzels, chips, cheese puffs.

'We got anything to dip with these?'

'This buttermilk still good?'

'Buttermilk can go *bad?*'

Don waggled the root beer bottle he'd been drinking from, set it down and leaned over to

283

pick up a folder from the top of the crate. 'Appreciate you guys coming in after hours like this. I know you don't have enough to do as it is.'

'Sheeit,' said Ferguson. 'Policin' is our passion. We live to pertect and serve.' He turned a chair around and straddled it, though he probably wouldn't be on it long. He was a freckle-faced joker who was always moving.

'Hell, yeah, Don,' said Will, lighting a Lucky with his Zippo. He threw one leg over the other. 'Idle mind's the devil's workshop.'

Vern took a swig of beer, belched and scratched under his arm. He was like a big woodchuck, with extra chins but otherwise not much sign of a neck.

'Anyway,' said Don, 'I'm glad for the help. There's never been a task force across divisions like this before, so we're making it up as we go along. Not exactly an easy sell, but for now Carsey green-lighted as many get-togethers on this as we need. We can keep the group intact until we hear different.'

'What about support?'

'We get OT and clerical help only as and when approved, flextime if we need it. And all the table scraps you guys can find around here.'

'Bring a tear to a glass eye, the generosity of that man,' said Will, pursing his lips like a puritan.

Another editorial belch from Vern.

'He's in a corner,' Don said. 'Everybody thought we had these killings cleared, and now this. He knows the press is gonna crack his bones and suck the marrow.'

Ferguson was eating cheese puffs in three quick bites: nip, nip, and in with the tail. No visible sympathy for the chief. 'Goddam perp out there chewing on the girl's windowsill,' he said. 'Can you fuckin' imagine?'

'Tells you something about the guy's state of mind,' Will said.

'What it tells us is he's got a full set of teeth,' Don said. 'Which we wouldn't know about if it wasn't for Jim.' He opened the folder and took a deep breath. 'So okay,' he said, rubbing his temples. 'Our hero Earl's off the hook and we still got murders to clear.' He looked around at the other men. 'By way of recap, anybody want to say anything about the Unrelated theory at this point?'

The men looked at each other. No one said anything.

'About even one of the vics?' said Don. 'Any doubt at all?'

Still no response.

After a moment Don ran a hand over his short hair and said, 'Okay. Me either. Meaning we're back to zero suspects.'

'Earl's gotta be good for something.'

'He's probably good for plenty,' said Don. 'All you have to do is look at what he tried to pull with the kids. But I was there when Doc Henley looked at his gums — he hasn't worn dentures in at least a year. And all indications, he's more inclined to boys anyway.'

Head shakes, shrugs and munches around the table. Dead ends clearly didn't faze these guys. Nothing new there. Neither did it seem to bother

285

them a hell of a lot that their former suspect had sat in jail all this time without having actually committed the crime he got locked up for. Ferguson ripped off a bite of cold fried chicken.

Don went on: 'What we're talking about is an unknown subject who I think probably lives here in the city and for his own nutball reasons committed all three homicides. Due to the age of the victims we can't rule out that the perp is also young, possibly even a teenager, which might've given him an in with them. Or they may have known him from somewhere, even though we came up dry on all our interviews. I'm told by our shrink it's likely the guy's been through the system already, probably isn't too successful with the opposite sex and has shown violent or sadistic tendencies in the past.' Don unfolded a city map and spread it across the table. 'Personal hunch here based on the girls' residences and the dump sites, he lives south of the Trinity within a mile or so of Marsalis Park.' He clicked his ballpoint and drew a circle on the map, taking in a couple of square miles. 'The murders, at least the ones we know about, occurred over a period of not quite six months. No idea why the guy chose these particular victims or why the killings were spaced out the way they were. All the victims lived in this area, but no other connection we know about. Victim One, Amanda Peyser, found behind the screen of a drive-in theater by the manager.' Don held up his thumb. Ferguson got up to look in the refrigerator again.

'Three and a half months later, Victim Two,' said Don. 'Marybeth Nichols, found at the back of the old Clarkson Lumberyard site by uniforms rolling on an anonymous call.' Index finger. 'Four weeks ago, Victim Three, Tricia Venables, found by our kids at the overpass.' Second finger.

'Which means — ' said Vern.

'He's pickin' up the pace,' said Ferguson.

'And somebody else's little girl is fixin' to die somewhere in that fuckin' circle,' finished Will.

A moment of silence. Then Don nodded and said, 'Afraid that's how it looks. Unless we can stop him.'

'What else we got?' asked Vern.

'Only deviation from MO we know about for sure is the partial absence of the characteristic mutilations on the first one, Peyser,' said Don. 'Which looks nonsignificant to me.'

He took out a handful of glossy eight-by-ten black-and-white photos showing various views of the nude bodies of girls lying in grassy areas. He passed them around, the men surely having looked at them before but looking again anyway because what you didn't see the first time you might see the second or third. Or tenth. Vern looked at each one right side up first, then again upside down and sideways, like a man trying to see rather than assume. All of the girls lay on their backs with their legs spread and their hands over their breasts. The only marks visible on them in the photographs were on their necks, wrists and ankles.

'This ain't no way to kill people,' said Will, stubbing out his cigarette in the small glass ashtray before him, a muscle jumping in his jaw.

There were a couple of grunts from the others. 'I mean, get drunk and shoot your brother-in-law over the six-pack he owes you or cut your cheatin' husband's gullers out with a razor, maybe kill a clerk at the Handy-Rob for three dollars and twenty cents — that's how it goes. I carried a stick in this town for four years, been in soft clothes for eleven, and this right here's the first thing like it I ever caught.'

'Fuckin' head case,' said Vern.

'Special kind of a twitch, though,' said Ferguson. He was chewing chicken and thinking out loud. 'It's not revenge. He's not after money.'

'He's after the hard-on,' said Vern.

'Exactly.' Don nodded. 'He had sex with them one way or another, but the killing was the main thing.'

'Ought to let me take care of the punishment phase. Time I got through with the cherry-pickin' sumbitch they'd have to put a new chapter in the Bible to cover what I done to him.'

Don returned to the file. 'No particular order here, so bear with me. Victims were thirteen to sixteen years of age,' he said. 'All three estimated to be between a hundred and five and a hundred and fifteen pounds, sixty-two to sixty-five inches in height, hair and eye color you can see in the photos, brown-brown or black. Per the families, all of them were wearing jeans, sneakers and sweaters or pullover tops when they were last seen. None of them wore glasses. Good kids, stayed out of trouble, had homes and families, went to school. Venables was an honor student.

288

Kind of interesting here: all the girls were more or less at the juncture of Tanner stages three and four.'

'What's that?' asked Ferguson.

'Sexual-development classification the docs use. Stage three going into four in females would mean some breast development but not adult volume yet, aureoles and nipples enlarged but not as much as an adult, pubic hair present but maybe still a little sparse, getting close to full development of characteristic feminine body shape, beginning of menstruation, things like that.'

'Yeah, that was Marcy around fourteen, fifteen,' said Vern.

'Uh-huh,' said Don. 'Says here girls can hit that stage anywhere from ten to seventeen in industrialized countries. Genetics along with nutrition and health can affect the timing.'

'What you're saying, the girls were different ages on the calendar but all developed to the same point physically.'

'Presto,' said Don.

Ferguson got up to look in the cabinet, returning with a box of raisins. He brought them back to the table. 'What does that signify?' he said, everyone in the room of course understanding his question to mean, *How does that get us the collar?*

'Wouldn't I like to know,' said Don.

'It ain't coincidence,' said Will.

'Right,' said Don. 'The guy had a picture in his head and he was making it come true in real life. No information on how he was able to

289

snatch the girls, whether they recognized him or he suckered them some way, or maybe just jumped out at them from somewhere. Sure would like to know exactly *where* he got them.' Don tapped his fingers absently on the folder, reworking old ground in his thinking.

'Figure he had some kind of wheels,' Vern said, because a cop always expects a perpetrator to do things the laziest possible way. 'Maybe marked like a service truck or even an emergency vehicle to keep from spooking the victims. Got up close enough to yank 'em in, controlled 'em however, got 'em out of sight and gassed it out of there.'

'Maybe it really *was* a service truck, or an emergency vehicle,' Vern said.

'Like a cruiser?'

'Meaning . . . '

A silence, then Ferguson said, 'Fuck that. It's not a cop. No way it's a cop.'

Another silence. Finally Don said, 'I don't care if it's the goddamn mayor. We bust the piece of shit no matter who he is.'

Grunts of agreement.

'What we needed here, we needed just one damn concerned citizen out walking his dog or something — but where the fuck are they when you need 'em? Just a partial plate number, vehicle description, anything — that too much to ask?'

'Been me out there with my fly open, there'da been twenty-four registered bird-watchers on hand to call it in,' said Vern.

'Somebody ought to send around a master list of these kind of calls,' said Will. 'Probably happens all the time, couple cases look just alike except they fell in different jurisdictions and nobody's the wiser.'

'Yeah, maybe have some kind of permanent network,' said Don. 'Not sure exactly how you'd work it but I've been thinking it'd be good for us to do something like that on our own, even if it's just the metro area. I've got a feeling this won't be the last time we need it.' He scratched his stomach and stared off into space, thinking.

If he had focused his eyes a little to the left, through the kitchen archway and across the living room to the top of the darkened stairs, he probably could have seen me there watching and listening, L.A. and Diana right behind me. We'd been up here when the men came in and were trying not to give away our position.

We had left Duck Lake less than an hour after my run down to the dock, and I'd only had a couple of hours of sleep since then. Tired as I was, I was still too buzzed to relax. But I had experienced two huge rushes of relief — finding L.A. and Gram safe was the first, and the second came an hour or so later on the back patio at Gram's where Diana met up with L.A. and me after a quick shower and change at home. She lightly touched the back of my neck with her fingers as she passed behind me and sat down with her knee against mine under the table. She and L.A. looked at each other for a couple of beats, there was a little bump in the flow of time and I felt some kind of adjustment happen between them that I understood had very little to do with me. Now L.A. knew it all, her expression telling me instantly that it hadn't come as a surprise to her and that she was okay about it. All my fear had been for nothing, and the feeling was like an illegal drug surging through my veins.

Later at the Chamforts' place Diana and I hadn't noticed right away when Don and the others came in, but of course L.A. had, radio or no radio. If you want to practice sneaking up on somebody, forget L.A. and try your luck with a fox. She had shushed Diana and me and we all had tiptoed out to the head of the stairs.

'Anyway,' said Don now, 'we sure as hell know about three of them right here smack in the middle of our midst, all by the same fuckin' artist.'

'The forensics and other stuff you wanted are pulled together in the blue folder,' said Ferguson.

'Thanks,' said Don. He picked up the file and thumbed through the reports and summaries, eyes narrowed in concentration.

'All the postmortem findings are consistent with known means-and-manners,' he said. 'Suggests a single perpetrator following a more or less fixed MO. None of the girls was menstruating at the time of death. Two of them, Peyser and Venables, were virgins when abducted. All three well nourished, normally developed and in good health, no surgeries, previous fractures, distinctive scars or birthmarks. No items of clothing other than the famous scarves and no jewelry found on or in association with the bodies, even though two of the girls had pierced ears. No leads from or matches on cigarette butts, empty bottles, hairs, fibers or anything else found at the scenes. One foreign hair found on the Nichols girl. Caucasian, medium length, brown.'

'Major breakthrough there,' Vern snorted.

'Right. But we may get a match when we collar this guy, so stay tuned. Anyway, I'm thinking it's obvious the victims were killed elsewhere — probably all in the same place, but who the hell knows — and dumped shortly thereafter at the locations where they were found. They were left where they probably wouldn't be discovered right away but beyond that no effort was made at concealment. Just the opposite: all the bodies being posed, like you see in the photos, says to me the doer expected them to be found and wanted them seen that way.'

'And wanted to keep that picture in his head. Think back on it, get off on it all over again,' said Will.

'Demeaning the vic, thumbing his nose at us,' said Ferguson.

Don got up and went to the fridge for another root beer as he read. On the way back he grabbed a breadstick from beside the toaster and took a bite, looked at it and tossed it into the trash. 'The nipples of Victims Two and Three severed with a very sharp knife or other edged instrument while the girls were still alive,' he said. 'Victim One's nipples were not cut off but had been severely bitten and probably also placed in some type of serrated clamps, possibly electrical, again while the victim was still alive.' Don flipped some more pages. 'On that subject, all three girls were kept alive at least twelve hours after abduction. Nichols may have been held captive for as long as four days.'

'Implies some kind of secure location,' said Vern. 'Isolated or maybe soundproofed.'

'Guy couldn't have had a regular job,' said Ferguson.

It was obvious from the way they talked that they'd worked their way out along this line of thought before, but that's how cops are. They just never burn out on going back over things they don't completely understand.

'Ligature marks on the wrists and ankles suggest all three girls had been tied, untied and retied several times,' said Don.

'Doing stuff with them, making them do stuff,' said Will. 'Posing them for photos, maybe?'

'That'd fit,' said Vern.

'On at least one occasion, presumably at the point of death, each victim had struggled violently against her bindings, which we think probably consisted of the kind of clothesline you buy in grocery stores, so no help there. Toxicology reports Miltown and Seconal taken orally in Peyser and the third victim, Venables. And whatever this is — I can't pronounce it — a muscle relaxant, I think, in all three.' Don took a drink of his root beer.

'To help him control them,' said Will. 'Not to make it easier on them.'

'You know it.'

'What'd the asshole do with the cut-off parts, I wonder?' said Vern.

'Dunno,' said Don. 'But off the record, the

ME says the first place he'd look is in the guy's freezer.'

'Godamighty,' said Will.

'Death in all cases was by asphyxia secondary to ligature strangulation,' Don said. 'Based on the location and appearance of the neck markings and on autopsy findings, the medical examiner believes all three girls were hanged.'

I flinched, my heart seeming to skip a couple of beats.

'Hyoid fractures in all three,' Don continued, 'but no fractures or major displacement of cervical vertebrae and no spinal cord injuries, so there was no drop. Just dangle-and-strangle, the ME said.' Don rubbed his eyes and pinched the bridge of his nose, then took a deep breath. 'This is conjecture, but it's possible the hangings were ceremonial or ritualistic in nature, based on the practically identical placement of nooses and bindings in all three cases. The noose, by the way, was apparently formed by use of a common slip knot, with the knot placed in precisely the same spot behind the left ear in each case. No concessions to convenience or circumstance there, I'd say.'

'Had to be just so,' said Will.

I was dizzy. L.A. and Diana had moved up tight against me and were looking over my shoulders. I could hear and feel their breathing, and L.A.'s hand gripped my arm. I didn't want to hear what was coming.

Don said, 'Although all the victims had been penetrated and injured vaginally, because of the absence of semen there's no direct evidence of vaginal intercourse per se. However, all three victims had performed oral sex, and semen was also present to indicate that all of them had been sodomized, probably repeatedly and probably both before and after death. Abrasions of the clitoris and adjacent tissues in all cases suggests the victims were repeatedly masturbated. He wanted them to come.'

L.A. sucked in her breath.

'And of course for our main trademark — and if you've got any ideas on what the hell it means, please enlighten me — each girl died with a white silk scarf tied in a four-in-hand and stuffed into her vagina.'

L.A. made a loud gagging sound as her fingers bit into my arm like a dog's teeth, and suddenly I saw everything — what had happened to L.A. and the other girls, and who had done all of it. My heart lunged against my ribs and my ears roared with a continuous thunder. I wanted to cover L.A. somehow and keep the world from hurting her any more. But she stumbled away and bounced off the wall as she ran down the stairs and out the front door. A few seconds later Don came up the stairs, followed by Will with his gun held down beside his leg, Ferguson and finally Vern, puffing and cramming in his shirttail as he climbed.

'Jim, Diana,' said Don, looking around. 'I didn't know you guys were here. What happened? Sounded like somebody was chok-ing.'

'It was L.A., Dad,' said Diana. 'I think maybe she got sick.'

The men asked more questions, the way cops do, but I wasn't really listening. I knew L.A. wasn't sick, at least not physically, and I thought I knew where she was going, but I didn't know what to say to Don and the others about it.

'I think she's going to be all right, sir,' I finally said. 'I'll find her.'

Will put his gun up as I ran past him down the stairs.

8

Turnabout

I ran half blindly, as hard as I could, but every block I covered seemed to take a century. L.A. was nowhere to be seen. When I bounced off a passing Volkswagen, went down and rolled against the curb, the concrete ripping the skin from one knee, it all seemed to happen in slow motion, the driver standing in the middle of the street behind me yelling as I scrambled to my feet and ran on, 'Hey! Are you all right? I never saw you coming — what the hell's the matter with you?' I didn't slow down, didn't feel any pain even though my jeans below the knee were already soaked with blood. All I could think about was how fast L.A. was and how many steps I had lost by falling.

Shit, I screamed in my mind, *shit shit shit*, gritting my teeth, trying to run faster, not giving a damn when I knocked some kid completely off his Schwinn on the sidewalk and heard him screaming and cussing behind me. More seconds lost.

By the time I made it to the front walk of Gram's house my legs were rubbery and I felt like I was inhaling fire. All I could think about was how far ahead of me L.A. had gotten. Fighting to catch my breath, I looked at the house, the dark windows, the open garage. This was market day, the Roadmaster nowhere to be seen, and there was no movement or sound anywhere around the house.

But it wasn't empty, I knew.

Opening the front door, I stepped inside, where I heard the kitchen radio playing faintly. Gram's station, Patsy Cline doing 'Crazy.' The radio being on wasn't unusual. Gram generally left it that way when she didn't expect to be gone long. That thought, along with the Roadmaster being gone, gave me hope.

But just inside the kitchen doorway I could see Jazzy's body lying slack and motionless against one leg of a chair, and the air buzzed with the most terrible energy I'd ever felt in my life.

I moved as quietly as I could across the front room and into the hall, trying to minimize the squishing sound my blood-filled sneaker made with each step. The bathroom door and the door to Gram's room stood open as usual, both rooms empty and dark. I couldn't see whether the door to my own room was open or not, but the hallway in that direction was unlit and felt cool and empty. I visualized my bat, leaning in a corner of my closet. I could almost feel the taped grip in my hands.

But there was no time for that.

Then I was at L.A.'s door. It was closed, which it never was unless she was inside. I swallowed hard and turned the knob, letting the door swing open on its own.

What I saw burned itself into my brain like a cutting torch, and I knew in that second that no matter how long I lived it would never leave me.

Reality began coming in stop-action flashes: *The killer pinning L.A. on the bed, one hand over her mouth and nose . . . his other hand tearing at the fly of her Levi's as he kneels between her legs . . . L.A. bucking and twisting, clawing at him, trying to kick him, her eyes insane as she fights to breathe . . . the killer seeming not to notice her struggles, his mind in some unknowable place, his veined pink cock out and erect above her . . . the killer catching sight of me, letting go now of her jeans, dragging the back of his hand across his mouth as if trying to wipe away something invisible, mumbling thickly, 'Bis — ' . . . the alien sound of my own raw scream as I dive at him, slamming the man who all her life has called himself L.A.'s father against the wall . . . driving one fist and then the other against the side of his head, again and again and again.*

'Kill you, you fucker,' Cam rasped, trying to block the blows, struggling to free himself of my weight. But I was nearly his size now, and crazy with rage. He covered his head with his arms, and I punched with everything I had at his ribs and kidneys, still screaming, trying to break his bones, crush his organs, stop his heart.

At the same time L.A., jeans and panties down on her hips, had twisted around on the bed, one hand darting under her pillow and coming out with my Swiss army knife. Quick as a cottonmouth, with exactly the same odd wrist motion the old woman had demonstrated that day at the tracks, she drove the blade into Cam's groin.

300

He shrieked like a jungle bird, looking down in disbelief and clapping his hands over the rapidly widening circle of red at his crotch. Blood spurting from between his fingers, he seemed to be trying to hold himself together as he scuttled sideways off the bed and ran stumbling from the room, whimpering and gagging. A few seconds later I heard the van's tires spinning and throwing gravel as he accelerated out of the alley behind the house.

L.A., panting, her lips already swollen and turning purple from Cam's blows, pulled up her jeans and rebuttoned them. She looked at me, her eyes filling, saying, 'He must have followed me here. I think he killed Jazzy.'

I was gasping for breath, and all I could do was nod. There was no way I could shield her from this, nothing I could do to fix it.

She shouldered past me on her way to the kitchen, saying, 'How'd you know I was here?'

'I knew you'd come for Jazzy before you ran away,' I gasped out. 'I saw it.'

She knelt over Jazzy and laid her hand on the little dog's chest.

'I can feel a heartbeat,' she said, her voice breaking. 'She's not dead.'

'What happened to her?'

'She bit him and he kicked her against the edge of the door,' L.A. said. 'Then he kicked her again when she tried to get up.' She carefully lifted the small furry body. 'Get my bicycle, Bis.'

9

Accountings

Jazzy wasn't permanently damaged, only knocked out, the vet said. We should watch for any sign of convulsions and keep her quiet. He accepted the eight dollars and change we were able to scrape up between us and agreed to send us his bill for the rest of his fee 'sometime when I get around to it.'

Later that day, after a desperate couple of hours of cleanup that took us from L.A.'s bed all the way out the front door, around the camellias and across the driveway, we faced Gram as she came in with her bags of squash, tomatoes, snap beans and cantaloupes. On the theory that simpler is almost always better when lying, we told her the best story we could think of, that Jazzy must have been hit by a car but was going to be okay. It was a touchy moment, and I held my breath as Gram eyed my torn and bloody jeans, bunged-up knee, and L.A.'s face, then looked up at me with one eyebrow raised.

'I fell,' I said.

'We both did,' L.A. said.

'I see,' Gram said. She examined Jazzy carefully, inquired about the vet's diagnosis and orders, gave both of us a stern look over her reading glasses and said, 'Are you two in any kind of trouble?'

'No, ma'am,' I said with every ounce of false conviction I could dredge up. And Gram seemed to buy it, maybe because in fact it remained to be seen whether we were in trouble or not, so technically there was no actual lie in my eyes at this point.

She sighed and reached out to take Jazzy from L.A., saying, 'Let's see if some warm milk will help.' One more hard look from Gram as she turned to take Jazzy back to the kitchen, and we were over that hump.

Cam was another story. He had apparently tried to make it to the hospital, but because of bad luck, bad driving or maybe just bleeding out, he lost control of the van and crashed into the overpass railing. He was already dead when the ambulance got there, so he'd lived less than fifteen minutes after we last saw him. To my amazement nothing was ever said about any unexplained crotch wounds.

Of course this simplified things no end from my point of view, and I decided to be grateful for the luck and let it go. But what I learned about the wreck afterward was puzzling. As for Cam himself, the damage was so bad that there was no way he could be spackled back into shape for viewing, which made the funeral a closed-casket affair. On the other hand, some things you might think would be fragile came through the wreck with hardly a scratch. One of them was the cheap camera Cam had kept under the driver's seat, which turned out to have a roll of film in it with pictures of the girls, all of the images hard to look at and impossible to forget, but also a couple of shots of a different girl, one none of us recognized. They were taken from a distance and it was obvious the girl, who I thought looked a little like L.A., didn't know anyone was taking her picture. It was Don who pronounced the final police consensus.

'She would have been next,' he said.

The pictures weren't clear enough to really make out her face but the short stretch of sidewalk and hedge in the background turned out to be only a block or so from the Crest, which was fairly close to the center of the section of town where all the girls had either lived, gone to school or had friends. All this, along with the fake uniform shirt with a Crest logo sewn on above the pocket the investigators found stuffed inside one of the van's door panels, convinced them he had grabbed the girls by posing as a theater employee.

Under the heading of odd news, Don said some homeless guy told the cops he saw an old woman with ragged clothes and a funny hat standing on the opposite side of the road watching as Cam crashed. He said there was a blue jay or something flying around her head, and swore the lady disappeared into thin air a second or two after the crash. But according to Don he was so full of gin that for all the good he did them as a witness he might as well have seen pink elephants.

Aunt Rachel laid low after the wreck, so nobody knew how Cam's death had affected her, but when Mom heard about it she gave me a big smile and a thumbs-up.

304

The gist of the reactions I heard generally came down to some variation of, *What goes around, comes around*, but all Hubert said as he bit into his chili dog was, 'Well boo-fuckin'-hoo.'

Gram's take was biblical. She said, "He that troubleth his own house shall inherit the wind."

As for me, I had my usual confused morass of thoughts and feelings. Somewhere in the process of trying to work them out, I watched a news clip of Amanda Peyser's mother on Channel 5.

'I pray to God no other parent will have to go through what we did,' she said, dabbing at her eye with a tissue. 'I'm thankful the monster who took Amanda is g-gone, and other girls like her ca-can be safe.'

I stared at the screen, hardly believing what I was hearing. I stood up and turned off the TV. 'How can she say that?' I asked L.A. 'How can she think there's any such thing as safe?'

After thinking it over for a minute L.A. said, 'She's just mad at everybody who didn't lose their kids.'

I sat back down, and neither of us spoke for a while. Finally I said, 'The only thing we know for sure is Cam's never gonna hurt anybody else.'

'So give yourself a gold star,' L.A. said. 'For once in your life take credit for something good.'

Take credit for Cam's death? It sounded ridiculous to me, but then if you looked at it from her standpoint the idea did make a certain kind of sense. One of the truest things Gram and Dr. Kepler had taught me was that knowledge is a two-edged sword, though I sometimes privately suspected it had a lot more edges, not to mention sharp points, than that. Either way, nothing could have made the basic truth of the concept plainer to me than my state of mind right now. Because at this moment, regardless of what it might say about me, I now knew for a certainty that I would have personally killed Cam a thousand times over to save L.A. from a hangnail, and done it with a song in my heart.

I don't really know why we even went to the funeral. I doubt Gram would have insisted on it, but maybe the force field created by her sense of the fitness of things compelled us. Or maybe it was guilt over feeling no guilt that Cam was dead.

Brother Wells preached over the casket just like he would anybody else's, except for not saying much about Cam being among God's children or walking with Jesus now or any bullshit like that.

'We are gathered here today to bid earthly farewell to Camden Lee Rowe . . . ' he said.

And there they were, all three names.

'His life's journey is done and he walks among us no more. As we are all imperfect vessels, unworthy of the limitless love of our Heavenly Father, we can make no claim to understand all that God has wrought . . . '

But I didn't catch the rest. Being in church brought back words and phrases I'd heard here over the years, like 'the blood of the lamb' and 'washed in the blood,' and even though I knew I didn't truly get the meaning of this any better now than I ever had, it was enough to catapult me backward in time, back to L.A. and me washing the bedspread and the knife in the hottest water we could stand, mopping the hardwood floor of her room and the hallway with pine cleaner and hosing away the splatters of blood on the porch and walk and driveway, praying to finish before Gram came home. The blood was everywhere, no visible difference between Cam's and mine, and for a crazy few seconds it seemed to me there wasn't enough water and soap in the world to wash it all away. And in a way I was right. It was still no trick at all for me to half close my eyes when I looked at, or even imagined, the floor or the sidewalk at Gram's and see it all again, bright and evil and in its own way absolutely unerasable.

After the service, as we walked out the double doors of the church into the white blast of afternoon heat and down the steps onto the blazing sidewalk where the long death cars waited at the curb, Gram, L.A. and I got separated. Gram and L.A. ended up with Mom in one car, and I rode with Diana in another.

The sun had overheated her in her black funeral dress, bringing out a little shine of sweat on her upper lip. A glow, I guess it was. Looking at it, I remembered the way her bare skin had sparkled with water on the island that day in Minnesota, and suddenly, in the middle of all this seriousness, I wanted to lick the sweat off her lip. But having that completely insane and undoubtedly sinful thought right here in front of the church, with Cam's dead and mutilated body so close by, caused a chilly shadow of guilt to pass over me. I tried to keep from thinking what

307

I was thinking, which of course only made it worse.

What finally distracted me from that was the unwanted memory of Don telling us about the other stuff they'd found in Cam's toolboxes and duffel bags in the van after the wreck. The camera and the uniform shirt hadn't been the end of it, not by a long shot. There were cords and ropes and blindfolds, surgical scissors and clamps, knives, rolls of duct tape, pulleys and other equipment he used, and a lot more stuff like that in the men's restroom inside the old Conoco station, which was where he had kept the girls locked up. Before he killed them. In the freezer of the little refrigerator he used for his beer they found the girls' nipples, wrapped in foil with several snips of dark hair. I could hardly believe I'd been as close as I had to all of it, even within touching distance of what was in the van, without feeling it.

And then it got even worse. When Don had to go take a phone call I managed to sneak a look at the pictures Cam had taken, and what he had written on them. In several of the pictures I recognized Tricia Venables, and you could see at least part of Cam in some of them too. In one picture, Tricia was tied in a chair naked and blindfolded, and a hand was holding a box knife against her left breast. At the bottom was written in black grease pencil, *SHE WAS READY!* In some of the photos, the girls were standing naked on a box with blood on their breasts and thin ropes around their necks, the way I'd dreamed of them. On one of these, Cam had written, *SHE COMES AND SHE GOES!* and on another, *MAKING HER WAIT IS THE BEST PART.*

The long black cars rolled silently away from the curb.

'What'd L.A. tell you?' I asked Diana.

'He did stuff to her, Bis, for a long time, like he did with those girls, except he didn't kill her and he only cut her a little.'

'A *little?*' I stared at her.

'She's still all there,' said Diana.

'Why did she wait so long to tell anybody?'

'He said he'd kill you and Gram if she did.'

My head was thumping and I felt the sting of tears in my eyes. L.A. had kept her mouth shut to save us. I tried to imagine what it must have felt like to hold that inside herself every day.

'So what changed?' I asked. 'Why'd she let on when she did?'

Diana looked hard at me for a minute, then said, 'You really don't know?'

I shook my head and wiped at my eyes.

Diana said, 'She started believing in you more than him.'

And the weight of complete inadequacy settled on my shoulders like sacks of cement.

We arrived at the cemetery and bumped our way back to the Rowe plot. There were a few black locusts and some crape myrtles back here but not much else to keep the sun off. The grave, along with a big gray pile of rocky dirt covered with a phony green rug that I assumed was meant to look like grass, was shaded by a blue-striped awning. Four rows of folding chairs had been arranged under the awning facing the casket, which was supported on a kind of frame draped with the same green material that had been thrown over the dirt. Sunlight reflected off the marble headstones all around us. From one of them a blue jay watched the movements of the people with a glittering black eye. In the distance, I saw Colossians Odell standing near the edge of the trees with his panama in his hand. He looked calm and focused, and I hoped the terrible storms that sometimes raged through his mind had let up at least for a while. There was no sign of Caruso, but I somehow felt sure he was sleeping safely in Colossians' pocket.

'I don't think we should make her talk about it too much until she's ready, Bis,' said Diana into my ear.

I nodded, taking a last swipe at my eyes and trying to straighten my tie, hoping nobody would get the idea I was shedding tears over Cam. I wondered how much talking was too much and how you were supposed to tell and why there wasn't a damn rulebook you could look things like this up in. For some reason I remembered what Dr. Kepler had said to me about true enemies, and thought of Jack in a coffin like Cam's. I wondered if an enemy was still an enemy after he was dead. Or had his teeth knocked out.

As everyone stood around waiting to be told where to sit, I saw L.A. standing stiffly next to Gram in her darkest blue dress and shiny black shoes, her hair tied with a black ribbon. I noticed a couple of the men from the church looking her up and down, their eyes full of hungry curiosity. I walked over and stood by her side for a second, wanting to offer her some kind of support but unable to think of anything to say or do that seemed the least bit helpful. I could smell the perfume she'd borrowed from Diana and the wine she'd been drinking. She stared at the casket with eyes like black diamonds. The power she was radiating was almost visible, but I didn't know what was in her mind. Maybe it was hate. Maybe satisfaction. Or something else entirely. All I knew for sure was that I wasn't going to ask her.

Diana took my hand as we sat in the third row of chairs, behind Gram and L.A. Mom, Rachel and Jack were in the second row, Jack looking like a sore thumb in his neck brace. For a few seconds I was lost in thoughts about right and wrong, justice and paybacks.

' . . . and in bringing Camden Lee Rowe here to this place of final farewell,' said Brother Wells, 'we humbly acknowledge our inability to fathom our Creator's will, or to truly know any man's heart. Camden walked in God's sunshine even as you and I do; he drank of the water God gave us and ate of the bread of the fields our Father prepared for us. We cannot know what separate country of the spirit he may have passed through while he was among us. That is between him and the Maker before Whom he now stands. As ever, we trust not only in the mercy but in the wisdom of that Maker, our Lord, the Ruler of heaven and earth.'

I visualized Cam, not free to just lie down and

be dead but cobbled and stitched back together like a chewed-up doll, standing in front of the great desk in God's office. But this time He looked bigger and more dangerous. This was the Maker of universes and Judge of judges, with world-breaking thunder in His face. Everything His eyes touched glowed and snapped with blue voltage.

Outside the windows behind Him strange violet lightning veined across a blue-black sky and I saw tall muscular figures armed with heavy swords gathering out there — dark angels empty of mercy. They began materializing one by one beside and behind Cam, their lion breath filling the air, their eyes as unbearable as the flames of arc welders.

I felt my hopes of getting a word in for Dad and Gramp and Dr. Kepler, not to mention the dead girls, slipping away, my tongue and my words locked down by the monstrous gravity in this place of ultimate judgment.

'Amen,' said Brother Wells from somewhere far away. I felt the blood returning to my face, and I breathed again.

And the last thing I heard as I came back to the moment was the long, despairing scream that ripped its way out of Cam's ruined throat as the irresistible blood-crusted hands of the dread angels closed on him and, as the old woman had promised L.A., he vanished into eternal night as the darkness took back its own.

10

Other Dreams

A couple of days later I threw the knife off the Cadiz Viaduct into the Trinity as the sun was going down behind the city. L.A. and I hadn't spoken about what had happened that day but what we knew about Cam's death naturally made for an extra weight between us, another thing we carried together in the world, the way Mr. Campion and I would always carry Dee's death.

But for L.A. the weight pulled a different way and seemed to reposition something in her heart. She didn't pay attention to every little sound and movement around her like she had before. I don't think she ever covered herself with pillows anymore, and she never hit me or got that wild look on her face again. She taped school pictures of the three murdered girls to her mirror. There was a changed light in her eyes now and she was somehow more beautiful, but older, and in a way you knew wasn't entirely good.

Something had changed in me too. Somehow the strange hungers I had never been able to satisfy left me. I almost never drank with L.A. anymore, and when I'd lit a Chesterfield in Gram's back yard the other day I hadn't liked the taste at all, crushing it out unsmoked.

Then on a Sunday afternoon Don, dressed in

loafers, khakis and a yellow pullover and not looking the least bit like a cop or a boss, visited Gram and me at home. Gram fixed him a big glass of iced tea, then poured cold buttermilk into a tumbler for herself. She got her pepper mill from the freezer, ground a little black pepper onto the buttermilk and sat down at the kitchen table. Then Don sat down across from her, and they talked about the heat and the government for a while, Don saying, 'Yes ma'am' and 'No ma'am' to her, exactly as I did.

After a few minutes he excused himself, stood up and said, 'Come on, Jimbo, give me a hand.'

We walked out to the front porch, where he set his sweating glass down on the porch rail and glanced up at the tinkling wind chime near the corner of the porch. He stretched, then reached into his pocket and brought out a small matchbox, opening it to give me a look. In the box were three yellowish teeth with blunt brown prongs at the bottoms. One of the teeth had a silver-looking filling.

'Cam's,' said Don.

We walked around back to what had been L.A.'s window, and Don fitted the teeth one at a time to the dents I'd found in the wood of the sill. He let me feel how when you held the tooth down in the right impression and tried to twist it there was no movement at all.

'Proves what you figured out — Earl wasn't our guy,' he said.

I nodded.

'But when you found these marks you didn't think it would do any good to call us . . . '

I swallowed hard.

' . . . and you were afraid of the possible consequences, am I right?'

I nodded again.

'You didn't want to scare your Gram or Lee Ann unnecessarily or take a chance on busting up your family.'

He looked at me for a while. I cleared my throat.

He said, 'Next time I'm thinking you'll know better.'

'Yes sir.'

*   ★   ★

Sometimes Gram would stop in at the gas station where Jack worked now to get the Buick gassed up, always saying something like, 'Jack, I wonder if you might just check the tires and see if you can get that little spot you missed back there on the window? Thank you so much.' At this point Jack would usually give me a homicidal glare, but the time when I was afraid of him was over. It wasn't just that his neck and eye were messed up, or that you could tell his reflexes and nerve were gone. It was realizing that it had never really been me he needed to destroy — it had been his own weakness. One time at the station when I got out of the car to go inside for a Coke, standing up in front of him just as he approached the car door, he flinched and brought his arms up to cover before he could stop himself, exactly as I had done with him so many times. At that moment I saw him as

315

he experienced himself — a lost boy too scared to cry, knowing there was no help for him anywhere and understanding that in the ways that truly counted he was the worst things there are in the world for a man to be: helpless and alone.

When Jack had been caught in the raid with Hubert and Shepherd Boy at the Triple-X Bookstore downtown, Gram said all it cost him was a fine. But Shepherd Boy didn't come to our church anymore, his name disappearing from the bulletins and newsletters and never again being mentioned by Brother Wells, or anyone else as far as I knew.

Hubert landed in juvenile court for the bookstore thing but just got remanded to the custody of his parents. I saw him around sometimes, wearing black clothes and letting his hair get shaggier and longer. He showed me a gun he said he'd stolen from somebody's car, a small chrome-plated .25 automatic with black plastic grips, and told me he'd started carrying it in his pocket everywhere he went.

'Wanta go out to the tracks and shoot it?' he said. 'I got shells.'

'Nah,' I said, knowing that a few weeks ago I would have gone without a second thought.

L.A. and I hadn't seen Fangbaby in weeks, finally admitting to ourselves she was gone for good. But I'd been wrong about her. She had let L.A. touch the tip of her nose the last time we saw her. Maybe it was the cheese L.A. was holding.

Dr. Kepler had died three weeks after the day

316

of the applesauce, and the funeral home cremated her according to the instructions in her will. They put her in a fancy silver jar that Gram called a funerary urn, which to me didn't look big enough to hold a cat. Since she had no family and there'd been no funeral service, Gram said putting her on our mantel beside the picture of Gramp in his black suit would have to serve as her last rites. I wondered what the ashes looked like but somehow couldn't bring myself to look. It was no problem for L.A., though. She took the lid off the urn, peered inside and said, 'Just looks like dry dirt.'

We gathered in front of the mantel and Gram read a poem called 'Our Saviour's Other Sheep' from one of her books while L.A. kind of stood at attention and looked very serious, even though she was like Dr. Kepler herself in having few if any supernatural beliefs. On a sheet of blue paper from the stationery box I printed the quotation Dr. Kepler had written inside the cover of the copy of *20,000 Leagues Under the Sea* she'd given me. It read:

— if you have seen the sparrow
almost blown from its branch
by the sweet winds of spring,
you have seen my true heart.

Folding the paper carefully, I put it under the urn. Then Gram made L.A. and me bow our heads with her for a moment of silence, and that was the end of it.

At first it was eerie having her up there on the

mantel like some silent witness to our comings and goings, but eventually we all pretty much got used to it. Sometimes when nobody else was around I even talked to her, which seemed to help me sort out my thinking and gave me the feeling she was still with us in some way.

In spite of not wanting to be away from Diana and spending more and more time with her at the end of that summer, I still kept going to the pool with L.A. whenever I could. Out there it was like the air was her real element and gravity didn't apply to her. When I watched her at the pool it seemed to me she was trying to fly away from what had happened to her, and I hoped the air was having some healing effect, because of course she was flying for me too.

After the newspaper did a photo series on her a diving coach from the university came down to watch her one Saturday, later visiting the house to talk to L.A. and Gram about the Olympic trials the year after next.

'She has tremendous talent,' the woman said. 'It would be criminal to let it go to waste.'

I couldn't believe my ears. 'You gotta do it,' I said to L.A. when the woman had gone.

'Maybe,' she said.

'Shit, L.A., I'm serious! You gotta!'

She shrugged.

She kept visiting Dr. Ballard occasionally for a while, but as time went by she gradually drifted away from us. I kept looking for some altered awareness in her, some sign that she was going to be all right, but there was nothing. We saw less and less of her, and she would never talk about where she'd been. A couple of times I'd seen her hanging out with Hubert after school and I knew she went down to Beauchamp's almost every day now, sometimes staying until Froggy locked up. Once when Gram was away for the weekend with some friends in Fort Worth I found L.A. passed out drunk on the floor in the bathroom and helped her to her bed. She seemed to have almost no weight. Sitting on the side of the bed, watching her sleep, I smoothed her wild dark hair back from her face and tried to think of a way to pray for her, but no words came to me.

Whoever or whatever had stood by my bed through so many nights never came again, and now when I dreamed about Dee or the dead girls, more and more often I saw them lying down peacefully in some safe place, their eyes closed and their hands folded. The girls were whole again, covered instead of naked and cold, and Dee no longer grieved for the father and the life I'd stolen from him. Somewhere in a diamond-clear dimension of truth Dr. Kepler forgot cancer and the ovens and the brownshirts, and under some forgiving sun Gramp laid down the terrible weight he carried and at last stood straight again. And on the deserted midnight highway that ran through the center of my heart, my own father finally walked free of the endless flames, his face fresh and unscarred.

Once or twice I even imagined that all of them, shining with a pure soft light, stood together in some high and blessed place, held out their hands to me across the dark universes and forgave me.

We do hope that you have enjoyed reading this large print book.

Did you know that all of our titles are available for purchase?

We publish a wide range of high quality large print books including:
Romances, Mysteries, Classics
General Fiction
Non Fiction and Westerns

Special interest titles available in large print are:
The Little Oxford Dictionary
Music Book
Song Book
Hymn Book
Service Book

Also available from us courtesy of Oxford University Press:
Young Readers' Dictionary
(large print edition)
Young Readers' Thesaurus
(large print edition)

For further information or a free brochure, please contact us at:
Ulverscroft Large Print Books Ltd.,
The Green, Bradgate Road, Anstey,
Leicester, LE7 7FU, England.
Tel: (00 44) 0116 236 4325
Fax: (00 44) 0116 234 0205

B